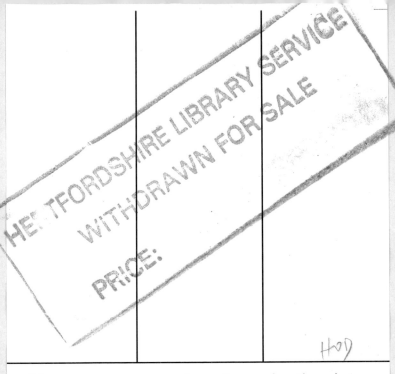

truth, not a factual or referential truth. And yet as more books are published and more stories get told, we increasingly seek out those writers who promise to give us something more than mere fiction'

Ian Sansom, *Guardian*

IN EVERY MOMENT WE ARE STILL ALIVE

Tom Malmquist

Translated from the Swedish by Henning Koch

SCEPTRE

First published in Sweden in 2015 by Natur & Kultur
First published in Great Britain in 2017 by Sceptre
An Imprint of Hodder & Stoughton
An Hachette UK company

This paperback edition published in 2018

1

Copyright © Tom Malmquist 2015
Translation copyright © Henning Koch 2017

The right of Tom Malmquist to be identified as the Author of the Work has been
asserted by him in accordance with the Copyright, Designs and Patents Act 1988.

A CIP catalogue record for this title is available from the British Library

Paperback ISBN 978 1 473 64002 3

Typeset in Sabon MT by Palimpsest Book Production Limited, Falkirk, Stirlingshire

Printed and bound by CPI Group (UK) Ltd, Croydon, CR0 4YY

Hodder & Stoughton policy is to use papers that are natural,
renewable and recyclable products and made from wood grown in sustainable
forests. The logging and manufacturing processes are expected to conform
to the environmental regulations of the country of origin.

Hodder & Stoughton Ltd
Carmelite House
50 Victoria Embankment
London EC4Y 0DZ

www.sceptrebooks.co.uk

The translation and publication of this work
were both supported by the

SWEDISH
ARTSCOUNCIL

In Every Moment
We Are Still Alive

THE CONSULTANT STAMPS down the wheel lock of Karin's hospital bed. In a loud voice he addresses the intensive care nurses, who are cutting open her tank top and sports bra: Pregnant woman, week thirty-three, child reportedly in good health, started feeling ill about five days ago with flu-like symptoms, fever, cough, slight shortness of breath yesterday which was put down to her pregnancy, condition severely deteriorating today, acute respiratory difficulties, arrived at the maternity unit about an hour ago. With powerful hands, he unscrews a cartridge-like bottle and continues: Sats about seventy ambient but responds to oxygen with higher saturation, RR about forty to fifty, BP ninety-five over fifty, HR a hundred and twenty. The midwife who helped with the oxygen in the ambulance stops in the doorway. She gently takes my arm. You're in Ward B at the ICU now, would you like me to write that down for you on a bit of paper? No need, thanks, I answer. She'll get all the help she needs now, she says. Yes, thanks. Okay, well, I'll be off, then. Okay, thanks. Karin has electrodes attached to her chest.

The monitor is beeping shrilly. What drugs have you given her? I ask. You have to ask Per-Olof about that, answers the intensive care nurse. Who's that? That's me, the consultant calls out: We're giving your wife Tazocin and Tamiflu, painkillers, sedatives and some other things – we've various different drugs on the infusion rack here, but there's no time to talk to you right now. We'll update you properly soon, just stay calm now and let us get on with helping your wife. What about the baby? I ask, but no one answers. I sink down onto the floor and lean against the wall beside a waste bin for used needles. I hug Karin's quilted jacket for a moment then suddenly drop it and run out of the room. I see the sign for the disabled toilet further down the sharply lit corridor and dive in and don't even have time to close the door behind me before I vomit and piss at the same time. I gargle with some water from the tap but my breath still stinks so I wash my tongue with liquid soap. The white double doors of Ward B are closed when I come back. I knock once, open, and peer inside. One of the intensive care nurses is sitting on a stool between Karin's parted thighs. Tattooed sword blades coil around his muscular arms. Karin is wearing an oxygen mask with a reservoir bag, her eyes are shut, and her face suddenly seems like that of a stranger. The nurse, wearing latex gloves, is prising open Karin's labia. He catches sight of me, drops the urinary catheter, stands and walks right up to me. His eyes are vacant. I have to ask you to wait outside, he says. Why? Privacy, he answers. Whose privacy? I ask. The patient's. The patient's? Yes, the patient's, he says, and stares at me, only not into my eyes but at one of my shoulders. I've lived with her for ten years, and she's carrying my child. There's still the matter of patient privacy, he says. If patient privacy is so important, why are you here alone with her? I ask. I try to step forward but he blocks my way and says: I have to ask you to wait outside. I'll come and get you when I'm ready. He shoos me out without even touching me, and closes the door.

There's a coffee machine opposite the lifts. I insert a ten-kronor piece but forget about the plastic mug. The coffee goes everywhere, all over the machine and down onto the floor, I get some paper towels from a cleaner's trolley and start mopping it up. The consultant comes out of the intensive care ward just as I'm rummaging about for some more coins. He glances down at the file he's resting against his belly. Haven't you passed out yet? he asks, apparently expecting me to laugh. When I don't, he says: Your wife is in a very serious condition. So it isn't pneumonia? I ask. Pneumonia can be pretty serious, he replies. It's curable, though, isn't it? Most of the time, but not always, he says and walks past me into the lift. He presses one of the buttons, nods at me, and adds that he'll update me as soon as they know more. I sit on a chair outside Ward B. Every inch of the corridor is greyish blue – the plastic floor, the skirting boards, the walls, the guard rails, even the food trolleys. There are three windows behind me but I can't see out of them, the evening darkness has turned them into mirrors. I stand up and knock on the white door, wait, and sit again. Eventually the intensive care nurse emerges. I notice his tattoos again, almost like warpaint. Can I go in now? I ask. No, he answers, then fetches something from a cupboard beside the door and disappears back into the room. I look at my telephone, answer a couple of text messages, then walk up and down the corridor until my legs feel tired. Again I knock at the door. This time the other nurse answers. Sorry, I say, but I don't understand why I can't come in. This is ridiculous, I know Karin wants me there with her. Oh, did no one come to get you? If they had I wouldn't be standing here, would I? I'm sorry, do come in. Karin is already a bit better, she says, and insists on getting me a cup of coffee and a cheese sandwich. Thanks, but I don't want anything, I tell her. Karin sees me and starts waving. An assistant nurse has loosened her oxygen mask and is dabbing her lips with a sponge stick. Karin is gasping for breath but seems happy to be free of the sweaty mask. I go over to her and take her hand. Darling? At least they've given you morphine. She points at her stomach – It'll be okay, I say, I promise, everything's going to be fine. She gives me a thumbs up. The guy with the tattoos is talking on the phone, he's sitting in an observation room, the windows of which overlook the ward. His face is stunningly beautiful, his thick hair perfectly combed, his skin smooth. I pick up Karin's puffer jacket. The consultant stands with his back to me waiting for a colleague who's pulling along something that looks like a defibrillator. He seems to be from the Cardiology Intensive Care Unit, taciturn and a bit odd. After a quick examination of Karin's chest he turns to the consultant: We need an emergency spiral CT. Is that serious? I ask. He gives me a look and turns to Karin: I've checked you over now,

4

Karin, and think it sounds like you've got serious pneumonia, maybe even a pulmonary embolism. It's difficult for me to say with absolute certainty at this point, we have to take an X-ray first. Could you repeat that? I say. The consultant answers while keeping his eyes on Karin: Pneumonia or a blood clot, maybe both, at least that's what we think at this stage. We're treating you for all the things we suspect may have caused your breathing difficulties, but this is serious; a young woman shouldn't be breathing like this even if she is pregnant. I try to establish eye contact with Karin but she's staring up at the ceiling, not passively but as if she's noticed something. I look up as well, but all I can see is a fluorescent tube and an immaculate, blindingly white ceiling, not a single crack in the paint. The consultant sees that I'm holding Karin's puffer jacket in my arms, and grimaces. There's a locker further down the corridor, you're welcome to use it, he says. No need, this is Karin's. Well, as I say, there are lockers available. No need, but thanks anyway, I answer and sit down next to her bed.

Karin is wheeled off into a room with a steel door, as if she's being taken to a bomb shelter. She coughs so hard that her chest bounces up from the bed. I sit at one of the tables in the corridor and can hear a droning sound through the walls. After about half an hour a doctor appears and asks if I am Karin's next of kin. Has something happened? I ask. He's bald, wears oval glasses, and introduces himself as the radiologist. He stammers while telling me this could take some time, because Karin, on account of her breathing difficulties, is having problems

5

lying in a horizontal position. Okay, I answer. So you understand it could take a while, then, yes? Okay, thanks. It's hot and stuffy in the corridor. I take off my cardigan and get my phone out. Sven answers on their landline. He listens as I explain what's been happening, then says: So the doctors suspect it's pneumonia? Yes, she's having an X-ray now. Thanks for ringing, Tom. It's not long before he calls back. Hello, Sven, I say. Lillemor must have been frantically pacing around their terraced house in Lidingö until Sven felt compelled to phone back. Sorry for calling you again, he says. Sven, I'm the one who called you just now – sorry, I only said that because you're apologising. Anyway, he continues, is there anything else you can tell us about her pneumonia? I've told you everything I know, I say. I see, he answers, and asks if it would be all right if they come in. That's probably not necessary, Sven, it's only pneumonia. Where are you now? he asks. Söder Hospital. Where exactly? I don't remember, Mum dropped us by the maternity ward. I don't know, somewhere below ground level. 'Centre for Nuclear Medicine and Imaging', it says here. She's probably only being X-rayed there, do you remember the name of the ward? No, Sven, look, can I check and text it to you? That's fine, thanks. I think I might have left a hob on in the kitchen, I burst out. Sorry, what? I made her tea, I probably forgot to turn off the hob. Oh right . . . Sven, I'm going to go, I have to call Mum, she has a spare set of keys.

The consultant has been waiting for me in Ward B, and wants to talk urgently. He rubs disinfectant gel into his rough hands from the pump-action dispenser by the door. Everything about him is grey, apart from his white hospital clothes. He has brought a doctor with him, and explains she's an obstetrician; she stands by a mobile ultrasound machine, which she plugs in by the hospital bed. The consultant shakes his hands dry and says: Karin, we just got the X-rays and have had a preliminary assessment of your blood tests, it's not looking good. Karin is strangely calm. I rub her feet. The consultant leans forward, so that he can look into Karin's eyes. Can you hear me, Karin? She nods. Good, I've discussed it with haematologists both here at Söder Hospital and also at Karolinska – they're blood specialists. You have a massive increase in white blood cells, it's highly likely that you have acute leukaemia. Karin looks at me and I hear her say something very faintly. Darling, I'm here, I say, reaching out to caress her cheek. We'll get through this, I promise, we'll get through this. Karin waves her hand. I try to read her lips behind the oxygen mask. She's asking about the baby, I say. Karin gives me a thumbs up. My priority now is Karin, says the consultant. The child is well protected in the uterus, adds the obstetrician, even against leukaemia. She has long brown hair and a straight little nose. She doesn't seem entirely comfortable that the consultant is there, and only relaxes once he's left the ward. She works an ultrasound device over Karin's stomach. You have a perky little baby, she's fine, I can't see anything to indicate otherwise, she says, wiping off the gel with tissue. At the door she turns to us, as if intending to say something else, but just stands there looking for a long time at Karin. Thanks, I say. She hesitates, then says: These days they're very good at treating leukaemia. Thanks a lot, thanks. A loose white thread curls up the neckline of Karin's hospital gown. I tuck it in under the fabric, and smooth over her fringe. She's drenched in sweat and tugs at my hand. Is everything all right? she asks. Are you really asking me that? She nods. Darling, of course I'm worried, but don't talk now, concentrate on your breathing. On a trolley I find a laminated sheet showing the emergency exits. I use it as a fan. Karin likes the air wafting against her. I don't know how long I've been standing there fanning her when she opens her mouth. She makes a smacking sound. I can't hear what she's saying, but it sounds like 'live'. She tries to take off her mask but I stop her. She groans. Darling, what is it? I ask. Her name, she says. Okay, okay, you want to call her Liv? She shakes her head and exclaims: Livia. Livia? She nods and lifts her wrist. Livia, she says. Okay, Livia it is, I answer. An alarm on the oxygen machine goes off and one of the intensive care nurses comes rushing in. What's going on? I ask. She calls out towards the monitoring room: She's working too hard. The consultant strolls in, he's chewing on something, he swallows it, clears his throat, pauses in front of one of the monitors with his hands folded behind his back. She's doing well with the oxygen, she's still managing, but we'll have to intubate if things don't improve, he says, and turns to Karin. I'm sorry to talk about you in this way, we don't mean to, it's just habit, but the situation is, Karin, in spite of the help we're giving you you're struggling to oxygenate yourself, so we may have to sedate you and use the respirator.

*

I suggest to Sven that he stop the car and pass the telephone to Lillemor. We're in a taxi now, but hold on and I'll put her on, he answers. I feel nervous when I hear Lillemor's deep voice. Hi, we've had a diagnosis, I say. Okay, she answers. I wanted to call right away, but it was difficult, I say. Okay. I thought I'd better call before you got here. Uh-huh, well? It's really difficult to say this. Well? It's not pneumonia. Lillemor goes so quiet that I have to ask: Are you still there?

The consultant is sitting on a stool by the bed when I get back. I just told your wife the child is causing too much strain, he says, her body is working at high pressure and her levels of lactic acid are dangerously high. He turns to Karin: I've just been on the phone with Central Intensive Care at Karolinska and it looks like we'll deliver the child by caesarean section as early as tomorrow morning. Karolinska has better resources in place to help you and the child, so you'll be put on the respirator tonight. You won't feel any pain, you'll be asleep, like a long, deep sleep after a hard day at work. Is she being moved? I ask. It's for the best, he answers. Tomorrow morning? Yes, as soon as they can get her a bed at Central Intensive Care. Why do you have to keep her sedated? It's better that way, both for Karin and the child; she'd have a general anyway for the caesarean. Karin tries to say something but gives up and shakes her head. She puts her hands on her stomach. I know it's difficult for you to talk, Karin, he says. I'll take that as you saying you understand.

Karin is in a sort of half-slumber. Her breathing gets worse, sometimes she opens her eyes and scratches under her mask, and the moment I stop fanning her she anxiously seeks my hand. Darling, my arms have gone numb, I tell her, I can't keep waving this bloody thing. I don't have the strength to stop her when she pulls off her mask. In a single breath she exhales: Love you in every possible way. A nurse rushes over and asks if everything's all right. Karin gives her a thumbs up. You mustn't take off your mask, she says. She knows, I tell her.

Lillemor is wearing her mah-jong clothes and Sven his old-fashioned suit as they march down the corridor of the ward. I feel Sven's broad, damp chest against mine. Lillemor seems uncomfortable when I embrace her. She stands facing away from me, peering at the doors of the patient rooms. She asks if they can see Karin. I walk ahead of them and call out from the doorway: Darling, your parents are here. Karin looks worried. Sven stops in the doorway. Lillemor hovers, then decides to go forward. She pats Karin's legs as she repeats: My darling girl. Karin starts sobbing and waves her arms. Lillemor stiffens and says: We'll wait outside. She grabs Sven by the arm and swiftly leads him out. Karin tugs at my jumper and looks at me. Darling, I understand, you don't have to say anything. I think they understand as well. I'll tell them you're happy they're here.

When I come out, Sven and Lillemor have just sat down on the sofa outside the ward kitchen, Lillemor has a tissue clamped against her mouth. Is everything okay? I ask. Fine, fine, says Sven. I mean it was the same thing last time, I say. Thanks, Tom, we understand, he says. Something's making a noise here, I can't stand it, says

Lillemor. She sits down, stands up, sits down again. What's making that noise? Maybe it's the dishwasher, says Sven. There's a lot of stuff making a noise in here, I say. It's something else, it's a very high-pitched noise, she says and shakes her head. I sit down next to them. Sven studies the pattern of the sofa fabric and establishes that it's supposed to be wind-tossed dandelion clocks. Lillemor shakes her head again and informs him that it's cow parsley. Sven folds his hands together over his thigh and asks: Did they say what kind of leukaemia it is? Lillemor glares at him. No, I don't suppose they know that yet, do they, he adds with a nod in my direction. They just said acute, I say, looking at Lillemor. I ask her if she's all right. Sorry, I just hate hospitals, and I can't stand that noise, she says and gets up. She rummages around in her bag for a mint, offers me one, then Sven, and then wanders off down the corridor with her hands covering her ears.

The consultant stands at the head of the bed and the obstetrician monitors Livia with ultrasound. Darling, I'm not leaving you, but I have to get home and pick up a few things. It'll just be tonight then I'll be straight back and stay with you the whole time. She looks at the door, then at me. Your parents are in the corridor outside, I say. She shakes her head. They understand, darling, don't worry. I told them you want to name her Livia. She makes a thumbs up. I stand by the wash basin. Karin moves her mouth. I don't hear her, but I can see that she's saying goodnight. Goodnight, darling, see you later, I call out. The consultant puts his hand over her mask. It looks as if he's injecting something into a valve attached to the oxygen tube. Karin's eyes close. The consultant counts out loud while checking his wristwatch: One, two, three, four, five. He is still going when I walk out of the ward. I get as far as the lifts before turning around and running back. The door to the ward is locked. I ring the bell. One of Karin's intensive care nurses opens it. Did you forget something? Yes, I say, pushing past and hurrying into Ward B. Is she sleeping, I ask, is everything going to plan? She's sleeping, everything went well, the obstetrician answers. Okay, thanks, I say, stroking Karin's ear. She's dark blue and bleeding slightly around the catheter in her arm. Will they start chemotherapy tomorrow? I don't know, you'll have to ask the haematologists at Karolinska about that tomorrow, says the consultant. The blinds are lowered but a little ventilation window is open, and through it I can just make out the slope down to the water across Årstaviken, the green and red navigation lights of the boats. I look around the ward. In the monitoring section sit the three intensive care nurses and an assistant nurse. They fall silent as I approach. Have you seen Karin's jacket? I ask. The assistant nurse walks over to a wardrobe. You mean this one? Yes, exactly, thanks. Go home and get some rest now, you have to sleep. Yes, I will, thanks, I just want to make sure you have my number. The assistant nurse, who has thinning purple dyed hair, turns to the computer and reads out my mobile number. That's right, thanks, I say. I'd like you to call me as soon as you know when she's being moved to Karolinska. We'll do that, she says. Okay, thanks, I answer.

Lillemor is waiting by the pond outside the main

entrance to the hospital. She's looking down at her reflection in the water, one hand on her stomach, making small, caressing movements. Now and then the hiss of a car can be heard from Ringvägen, but apart from that it's silent. The taxi will be here shortly, says Sven, tucking his mobile into his inside jacket pocket. What's the time? I ask. Just before four, he answers. In the taxi I hug Karin's puffer jacket. I lean my head against the cool window and look out at the asphalt, the gutters, kerbs, pavements, and traffic islands. Before I get out by the steps to Lundagatan I say: It's going to be okay.

Mum parks the car at the bus stop outside Karolinska University Hospital in Solna, I jump out, she calls out but I don't hear what she says, I run inside to the information desk, a woman gives me a map and points, I sprint through the lobby along a twenty-metre-long corridor leading into a hall, past a shop, two bed lifts and a stairwell, turn right and run through yet another automatic door into a corridor twice as long and across an inner courtyard, I share a bed lift with two doctors wearing surgical caps, I get out, run through the stairwell, follow the arrow-shaped sign for Central Operations, I pass an open steel door and some green pillars, I run across a garish green plastic floor down a forty-metre-long corridor ending in a T-junction, I read the signs, I hang a right towards Central Intensive Care and run alongside some windows, on the right is the hospital park, walls of white fabric, I run down a hundred-metre corridor, I stop by a video entryphone, signals ring out, I look into the lens. A man's voice: Good morning, what can I do for you?

Hello, my wife, she's come by ambulance from Söder Hospital, she's pregnant, she's having an emergency caesarean. At Central Intensive Care? he asks. Yes, F21, I answer. What's her name? Karin Lagerlöf. Wait a moment, he says. After a few minutes the automatic doors open. The doctor is tall with dark, slicked-back hair, and wears a white uniform. He introduces himself but I'm only really conscious of his eyes, which never want to look directly at me. He says my wife has just arrived and they're installing her in Room 1, which is a single room. He emphasises that he doesn't know anything else. Who *does* know, then? I ask. As soon as they've got her installed you can talk to someone who knows, he answers. Is she okay? They're installing her now, as soon as that's done we'll come and get you, he says and walks past me into the corridor. He keeps his eyes on me, so I follow him. Do you know about CIC? he asks. What do you mean? He punches in a code to open a door and says: At CIC we treat patients who need extra-intensive care. We have thirteen beds, specially trained doctors and nurses. He turns on the light. Right, okay, I answer, and peer into the room which is about twenty metres square. A sofa, chairs, an armchair, a round table, and a simple kitchenette. Not exactly the Waldorf-Astoria, he says, but better than nothing. When is the caesarean being done? I ask. Unfortunately I don't know, your wife has to be stabilised before anything can be done. How long will I have to wait in here? Difficult to say, maybe an hour? I really don't know, but you don't have to stay in the family room. It's fine, thanks. Okay, he says, and leaves me at the door. A TV is suspended from the ceiling. There's another room adjoining the bigger one with a bunk bed and a small toilet. The translucent curtains are drawn across the window facing into the corridor. Abandoned coffee cups. A waste paper basket filled with scrunched-up tissues. I sit at the table. There's a plastic yucca plant in front of me. Someone has pressed a bit of chewing gum onto one of its leaves. I decide to head back into the corridor but realise that the door has a combination lock. They haven't given me the code and I don't know where else I can wait so I just stand in the doorway. A doctor emerges from CIC. Excuse me? I say. She glances at me but strides past. I call out to her. She stops and turns around. Do you have the code to the door? Don't you have it already? No, they let me in but didn't give me the code, I answer. She gets out a little notebook from her top pocket and flips through the pages. Twelve twenty-one, she says. Okay, that's the year and the ward number, I suppose? Never occurred to me, she answers. That'll help me remember it, I say. She blinks, and says with a knowing glance: Is it your wife who's pregnant? Yes, she's pregnant, I say. She comes closer. If it weren't for the wrinkles that appear around her eyes I would have taken her for a teenager. She's standing right beside me when she says: I've got a girl myself who was born a month and a half premature. You should be glad it's a girl, premature girls have a better chance than premature boys of surviving and avoiding any long-term damage.

Mum buys me a salad from the hospital shop. The machine-peeled prawns are drenched in Rhode Island sauce. Go easy, you're wolfing it down like I-don't-know-what, says Mum. I've never changed a nappy in my life, I say. You'll manage it. Even your father managed it, she says, standing up, looking at me and adding: Sweetie, what's the matter? I think I left the hob on, I answer. No, Tom, that's what you thought yesterday, but it wasn't on. I'm positive I forgot to turn the fucking thing off this time, though. Sweetheart, yesterday I dropped everything and bolted round to yours, and it wasn't on. What do you want me to say? Do you want me to go and check again? Maybe it would be best, I say. Mum turns abruptly towards the door just as Sven and Lillemor arrive. She adjusts her cardigan and says: Lillemor, Sven, I don't know what to say. They hug Mum and ask how things are with Thomas. Not good, answers Mum. They are silent. Mum seems to become nervous, as if she's said the wrong thing. You found it, I say. It wasn't very difficult, you gave us good directions, says Lillemor. Mum can't get the TV on, just fiddles with the remote control. Lillemor asks if I've managed to see Karin yet. No, they're installing her now. *Installing* her? That's how they put it, I say. Mum starts leafing through the paper, her reading glasses hanging by a cord around her neck. Mum, can you even see anything? It doesn't matter, she says, then adds: Do you still want me to go home and check the hob? No, forget it, I'm probably just being neurotic, I reply, and walk out into the corridor; I keep walking until I find a bench. A doctor speeds past on a kick scooter. What would Karin have wanted me to do if she could see me sitting here? I scroll through the telephone numbers of Karin's closest friends, Caro, Johanna and Ullis. Hi, it's Tom, have you got a moment?

When I return, Sven is leaning back in the sofa, reading on his tablet, Lillemor is rummaging around in her handbag. Bisse said she'd go back and check your hob, she says. Okay, but I did tell her she didn't have to go, I answer. Måns is on his way, she adds. What, from Örebro? Yes, he's coming on the next train, she answers. I sit on one of the chairs. A doctor came by, says Sven. What did he say? Karin's readings have stabilised now, they plan to do the caesarean this afternoon. Okay, that's good, thanks, but in future I want all information to come to me first, if that's okay? You weren't even here, says Lillemor. No, but that doesn't make any difference, this is how we want it. We? she exclaims. Me and Karin, obviously. Right, but he came here asking for you and you weren't here, and we thought it might be important. Okay, so I'll run through it one more time, this is something Karin wanted, info to me first, that is me and Karin, and by the way we did talk about this only yesterday. A knock at the door makes Lillemor jump. Sven, she says, and looks at him expectantly. He stands but I'm already at the door. The nurse is shy and tries to smile as she asks: Are you all here with Karin Lagerlöf? Yes, is the caesarean being done now? I ask. No, not yet, I just wanted to say you can come and see her if you'd like to, and meet the doctors in charge. I look over at Sven and Lillemor. Tom, you go, we'll wait here, says Sven.

Only when the nurse opens the door to Room 1 do I stop, I look down at my hands, spread my fingers wide and try to remember Karin's face, but something about it is unclear to me, parts of her are missing, and I have an unpleasant sense of not having seen her for many years. Are you coming? asks the nurse, who's standing by the open door. I look up: first I see the oxygen tube, light blue, looking like part of a toy as it hangs down between Karin's oxygen mask and the respirator, which makes a recurring crunching sound as it synchronises with Karin's rising and sinking chest, then I realise that Karin is naked, only a small blanket over her breasts and lower abdomen; I can see between her legs, where they've shaved her, a catheter hangs out of her urethra and her eyelids look glassy. Come in, says the nurse, unfolding a sheet which she tosses over Karin's thighs. She pats her hand and says: I just told your wife you're going to be parents. She already knows, I answer. I mean you're going to be parents today, soon. Yes, okay, thanks. She fetches a stool and puts it by the bed. I sit down. Another nurse is standing there, fiddling with the infusion stand. A doctor sits in the corner of the room tapping at a computer. Outside the window on the other side of the street a brick façade rears up, three windows in line, pitch-black foundations. I recognise the building. Is that the Cancer Research Institute? I ask, pointing at it. That's right, you know it? Yeah, my dad's been going there for check-ups for the last ten years. Oh, right, she says, standing next to me, also looking out of the window. Lovely spring weather, I reckon I'll have lunch in the park today, she says. The doctor has a pointy face, brown hair, a straight fringe, small rectangular glasses. A limp hand-shake. He seems shy. John Persson, he says, I'm the senior physician here at CIC, ultimately I'm in charge of Karin's time here at the intensive care unit. Okay, my name is Tom, I reply. Is it just you here, Tom? Well, I'm the next

18

of kin, or whatever you want to call it. I was under the impression that Karin's parents were also here? Karin has stated that she'd prefer to have information come to me first, and then I'll relay it to parents and friends after that, I say. Right, that's good to know. I suggest we sit down and talk to the haematologist right away, he's the one who'll be handling Karin's treatment; the obstetrician delivering the child will also join us. Okay, sounds good, do you mean right now? Yes, unless this isn't a good time? No, no, thanks, it's fine. He walks very slowly across the corridor into a sort of office he refers to as the Atlas Room. Computers, printers, a bookshelf with medical books and a stack of blank paper. The haematologist is already waiting for us there, he finishes off a call on his mobile and introduces himself as Franz Callmer, professor and consultant at the Centre for Haematology. Thick and tangled grey hair, wrinkled throat, friendly eyes. In addition to Persson and the haematologist, a junior doctor sits on one of the desks, his hands in his pockets, and an anaesthetist is leaning against the doorpost, chewing gum. They explain that the junior doctor is part of the Room 1 care team, and that the anaesthetist will be administering the anaesthetic during the caesarean operation. We're also waiting for Agneta, says Persson, she's the actual surgeon, but I think we can get started. I sit on one of the office chairs and look down at the fabric, light blue denim. Persson continues in the same calm voice: Tom, your wife is very seriously ill and is deteriorating rapidly, which is why we've decided to go ahead with the C-section. The child is well, it's Karin we're worried about, or to speak plainly, she's the one we need to get through this, and the slightest intervention has a measure of risk attached to it. It seems that Karin's internal organs aren't managing to work as they should. The intensive care situation is critical for a number of reasons, the most obvious of which is that she can't oxygenate herself, also there's the imbalance between blood flow and blood pressure in her body, and her lactate is at fifteen and rising, which is extremely high for a person at rest. The haematologist interjects: That's the sort of reading top athletes have when they're straining to the point of collapse; normally if we're out for a walk we'll have a lactate of one or two, so it's an understatement to say that Karin's body is exhausted. What does that mean? I ask. The haematologist answers: Well, what it means is your wife is pregnant and gravely ill, there's the lactate reading, as John said, and the imbalance between blood flow and blood pressure, which seems to hint at sepsis, I mean blood poisoning, but we aren't going to speculate. Certainly Karin's general condition is a result of her disease. He's choosing his words carefully. I want you to be as honest as possible, I want to hear everything now, I say, and I notice that the haematologist is getting a little irritated by the way I'm swivelling on the chair. Of course, Persson responds, we have to be honest with you. Is she going to make it? I ask. Persson rests his elbows on the table and gives me an authoritative look: Tom, we're working on improving Karin's condition, but if we're being honest I can't deny that the intensive care situation is highly critical, as I explained. Just how critical do you mean? We've got the ECMO Unit on stand-by, he says. I recognise the name, but no more than that, I say. The haematologist answers: ECMO stands for Extracorporeal Membrane Oxygenation, it's a heart and lung machine, we have a unit here at Karolinska specialising in the care of patients on ECMO, and while we don't want to assume the worst and will do everything we can to avoid it, the situation *is* critical so ECMO is a Plan B, from my point of view as a blood specialist we have to win time when dealing with this type of illness. It's leukaemia, isn't it? It is, yes, he answers. What kind of leukaemia does she have? If you stop spinning on the chair for a minute I'll be able to hear you a bit better, he points out. Okay, sorry, I reply, and repeat the question. He looks down at his white gym shoes which are long and tightly laced. He mumbles his answer: Well, it's called acute myeloid leukaemia. He raises his voice: But as I was saying, we have to gain time here, first an emergency C-section, then we go in and reduce the high number of leukocytes – the white blood cells, a product of the leukaemia – and once that's done, hopefully tomorrow, I want to start the chemotherapy, which will take time, and time is what we don't have. I put my hands across the back of my head. Tom, I understand this is a lot of information for you to take in, says Persson. A week ago, I reply, the doctor at the maternity hospital took a blood test, she said everything was looking fine, and two days ago we were watching a movie together. The haematologist looks down at the table, and answers: It was probably looking fine then, but it's moved fast. He peers at me and goes on: I can't even imagine what you must be going through, now you're going to be parents and everything, it's just awful. The junior doctor reaches out to offer me a tissue. Thanks, I say, and start rolling the paper between my fingers. Myeloid leukaemia often varies from person to person – in your wife's case there's probably a connection between the speed of the disease and her pregnancy – but as John said, what we're working on now is making her better. I interrupt Callmer to ask if the chemotherapy has side effects? Cytostatic drugs do have side effects, yes, but not like they used to, we've got better at medicating against them. Okay, that's good, I say. It's worth bearing in mind, though, that even if the cytostatic treatment has the desired effect the risk of reoccurrence is high. Life is going to get tough, with a lot of ongoing treatment, but at least it's life, he says. Persson adds: But right now we're here, Karin is in the ward outside, and we're going to do everything we can to make her well again. He looks up over my shoulder and says: And here's the doctor who'll be doing the C-section. A stout woman with a bob of dark brown hair stands in the doorway. She's panting and sweating. Sorry, I got held up. I assume you must be the father? She steps forward and gives me a firm handshake: My name is Agneta, I'm the consultant at the Women's Health Clinic. She doesn't let go of my hand: I'm going to be operating on your wife. The baby is fine but your wife is seriously ill. The operation itself is not very tricky, but given the circumstances it's obviously a bigger thing, there will be more intensive care staff involved than in a normal section, as a safety precaution, but apart from that nothing out of the ordinary. She lets go of my hand. Do you have any questions? She looks at me and waits. I'd really like to be there during the delivery, I say. You'll be waiting in the room next door, then a nurse will bring you the baby. We'll have staff on standby from Neonatal, they'll take care of the baby. Your daughter will be about a month and a half premature; your wife must be in week thirty-three plus a few days. Yes, I reply. Good, well at least you're a bit more up to speed now, she says, putting her hand on my shoulder and adding: we'll see you in a moment, Tom. I'm not sure I understand, why can't I be there in the operating theatre? I ask. She looks at the anaesthetist as she answers: You'll be in the room next door, there's a window overlooking the operating theatre. So I'm not allowed to sit with Karin? Family members aren't allowed in the operating theatre, she answers. I'd rather not leave Karin right now. You'll be able to see your wife, that's just how it's done, she says, then explains that she has to go, she has an operation to get on with. The anaesthetist blinks between his silver-rimmed spectacles, spits his chewing gum into a bin, and says: I'll see what I can do, hang tight and we'll fetch you when the moment comes. Thanks a lot, I say. He nods at the other doctors, then also leaves. The haematologist leans forward as if he's about to get up: I imagine you've heard more than you can process for now, but is there anything else I can tell you? Persson looks at me, waiting for my answer. I peer down at my notepad, trying to make sense of what I have written down.

I'm sitting in the corridor outside F21 when an anaesthetic nurse holds out her porcelain-like hand. Jaleh, she says. I stand up. Has something happened? I ask. I'm supposed to fetch you and bring you to the operating theatre, she answers. For the Caesarean? Yes, the Caesarean. Now? She twists a white pearl earring. Yes, now, you can come with me, it's over there, come on. I follow her as she bounces along the corridor in her camouflage Crocs. Post-op is a large room with about twenty beds in it, separated by partition screens. Wait here, I'll just check if we have a green light, she says and goes up to a staff desk in the middle of the room where she starts to talk to someone wearing some kind of goggles who seems to be in charge. She gestures, they both look at me. His head drops forward and he picks up a telephone. She comes back and whispers: It can be a bit like that, the doctors all have their own territory. With a wink, she walks over to a storage room and searches the shelves. This one should fit you, she says, handing me a dark blue set of scrubs and a turquoise cap. Then she stands waiting in front of two steel doors that lead into the Central Operations Emergency and Trauma Unit. I feel silly, like a kid in fancy dress, especially with the ridiculous cap. Do I really have to wear this? I ask. She's walking backwards into the ward when she answers: Things have to be sterile in the operating theatre; it's not that bad, is it? So I can come into the operating theatre? Exactly. Next to Karin? Exactly. Thank you, thank you so much. The fluorescent lights reflect against the smooth plastic floor, forming a central line in the corridor. Along the sides are bright yellow refuse bins and trolleys brimming with emergency equipment. She stops and says: This is us, Emergency Room 11. Do I have time to go to the loo? I ask. Yes, she says, pointing towards a corner of the corridor. On the right, it says staff toilet but you can use it, she adds, then calls out behind me: No need to run. Only a few drips come out of me, I zip myself up and avoid the mirror. I sound like an animal when I put my fingers down my throat over the washbasin, but the contents of my stomach don't come up, it's just a dry retching. I take off my cap and rinse my face. In the vestibule by Emergency Room 11 is another washbasin, I wash my hands again. The anaesthetic nurse holds the door open for me while I knead disinfectant gel into my fingers. Don't forget the cap, she says. I put it on. The effect of the room seems to force itself on me, the burning surgical lighthead, the operation table lift, the pale blue walls, the floor pattern of rectangles and rhombi, the steel trolleys, infusion stands, monitors, an almost big-city feel of nearly twenty doctors and nurses getting themselves ready, and then Karin, wearing the same cap as me, lying in the middle of the room, her stomach obscured by a green curtain suspended between posts on wheels. You can sit here, says the anaesthetic nurse. Okay, thanks, I reply and sit by Karin's left arm. It's on a steel armrest padded with nylon. Hold her hand, she says. Okay, thanks. I work my hand into Karin's, my palm wet. On my right the anaesthetist stands by a monitor, on the phone. He takes a few quick steps forward and taps me on the shoulder: Hi there. I'm worried I might knock her somehow and interfere, I think my hands are shaking? I ask the anaesthetic nurse. She looks down at Karin's arm and turns to the anaesthetist: It's okay if he holds her hand, isn't it? He peers over his glasses and answers: No problem, the arm is good there,

25

she's strapped in as well. He looks at me and adds: Of course you should hold her hand. The staff behind the curtain are wearing surgical masks and caps covering their ears and throats, sort of flimsy balaclavas. One of them, the theatre nurse, turns around and says: Okay, let's have the run-through, surgeon goes first. The consultant answers: Agneta Arvidsson, obstetrician, consultant at the Women's Health Clinic, I'll be operating today. It's an emergency section partly because of the mother's condition, recently diagnosed with leukaemia, and partly because we're concerned the child might otherwise risk developing breathing difficulties because of high numbers of blasts in the circulation. The mother has been kept sedated since yesterday, intubated on a respirator, I'll come back to that. She returns to her preparations. One by one they introduce themselves: the nurses, assistant nurses, midwives, and doctors. I tense up about also having to introduce myself, having to stand up in my silly operation cap and give away how close I am to collapsing and maybe being carried out and separated from Karin and Livia. Only when it's the anaesthetist's turn to speak and he explains that I'm the father of the child do I feel calmer. Behind me, by one of the doors, stands a man in a white hospital uniform. He's the only one who's not wearing scrubs, apart from his cap. He stands rigid, almost like a skier: straight, strong back, firm legs, tight shoulders. When it's his turn he says: My name is Holger Kinch, I'm a doctor from ECMO, the patient has had acute respiratory fluctuations since yesterday, I'm here in case a full gas substitution is required. An assistant nurse stands next to me and reads out what it says on Karin's identity tag. I hear a voice from the other side of the room, repeating her social security number. More nurses come forward and read from the identity tag and more voices echo them at the other end of the room. I forgot, whispers the anaesthetic nurse. She's holding a surgical mask: Put this on. I try but get it stuck around my throat, You have to put those behind your ears, she points out, helping me extricate myself from the rubber bands. When I manage to get it on the sound of my own breathing drowns everything else out, I have to hold my breath to follow what's being said around me. Someone calls out: Pre-Op Skin Prep completed, sterility confirmed. I squeeze Karin's hand. The anaesthetic nurse puts a glass of water on the floor. Thanks, I say, pulling down my mask and drinking. She squats while the consultant talks about the blood loss they can expect. How are you holding up? she asks. I had a splitting headache before, but it's better now, thanks. Okay, let me know if you want to ask anything. Thanks. I try to dry my hands on the hospital gown, but all I do is spread my sticky sweat over the plastic. The operation nurse raises her voice: Are we all agreed that we'll check status whenever necessary? They respond in unison: Yes. The consultant says: Making the first incision now at 14.21 . . . today . . . She looks around. After a pause, the assistant nurse says: Twentieth of March. Someone laughs. Well, that's what happens when you're overworked. Right, the twentieth of March, says the consultant. The anaesthetic nurse hurries over to a pump rack and starts turning a valve on some sort of cartridge, then adjusts the cannula in Karin's arm. The anaesthetist says: Well done, Jaleh, that's looking better. A nurse holding on Karin's breathing mask says: Coughing, thin, bloody slime. Karin's body starts shaking imperceptibly, but I feel it too, like tiny tremors running through my hand. I hear them talking behind the curtain, there's a clattering of steel, a sucking sound, I squeeze Karin's hand tighter and I whisper: I'm here, darling. I bend forward, I close my eyes, hear some scattered applause and a scream, shrill and horrible but also beautiful, sustained, so incredibly loud; I recognise the consultant's voice: The time is 14.35, enter as time of birth. I open my eyes and stand up without letting go of Karin's hand. The consultant is holding Livia by the legs, as if she's bleeding prey. If the father can hear me now, a baby that doesn't yell is a bad sign, this is excellent, you have a strong voice, yes you do, you're a lovely girl, says the consultant. I don't have time to process what's happening, I'm suddenly chasing after the team from Neonatal, one of them carrying Livia in a white towel, she's pink and sticky, and the other pushing a cart with the placenta in a kidney dish. The anaesthetic nurse follows me out and as we reach the door she points: That's the nurse from Neo, that's the midwife, and the one by the oxygen is the children's doctor, the paediatrician. They've put Livia on a bench that's apparently known as a neonatal resuscitation table. Livia is given oxygen via a mask, the paediatrician listens into a stethoscope. The heart sounds good, she says, then adds, with great composure: She's a really beautiful little girl, congratulations. The others agree. I suppose you say that to everyone, I say. Yes, she responds, but one doesn't always mean it. There are two clamps at the end of the umbilical cord, which is light turquoise and about twenty centimetres long. The nurse looks at me and asks: Can I give you a hug? Okay, I say, and she embraces me. Do you have a name for her? she asks. Livia, I answer. Olivia, that's lovely, would Dad like to cut Olivia's umbilical cord? Will I hurt her? I ask. No, it's just blood vessels and connective tissue, it's like cutting your nails, she says, handing me a pair of surgical scissors. No, here, you cut here, she says and points. I cut, she applauds. Tom, someone wants to talk to you, says the anaesthetic nurse and nods towards the emergency room. I turn around and see the anaesthetist on the other side of the small rectangular window; he pulls down his mask and gives me a thumbs up, but just before I realise it's him standing there I have a sense that it's actually Karin, and in that instant I almost call out: Everything's fine, darling. The midwife holds up the wet placenta. She points at the umbilical cord, which points upwards like an old Chinese drawing of a tree trunk, the veins like branches and the amniotic sac the crown of leaves, and she says: You can understand why it's called the Tree of Life. Yes, I answer. Do you want to keep it? Keep it?! I exclaim. Yes, she answers. No thanks. Don't panic, I usually offer, some people want to eat the placenta. Are you joking? No. I certainly don't fancy a bit of placenta, I say. No, fair enough, it's usually the mothers, it's supposed to have a number of positive effects, stimulating milk production and balancing the hormones. Anyway, I was only asking. Right, well I had no idea it could do that, I say, and lean over Livia. Can I hold her hand? Yes, of course, says the paediatrician. It's so small it doesn't even reach around my finger, light red nails, so tiny. The paediatrician peers at me: I'll tell you one thing, your daughter is a real whopper bearing in mind she's one and a half months premature, but she needs to go into Neonatal for some help just to get started.

It's dark apart from a bright lamp over Livia's incubator. Her face isn't pretty, isn't sweet; it's thin but also swelled up, wrinkled, chapped like an old, sick person. I see no trace of Karin's sanguinity in her. It's as if Karin's blood disease has corroded her. She's got a nappy on, and a pale lemon-yellow hat, and a silicone band across her nose with an oxygen tube curling over her little head into her nose, like a space mask. We'll be feeding your daughter intravenously with PreNAN Discharge, says the nurse. Uh-huh, and what's that? I ask. It's like breast-milk with a bit of extra zing; you should google it if you want to know more. I'm sure it's fine, I don't have the Internet on my phone anyway, I say. Sounds sensible, these days people just sit about fiddling with their phones, she says. I tell her it's mainly because I can't afford it, then, while we're talking, Livia goes quiet and starts moving her head around as if she's looking for something. Did you talk to your daughter while she was in the womb? asks the nurse. I suppose I did, now and then. How did you do it? What do you mean, how? Because she recognises your voice, she points out. No, really? I don't think so, I say. Oh I do think so, you know I've picked up a few things while I've been working here, which is a long time. Okay, if you say so, I say, keeping my eyes on Livia. She says Livia's not just reacting to the sound of our voices, she's listening, it's quite clear. The other nurse comes over from an incubator at the other end of the ward, and asks: Did you talk right up against the bump? Yes, but mainly I just sang, it calmed Livia's mother down, I answer. Just imagine, even in the womb we're so receptive, she says. Absolutely incredible, says the other nurse. Excuse me a moment, I say, and hurry into the corridor.

In front of the bathroom mirror I notice I'm still wearing the dark blue scrubs and cap. I throw the entire get-up into the bin and sit on the toilet lid. I check my phone: fifteen missed calls, one from Mum and four from Dad. I read the texts and reply to a couple of them. Livia has fallen asleep by the time I come back. Her right foot has been bandaged. I had to put some dressing on her foot, she kept wanting to kick off the catheter the whole time – a determined little lady. Do you want to hold her? Won't that wake her up? I'm sure she'd like to sleep close to her dad for a while. Okay. She fetches a shirt, which she refers to as a nursing smock. Everything has to be sterile, this is all we've got, she says. Okay, fine. I take off my T-shirt and put on the soft top, which is open down to the navel. She places Livia across my chest. After a while I call the nurse over, she asks how it's going. I'm breathing so fast, I say, do you think it might wake her? Oh no, it's fine, she looks quite happy. Uh-huh, yeah, but isn't it getting a bit hot? I'm so bloody hot. She puts her hand on Livia's throat. No, she's sleeping really well. Someone's looking for you, says the other nurse, gesturing towards the corridor. It's the anaesthetist from the emergency room. Hello there, hi, he says, just to say Karin's

31

readings are looking a lot better, she's back in CIC for dialysis, I thought you'd want to know. Thanks a lot, I answer. He rubs disinfectant gel into his hands and comes closer. He caresses Livia's back with his finger. Amazing, has she opened her eyes yet? I look at the nurse, who smiles: You're the father, not me. I don't think she's opened her eyes yet, I answer. It's just the best when they do, he says, and gives me a thumbs up on his way out. The nurses give him slightly smitten gazes: That doesn't happen every day, doctors from other wards visiting. Or maybe you know him? No, I answer.

In Room 1, a bag of Karin's blood is suspended in the dialysis machine. Blood is pumped out, blood is pumped in. The doctor in charge of it is as grey as the consultant at Söder Hospital, but bony like me and my father. He becomes animated when I ask him about the machine. It removes the waste products from the blood, it's the same principle as in Laval's separator, you know, the guy who separated the cream from the milk, he says. Uh-huh, okay, I answer. A nurse from Neonatal has taken a photo of Livia, which she's already developed and laminated. In the photo, Livia is lying in the open incubator with the oxygen tube. She has her mother's mouth, the same vermilion colour, the pronounced Cupid's bow, and under the photo is written in marker pen: Livia 20/3-12. I look for a place to put it. The nurse watches me. Here, she says, reaching towards a console and handing me a roll of surgical tape. She suggests I stick the photo up on a horizontal aluminium beam behind the bed. But then Karin can't see Livia, I point out. No, I suppose that's true, what about here? she suggests, pulling out the adjustable bar of the table lamp. The photo ends up taped slightly wonkily above Karin. I sit on the stool and take her wrist in my hand. Hi, darling, I wanted you to know that Livia is well. In the corner of my eye I can see Persson in his light blue hospital issue shirt. It's good that you're talking to her, I often recommend that, he says, looking at the photo. Congratulations on your daughter, he adds. Thanks, I answer. Tom, can I talk with you for a moment? Has something happened? Stay calm, this is about you, he answers. His hands are folded across his belly, like a vicar, as he squats down. I've been through similar situations, I've sat there just as you're doing now, he says, eyeing me compassionately. Uh-huh, okay, thanks a lot. There are three things you need to remember now, just three things, three important things, he explains and shifts his position, going on in a voice of unrelinquishing gravity: First, sleep, you have to sleep or you won't be able to sustain this, second, food, you mustn't forget to eat, or you won't have the strength, third, get out of the hospital as often as you can or you'll start going round the bend.

I run into David outside the elevators to the Neonatal ward. He's sweaty, puffing, his hands shaking as usual, a sort of congenital nervousness which in some curious way disappears as soon as he meets people he doesn't know, after which he becomes self-confident and talkative. He's brought a teddy bear for Livia, which he takes out of the plastic bag as if it's some kind of curiosity he found on the way. The nurse puts the teddy on a shelf above the incubator. Thanks, David, that's really nice,

I say. He sits there watching me holding Livia in my arms. He asks the nurse a couple of questions. Then she asks: Do you have any children yourself? A daughter, she turned two a couple of weeks ago. Tom is her godfather, he adds. David, sorry, that's so embarrassing, I say. David laughs and replies: If you were the type who remembered your own birthday, then it might be a problem. He turns to the nurse: Tom's going to be thirty-four in a couple of days, he's probably forgotten. Actually, only a few days ago Karin was asking me what present I'd like, I say. David ejects his portion of snuff with his finger and runs his hands over his shaved scalp. When he's sad or serious he looks like a seal.

The Neonatal family room is opposite the lifts. Unlike the family room at CIC it's spacious and generously furnished. A large mint-green settee by an oval table, a flat-screen TV, two rectangular dining tables, a bar counter, dishwasher, freezer, fridge, kitchen sink, several microwave ovens, and masses of toys. The bedroom's next to the kitchen, a bed and locker is all that fits in there; it has a view of the inside courtyard, bushes, trees, and street lights surrounded by high brick walls. David is lying on the sofa, tapping on his laptop. How are things with Karin now? he asks. No change, I answer. Have her parents met Livia? Not yet. They haven't seen Karin either, they're obviously desperate to. I've told them they can visit tomorrow, but it makes me feel disloyal to Karin – she only wanted me to be with her. Okay, but don't you think it's heavy going for them not to be able to see her? She's not a child, David. We're a family, it would feel pretty weird if they spent their time sitting in there;

that bloody room she's lying in has become like a part of our flat. But she's still their daughter, he replies. She's my Karin. Yeah, that's true, he concedes. It has to be my decision and Karin's, I say. I know this is important to her as well; she wanted it to be just me by her side. Tom, I know you, I can understand this is just unbelievably hard, the whole thing is nuts, but I think it would be good if you let them see her. It's not as simple as that, David. What's not so simple? You have a good relationship with them, don't you? Yeah, we do, but David, I can't talk about this any more now, I'm so tired. I think it'd be better if you let them see her, he says. I reckon Karin would have wanted that too. I sit down next to him. He takes off his headphones. Can you stay the night tonight? I ask. If you like, yeah, sure, I'll just let Kristina know. Thanks, David. You remember I snore really badly though, yeah? It doesn't matter, I answer. Tom, go and lie down. I have to work a bit longer, and if I can't stay the night then at least I'll stay until you're asleep. You shouldn't be on your own right now. David has turned onto his side, watching me. Shit, Tom, you're so tired, your eyes are completely bloodshot. Last weekend Karin was painting her toenails and laughing at an episode of *The Sarah Silverman Program*, I tell him. This has gone so bloody fast, I don't get it. Yeah, it's unbelievable. She was laughing, I stress. Does she like Silverman? She was laughing, I tell him again.

At quarter past twelve I wander down to CIC to say goodnight to Karin. The automated female voice in the lift says: Level zero two. And then: Level zero zero, entrance level. I hurry out as soon as the doors open. In F21 I ask the doctor who lets me in if I can't just have the code to the door; it's a nuisance always to have to ring the bell and explain why I'm here. I feel as if I'm disturbing them, I add. I'm not allowed to give the code to next of kin, he answers, but really, you're not disturbing anyone. I get stopped again at the door to Karin's room: We're just changing the sheets, you can come in in a minute, says the nurse. Is everything okay? I ask. We're just washing her, she answers. John said I could be with her as long as she's not in surgery, I say. We won't be a moment, you can come in shortly, she says and closes the door. I stand for a while in the vestibule before returning to the corridor, but then I turn around and hurry back. I knock, open the door, and step inside. Look, sorry, I completely get that you have your work to get on with and your procedures, but I was shut out at Söder Hospital and it's not bloody happening again. I go on: I sat with Karin during her Caesarean, and believe me, it wouldn't be the first time I've seen her taking a shit. I sit on the stool at her bedside and adjust the lamp so that the photo of Livia ends up in front of her. The nurses study me but after a moment get back to their work. They lift one leg at a time, discard a sticky underlay, and wash her with wet wipes. I stroke Karin's fringe as gently as I can.

The Family Room. Lillemor stands in the doorway to the sleeping alcove. She's wearing a faded nightie and says she's taken a sleeping tablet. She's made her bed in one of the bunks and put Norén's *Diary of a Dramatist* on the pillow. How are you, Lillemor? I tried to read, it didn't work, she answers. I can imagine, I say. Sven and Måns are on Lidingö island, she says. Right, okay, well it's so great that Måns came, it was really good to see him. There's a room called Livia's Room on Gotland, she says, the gallery in Körsbärsgården, maybe that's where Karin got the name from? I don't know, she never actually mentioned the name before. She likes that gallery. Yes, she does. Oscar's wife is called Livia, you know, the actress. Yeah, no, actually I didn't know, Lillemor. It's a lovely name, Livia, Livia Lagerlöf. Yes, that feels right. Lillemor clutches a little grey ball made of suede, no bigger than an egg, it looks like a pincushion. I look down at it. Are you sewing? I ask, trying to smile at her. She glances down at it – Oh, no, apparently it's called an anti-stress ball. Right, okay. It's silly, perhaps, but I've started holding it when I'm walking about, it's nice to squeeze it. It feels a bit like Karin's hand when she was small and I would walk her to school. What primary did she go to? I actually don't know. Bo School, she replies. Oh that's right, okay. Lillemor hides behind the door and says: Goodnight, Tom, call me if you want to, I'll leave my phone on. Same to you, Lillemor, goodnight, I answer, and wait until I hear her lock the door.

I've learnt to like the plastic floor in the corridors at Karolinska, smooth and white as if covered in condensation, like artificial ice. As a child I wanted the whole of Huddinge to be covered in ice. I was fascinated by the Ice Age, I fantasised about a new Ice Age so I could skate everywhere. On my skates I was strong and even quicker than the birds. I'll avoid lifts from now on. I want to be able to glide away whenever the urge arises. In the lifts I'm locked in with mirrors or people I've never met who somehow remind me of Karin. Only fleetingly, never more than an arm movement or a tone of voice, but there she is, just as always, next to me in the lift, only she doesn't know me, she has no idea who I am.

Livia's incubator is no longer in Room 15. I stop one of the Neonatal nurses I recognise from yesterday. Livia's not here, where is she, what's happened? She answers me in a whisper: She's fine. So where is she then? I burst out. We moved her out of Neo-Iva because she no longer needs breathing assistance, she answers. Okay, but you might have called and let me know, I was only in the room over there. Well in that case we're sorry, I suppose we just thought there was no need. We only moved your daughter a little further down the corridor, we did it early this morning. She's in Monitoring Room 9 now. Where's that? I ask. Just follow the corridor straight ahead to Neonatal, past the entrance, and then it's the room directly on your right. Okay, thanks, I reply, and break into a run.

On the floor inside the door of the Neonatal section big letters proclaim: *Stop!* And then, in smaller letters: *Wash your hands*. Hanging from the ceiling is a large sign written in both Swedish and English: *Please wash your hands*. The assistant nurse, who comes to meet me, walks very slowly and talks in a low voice, her forehead flaming red with acne. All the staff in the section move quietly, a reassuring calmness about them. Livia's incubator is by the window. There are another two incubators in this part of the room, and four incubators in the adjoining room. In real terms it's one big room divided by an open area and a small reception. A piece of fabric has been draped over Livia's incubator. I was going to feed her in a minute, maybe you'd like to do it. Thanks, but I have to go down to CIC. That's where Livia's mother is, I say, lifting the fabric. How's Livia's mother doing? she asks. I don't know, I mean, things aren't good, I answer. Livia lies there with her arms and legs stretched out; she has a small yellow dummy in her mouth, and is wearing a pink babygrow, and a white hat with sort of teddy bear ears on it. While keeping her eyes on Livia, the nurse says: The doctor is coming by to have a look at her today or tomorrow. Where did you get the clothes from? I ask. We have them here, she says. Livia's mother is a bit allergic to pink, I point out. I just grabbed what was there, you can change them if you like? I wouldn't mind a different hat . . . If you've brought your own clothes you're obviously welcome to use them, she says. Forget it, I only just woke up, I'm talking off the top of my head, it's fine like it is, thanks. She leans her chin over the incubator and inhales through her nostrils. There's a bit of a smell, I think, maybe you'd like to change her? she asks. I don't know, I answer. She lifts Livia's legs and instructs me. I'm so tired that I just do exactly what she tells me. She looks down into the nappy and explains: That's called meconium, poppy juice they used to say in the olden days, it's what's formed in the child's intestines while it's still in the womb. Uh-huh, okay. Was that the first time you changed her? she asks. I don't want to keep the nappy. She looks back at me, confused, almost scared, then turns and discards the nappy in a refuse bin by the door.

Persson is just coming out of Room 1, he almost bumps into me: Hello, how are things with you and your daughter? We're fine, how's the night been here? The lactate is still rising, which we don't want, so we're working on bringing it down. Okay, I say. It's almost certainly a result of the leukaemia, we're X-raying her today so we can rule out anything else. I get out my writing pad and say: Karin's father is basically a doctor, what should I tell him? I'm not sure I follow, he says, just tell him what I told you, he's welcome to talk directly to me if he prefers. It's Karin's wish that I talk to you direct, I say, but I figured if I tell you my father-in-law is a doctor I might get straighter answers out of you. We're not withholding anything, Tom. No, I'm not accusing you of that, but you're very careful about how you present things, you say the glass is half-full, not half-empty. He considers this thoughtfully then looks away down the corridor. I go on: Only a glass that's being *refilled* can be half-full, if the liquid is about to disappear then it's half-empty, and . . . oh forget it, look, I want you to talk to me using the proper terms. I don't want you to interpret those terms for me, talk to me as if I was a doctor, that's all I'm asking. I think I understand what you're saying, but we can't and we mustn't guess, he says. Which is exactly what I mean, so what can I tell Karin's father? He looks down at the floor and answers: Karin has an extreme and sustained lactic acidosis and a very high lactate, as we've told you. I can understand it's a lot for you to take in and I'm more than happy to run through it again with you. My view is that her illness has been a complication of acute leukaemia, but it could very well be combined with acute infection. We're starting the cytostatic treatment today, but Tom, your wife is gravely ill, both in the short and the longer term, and all we can do now is help Karin pull through. In passing he also mentions something that sounds like ARDS or it may have been an English pronunciation, as in RDS.

The nurse dabs Karin's lips with a sponge. She scrutinises Karin's face. There, dear, I won't bother you any more, she says, then catches sight of me: Hi, come in, I should tell you right away that Karin is bleeding from her vagina after the C-section, they've been here from Gynae to have a look, just so you know. Okay, I answer. You may notice bleeding, I mean, just so you don't worry. Okay, now I know, thanks. I sit on the stool. She looks at the photo of Livia: I have to say, your daughter is so lovely. Yeah, thanks, I say. Livia, that's a nice name. Yes, it is, thanks, I say. She smiles, I smile back. She puts her hand on Karin's arm. Karin, you have such a lovely daughter, and a fine man who's here with you all the time, she says. Karin's weight must have gone up by forty kilos since I saw her yesterday. I learn that this is because of the copious amounts of blood plasma, sodium bicarbonate, and glucose that the doctors are trying to get into her circulation, although most of it accumulates under her skin. With the thin sheet over her she looks like a gigantic jellyfish. She has a support cushion under her right arm, and a saturation sensor on her ring finger.

Sorry, but does she have to have that gadget on her ring finger? I ask. The nurse looks a bit puzzled, asks what I mean. It's almost a bit symbolic, I tell her. Oh, you mean like a wedding ring? Yes. They're usually worn on the left hand, she says. Oh sod it, it doesn't matter, forget what I said. Karin's belongings are kept locked up in a cupboard, if that's what you meant? Okay, thanks, but she doesn't even have a wedding ring, I say. She smiles at me again. The specialist is sitting by a computer, writing, a dictionary open next to the keyboard. I turn the pages of my writing pad. My notes are careless, sometimes small, squiggly, hardly even legible, sometimes firm and angular. Anders, sorry, I say to him. The specialist turns to me. He seems awkward about my knowing his first name, and then, more as a statement than a question, I blurt out: RDS. He stands up, puts his hands in his pockets, and comes towards me. We generally just have to hope it sorts itself out, he says. 'Just have to hope'? He continues hesitantly: It can only heal itself spontaneously. You should probably talk to John about this, what has he told you? More or less what you just said, I answer. Okay then, if there's anything else just ask, he says before sitting back down and resuming his writing. Anders, again, I'm sorry, I need to hear this over and over, how serious is RDS? He leans his elbows on the table, turns his head towards the window, and answers: It's certainly serious. Most people who develop the condition are already gravely ill with something else, I mean, it's an inflammation of the lung with emission of fluids and deflation of the alveoli; the inflammation causes damage to the body, oedema, fluid in the lungs. He looks round at me, then goes on: It's especially serious bearing in mind that it's caused by leukaemia. I make a note and say: What's the disease actually called? It's called Acute Respiratory Distress Syndrome, ARDS, people used to call it lung shock. I get a feeling the cytostatic treatment is going to be important now, I say. Yes, we want the cytostatic treatment to turn everything around, we're starting it today. It won't cure her ARDS, but hopefully it'll help your wife to recover enough strength to start self-healing.

On the way back to Neonatal I stop off at the family room. Sven and Måns are sitting in the sofa, talking. Lillemor is sitting at the kitchen table, leafing through the evening paper. I sink into one of the armchairs and say: I just wanted to update you a bit. Okay, thanks, answers Sven, his hernia brace creaking slightly over his stomach. I more or less start reading out the notes from my writing pad, and try to explain as best as I can. Lillemor stares at the floor, and Sven corrects me a couple of times on my pronunciation of certain medical terms. Måns directs his questions to Sven. He has the same high brow as Karin, but a larger head, the hard cranium of a bull. They check everything on their smartphones and tablets as I talk. I hope you understand me, why I've been uncommunicative, I say. We understand, answers Sven. Karin could hardly have expected this, says Måns. Who knows, maybe she did, I say, either way I was going to suggest that you visit her today, I've told them you're coming, and Måns responds: So let me get this straight, you're saying we can only visit Karin today, just a short one, then that's it? Please, Måns, sorry if I use

Lena as an example, but if she was lying in there and had told you before she was put to sleep, *only you can come in Måns and no one else*, then surely you'd be saying the same thing to Lena's parents? We understand, said Sven. A moment later, Måns calls out after me in the corridor. He embraces me. I don't want us to be on bad terms, he says. I don't feel we're on bad terms, I answer. He hugs me again and says: Tom, if you need anything, anything at all, we're here. Thanks, Måns. I'll take Mum back to Lidingö tonight, she's ready to pass out, you know how she gets, she blames herself for all sorts of things. Yeah, okay, good, do it. I'm just so tired, Måns. Yeah, I understand it's chaotic. Thanks for letting us visit Karin, Mum really needed to. He embraces me again: And when it's a good time for you, Mum and Dad really want to meet Livia, it would be good for them to have something positive to focus on.

The midwife from this morning catches sight of me by the entrance to Neonatal. She waves a key and says: We've got you a room. She seems incredibly nervous so I ask her if something's happened. No, but, I mean the room is really for mothers recovering after giving birth. She leads me to a lavender-blue door with a round window of frosted glass, and a sign: Family Room 1. I look inside, and notice a bare burnt-ochre wall right outside the window. How long can I stay here? I ask. Until further notice, a week or two, until your daughter can go home. Okay, even if Livia's mother is still here? I can't answer that, she says. Okay, thanks. But if someone from Maternity comes along and needs the room we'll have to find you something else, she says. I go inside and look around. My own shower, toilet, a patient bed with valves overhead for oxygen and air, a fold-out bed against the wall, a refrigerator for formula and breast milk, a noticeboard, a changing table. She hands over the key and leads me to the monitoring room. Someone has stuck a laminated sheet to Livia's incubator. It says: *Livia Lagerlöf. Mother: Karin. Father: Tom.* The midwife pushes over an armchair with a footrest. I take off my T-shirt and sit down. Have you done this before? she asks. I've got the fact that it has to be sterile, I'm with you that far, but I've never fed her intravenously, I say. She picks up Livia, who's only wearing a nappy, and puts a blanket around us. She fills a syringe with milk replacement and connects it to the tube going into Livia's nose, and says: Press in one black mark's worth per minute; if you do it too quickly she'll only vomit, but if you do it too slow she'll scream, and make sure there aren't any air bubbles in the syringe, or she'll have gas in her tummy. Okay, I think I've got it. My weight has come tumbling down, I was skinny before all this, my ribs stick out, I'm horribly pale, full of veins and blackheads, the sun hasn't touched me in over a year. Livia sniffs at me. Mine can't be a very nice breast to lie against, I whisper to her, but it's all I've got. She puts her ear against me and sleeps for almost an hour before the midwife comes back and asks how it's going. Quite well, I think, but she's still sleeping. She looks at the milk-filled syringe and says: You can keep feeding her even while she's asleep. Oh, okay. She squeezes the syringe and adds: The milk's gone cold, I think we'll have to do this again. Back in Family Room 1, I pull down the folding bed and lie down on it. I look at the perfectly made patient bed on the other side of the room. I go to the window; obliquely to the right I can see the grey sky between pitch-black metal rooftops, and to the left a gravel terrace jutting out, a work of art on it, large, colourful glass eggs piled up on a pool-like mirror. I can hear the TV from Family Room 2.

Callmer has brought two specialists with him into the little room in F21. A table and four plastic chairs occupy the whole space, the white walls are bare. The two young women seem afraid of me, they maintain a slight but nonetheless noticeable distance when they shake hands. Callmer asks if it's all right that they take part in the conversation. Sure, I answer. How are you feeling, Tom? he asks. How do I answer that? Well, you tell me. I guess I'm okay, I say. You don't have to be a doctor to see that you're having a tough time: you're charged with adrenalin and showing all the standard symptoms, dilated pupils, quick movements, eyes darting around in all directions. That sounds like what I'm normally like, I answer, otherwise I'd take offence at that. Tom, I'm only saying it so you don't forget about yourself. Yeah, I got that, thanks. Callmer looks away and explains something to the specialists, pointing with his ballpoint pen at something in their files. A cold light from the fluorescent tubes overhead. I've already prepared myself that Karin may not pull through, I say. Callmer lifts his chin towards me, tucks his biro into his breast pocket, and says: Right now that's not where we are. He leans back in his chair. Two deep folds of skin separate his jaw from his cheeks, and there's dried blood on his throat from shaving. He scratches the corners of his mouth, then continues: As John said yesterday, Karin is with us here at CIC, she's certainly ill, seriously ill, but she's alive, Tom, and anyway I don't know that anyone can really prepare themselves for something like that. Okay, I'll rephrase that, I say. I'm choosing to make the assumption that Karin is not going to survive in order to prepare myself mentally; nothing is more frightening to me now than the idea of being surprised, I can't handle it, it's about having some semblance of control in a situation where I'm totally powerless. He rests his elbows on the table and looks curious. Do you work as a therapist or some-thing like that? he asks. What? It's not an unusual profession, he adds. Karin has been ill before, that's all, I tell him. He looks down into his plastic folder, picks up a thick wad of notes, skims the pages and says, while occasionally looking up at the specialists: AVM which was embolised, that was in the nineties, and then she had gamma knife radiosurgery in . . . 2001. I was with her when she got the cyst, that was in 2004, I say. He keeps looking through the notes. It developed in the scar tissue from the gamma knife, I add. Was it surgically removed? Yeah, they operated, I answer. Do you know if it was done here at Karolinska? Yes, the surgeon was called Marsala, it was a massive cyst, grew rapidly. Taavi is incredibly skilled, we were students together in fact, anyway, well, and now this, poor girl . . . but the child is fine? Yes, she's fine, thanks. What about Karin's parents, how are they handling all this? They're in shock, but they have each other for support, I answer. Callmer replaces the notes in the file and says: I've said it before, I'll say it again, against this type of blood disease one has to gain time. He says nothing else that I haven't heard before. They sit in front of me in a semi-circle, their hands on the table as if they're preparing to grab me in case I collapse or make a lunge at them.

In Room 1, the nurses are changing the sheets. They notice me looking at the imprints of their hands, which stay on Karin's body. She has so much fluid under her skin, that's why it gets like this, says one of the nurses. I get out a little orange blanket from my bag. The midwives at Neo said I could leave it with Karin, it's been with Livia, it has her smell on it, I say. They look astonished, and exchange a glance, but then help me spread the blanket over Karin's breast under the unwieldy respirator tube. Did you get a sleeping tablet? asks the same nurse. Yes, thanks. Good, you need to sleep. They change the oxygen mask and calibrate the respirator. Persson appears in the doorway, in casual clothes: jeans, a windbreaker, a chestnut leather briefcase in one hand. He casts his eye on Karin, nods to the nurses, and says he's had a response from the cardio X-ray. I can tell by the way he says this that something is wrong: What's happened? Karin's heart is struggling, she's getting medication for that as well, he answers. So it's her heart now? This is how it is, everything in the body is connected, if one organ starts going on strike it's not unusual for others to do the same. Is it serious? She has what's called a dilated ventricle on the right, it's been stretched, it can't function as it's supposed to, which also affects the left

48

ventricle, so we're giving her medication to counteract the problem. What sort of medication? He seems surprised by the question but answers as calmly as ever: It's called Levosimendan, it's what you administer in situations like this. He puts down his briefcase, removes his glasses and polishes them with a corner of his shirt, then one of the nurses who has stayed behind says to me: Tom, if I don't have time to come back before you go, goodnight, hope you get some rest. She also leaves the room, carrying the sheets. Are you making those notes for your father-in-law? asks Persson. No, I want to be able to explain it all to Karin if she wakes up. You know, Karin can see our medical reports any time, he says. I know that, but that's your version, I point out. He peers sceptically at me. It's stressful taking notes all the time, Tom, you need to rest as well, remember, eat, sleep, and get out of the hospital as often as you can. But I have a baby lying up there, I can't leave the hospital, I answer. He puts on his glasses, picks up his briefcase, and says on his way out: Just a walk in the park at some point in the day, you can allow yourself that. Later, on my way to Neonatal, I take a detour and stop at the sculpture, those large, colourful glass eggs I saw from the window of Family Room 1, now shining in the dark. On a copper plaque it says the work is entitled *To Mother*.

Stefan has brought twelve pieces of sushi with him. He scrutinises my gym shoes while I sit eating on the guest bed. I stare at the brick wall outside the window. Tompa, he says, those shoes of yours reek, I can smell them from here. I don't think anyone cares, I answer. Didn't you bring a spare pair? No, I don't have any others. He washes the insoles under running water and puts them on the windowsill to dry. Livia, she's so bloody lovely, Tompa, she looks like you, has your mouth. I think she looks like Karin, especially the mouth. Yeah, I guess she does, he answers and lies on the other bed. What was that tablet the doctor gave you? he asks after a while. I don't know. Can I have a look? he says, reaching out. I give him the tablet with a bit of the foil casing. He inspects it under the bedside lamp. Shit, Nitrazepam, he says. Is that good? I ask. It's what my clients call a dry booze-up, it's good shit, Tompa. I don't like his nickname for me, but Stefan is the only one of my mates who calls me that, he's also my oldest friend, we've known one another since we were babies; when he says Tompa it's with a voice that resounds through my whole life. I lie on the guest bed but I'm so tired that I don't have the strength to get up and fetch some water. I chew down the sleeping tablet.

Stefan yells behind me: Run, Tompa! He sprints behind me, carrying my gym shoes. I hit the entryphone button. Stefan is out of breath. Put these on, Tompa. He puts the shoes down and steadies me. Inside Room 1 I can see nothing but white, light blue, and green uniforms, Stefan holds onto me by both arms. On the white polished floor by the metal legs of the bed among all the orthopaedic shoes I catch sight of Livia's orange blanket. Then I recognise a straight, strong back from Emergency Room 11. I call out, or rather Stefan calls out: What's going on? Kinch turns to us: We're flat out here, he answers. One of the nurses helps me to a chair.

I took a sleeping tab a couple of hours ago, I tell the nurse, I'm just out of it. Crap, okay, wait here, I'll fix it, just sit there, he answers, then returns holding a small silvery bag with a nozzle at the end. Its contents are like jelly. Get that down you, he says, pressing firmly on my shoulders. He has a heavy, square body, and flowing locks. He reminds me of a hockey coach I used to have. I hear Stefan's voice: Tompa, I'll wait outside. Persson sits down in front of me, he has hurriedly thrown on a white doctor's coat over his normal clothes. His mouth and eyes are scrunched up, he holds onto the chair and leans back. Tom, it's good you came so quickly, Karin's condition has deteriorated in the night, first her circulation and then also her respiration. Okay, okay, is it serious? Tom, we can't wait any longer with the ECMO treatment. He pats me on the arm and adds: We're in a difficult situation here. Okay, thanks. The nurse gives me a glass of orange juice and a cheese sandwich. He stands next to me muttering to himself while tenderly squeezing my shoulder: Shit, oh shit. Kinch takes my hand and gives it a shake. So I understand this is your wife, he says. She's my Karin, right, I answer. Holger, ECMO Unit, he says. I'm Tom, sorry, I'm so bloody groggy. Kinch lets go of my hand, he stares at me as if he has just noticed something in my eyes. He took a sleeping tab a few hours ago, the nurse interjects. But you know where you are and what's happening? asks Kinch. I know where I am, but not what's happening, I answer. Your wife has lactic acidosis, ninety saturation with ninety-five in oxygen supply, serious hypoglycaemia, low blood pressure despite medication, haemodynamically

51

worsening despite medication, we now also suspect lysis of the red blood cells. Sorry, I didn't follow a word of that, I say. He shakes his head: Tom, I'm the one who should be apologising, I was told earlier that you wanted detailed information, which in all honesty I just don't have right now. Let's try this, then: your wife is in such a bad state that we're here from the ECMO Unit, okay? Okay. What's going to happen now is that we put your wife on ECMO, we have to do it right away, it can't wait, one needle in her groin and one in her throat, we take over the entire gaseous exchange, then we'll bring your wife across to our unit, okay? Okay. This must feel so unreal to you, he says, peering at me over the top of his glasses. Earlier you told me ECMO was Plan B, I answer. He puts his hands on my knees and says: We're in proper hell now, you're right in the middle of it. Thanks for being honest about it, I answer. He stands up and goes back to the circle of doctors. Two people in surgical scrubs come into the room. The nurse comes and takes my glass. Who are they? I ask him. That's the perfusionist, he's specially trained in ECMO, and she's the operation nurse, he answers. They've brought a sort of multi-level trolley with a computer on it, a bit like the dialysis machine but more complicated, with tubes, pumps, cylinders, monitors, displays. One of the doctors speaks up: Ready for cannulation.

I peer up at the beige suspended ceiling in the corridor, tiles of mineral wool; in the doorway of an adjoining room stands a man wearing a hospital uniform much the same as those worn by Karin's nurses. He stares at me. Next of kin can't stand in the corridor, he says at last. Okay, and who are you? Does it matter? I haven't seen you before, I point out. He scratches his throat, steps into the corridor, and glances over towards Room 1. Is that your wife in there? Who are you? I ask. He changes tack, suddenly seems a little ashamed of himself and starts explaining that he's doing a bit of overtime, but is interrupted by voices in the anteroom, the perfusionist, Kinch, and another three people come out, and when I look back at him he's gone. Kinch is holding an internal telephone which is ringing and blinking. He comes up to me and says: This is very embarrassing, we have a bed shortage in the ECMO Unit, I was just told about it, but not to worry, we've spoken to TICC, they have space, they are well accustomed to dealing with patients in ECMO, excuse me. He shuffles off and answers his telephone. You're standing up, says the specialist. Yes, but I took a sleeping tablet a few hours ago, I answer, I feel as if I'm wearing a diving helmet. Maybe it's not just the tablet? he points out. TICC? I ask. Yes, Thoracic Intensive Care Clinic, he answers. Chest and things like that? Precisely, heart and lung and related organs, he answers, adding: They're highly competent, one of the most prestigious units in Sweden to work in. Kinch positions himself between us and, while hammering the internal telephone against the palm of his hand, says: We have to bring her through the basements, it's the only way. It must be a kilometre to TICC, says the specialist. Kinch looks at me when he says: Moving her is not going to be a walk in the park, we have to push your wife through the underground passages with ECMO, medicine bags, oxygen, the whole lot, TICC is at the other end of the hospital. It sounds far, I say. It's not only that, it's also a priority not to bump into anything, he says, and while Kinch frets about the size of the lifts and the tight corners in the basement passages, Sven comes striding down the corridor, his idiosyncratic posture making his back flex slightly as he walks. He almost trips up on a floor-polishing machine. He doesn't see me. Stefan is moving along behind him with his hands held out. Without introducing himself or any other preamble, Sven launches into a monologue on an article that Måns has found on the Internet about the use of dichloroacetate in the treatment of lactosis in children with metabolic illnesses. I grab Sven's arm. His heavy body feels impossible to budge. Well, it seems we've read the same article, answers Kinch. Sven wants to go on talking about dichloroacetate and I notice Kinch is getting impatient. Stefan doesn't know what to do with himself. I think they know what they're doing, Sven, they're doing everything they can for Karin, I say. He ignores me. Stefan and a nurse help me lead him away down the corridor; after a few metres I realise he's gone. You can come in now, the specialist calls out to me. It's hot and stuffy in the room. The ECMO cannulas are transparent, one of them is hanging from Karin's throat just above the collarbone, another is coming out of her groin, they're as thick as garden hose, there must be many litres of blood flowing through them. I lean forward and push my way through a wall of hips in front of me, I pick up Livia's blanket, shake it off, and put it in my back pocket. Where's the husband, I suppose you'll be wanting to come with us? Kinch calls out. Yes, please, I answer. Are you feeling more awake now? he asks. Yes, I am. He asks me to hold onto the cannula jutting out of Karin's groin. Don't you let go of that, if we walk into anything and knock the cannula it's all over, instantly, he says. The cannula is as warm as her body.

Kinch steers the bed down the corridor while holding onto the throat cannula, which is partially taped to the side rail of the bed. A nurse pulls the infusion rack and keeps a hand on Karin's oxygen mask. Another nurse pushes along the ECMO machine. Catheters are trailing and lying all over the bed. Carefully, the nurse rocks the ECMO machine from side to side to manouvre it between the oxygen tube and the lift doors, there's no space for him inside, and he's just sprinting off towards the stairwell when Kinch calls out for him to wait. The nurse runs back and jams his arm between the closing doors. Kinch leans over Karin, and says: We can't get to the buttons, you have to run down to the basement and call down the lift from there. The nurse has broken into a sweat, he's complaining about his fitness when the doors open in the basement. Slowly he coaxes out the ECMO machine and then starts tugging at the bed. Wait, hold on! Kinch calls out and lifts the urine catheter, which is sandwiched between the bed and the side of the lift. The floors in the basement are made of rough concrete, there are guard rails along the walls, sometimes the floor slopes down and sometimes up, but mostly down, some of the passages are so narrow that we can barely get through, others are as wide as dual carriageways, even though we're creeping along step by step we have to stop for a breather every ten metres, Kinch glares up at the traffic mirrors on every corner, his temples shiny with sweat, all the time we run into doctors or messengers on kick-scooters or janitors on bright yellow trucks towing a line of wheeled baskets. Stop, the nurse cries. She's suspended with outstretched arms between the oxygen mask and the infusion stand, which has got stuck in a crack in the floor. Kinch throws himself at the oxygen mask. Damn it, he yells. My hand, grasping onto the cannula, has turned white, my fingers are burning. On the ceiling are ventilation drums, cable ladders, copper tubes, there's a whining of capsules in the pneumatic tube system, the basement seems to be getting more modern, the floors look newly painted in light grey hues, the walls are white and clean, sturdy pillars, we pass a pressurised chamber, emergency supply cupboards, a seminar room, specialists and students, changing rooms, steam issuing from laundries, medical and surgical archives, fire doors with explanatory signs on them, from time to time daylight entering through gaps in the ceiling where one can see the sky between steel beams, and then after walking for about an hour the floor starts sloping upwards quite steeply and we have to push the bed with our bodies, the passages getting colder, in places the beams flaking with rust and paint, it gets warmer again, the air turns drier, whenever we turn into a new stretch of corridor Kinch punches a button to start a flashing siren light, people move out of the way and stare at us, the trucks apply their brakes and reverse, on a couple of occasions Kinch stops to make a telephone call, at other times he yells loudly into the corridors: Emergency patient transport! I have not dared to look at Karin even once since we left F21. Opposite the Thoracic Intensive Care Clinic is an open refuse room, there's a stink coming from some brown sludge running onto the floor and dripping into a drain. The bed lift is tiny. Kinch and the nurses swear as they wiggle the bed to get it out. The nurse who was struggling with the ECMO machine stretches to press the button. Good luck now, Tom, he says before the doors close. I don't know his name, I never looked at his name tag, I didn't ask either, and I'm ashamed about it and I'm ashamed that I didn't have time to say thank you. Your wife will be well taken care of now, says the other nurse. Thanks, but we're not married, I answer. Oh, I thought you were. We were thinking of getting married before Livia came along, I say. When was your daughter due? Early May, I answer. Two doctors and two nurses are waiting for us on level 4. On a lime-green steel door is written: *Welcome to the Thoracic Clinic.* Could someone help me? I ask. I'll take over, answers one of the doctors. Only now that I can drop my arms as I jog along next to the patient bed do I dare look at Karin, her nails, the colour of her hair, her ears, eyebrows, eyelashes, nose, and that little indentation in her skin by her right nostril, that's the only thing that's still the same, but it's enough, it's Karin. The section is called N14 and we're going to Room 2, one of the doctors says to me. I write it down in my pad without stopping. I am left standing in a long, windowless corridor, I hold the door, five people help move Karin to an intensive care bed. She faces a large window, which is slightly open. I see the scar on her stomach for the first time. The nurse who helped us get through the basement pushes the bed into the corridor. Something on the sheet looks like a mixture of excrement and blood. She looks at me. Thanks, I say. She embraces me. The doctor in charge must be two metres tall, with maniacal eyes, he charges back and forth between Karin and a computer. Tobias Sax, it says on his name tag. He has a powerful voice: Talk to me, what's our status here? ECMO and oxygen working well, someone says. A nurse squeezes Karin's lower arm and calls out: Acutely oedematous, bleeding from punctures and tubes. He yells out: Top priority now drain off fluid, drain off fluid, come on go. In the corridor a few metres behind me one of the older doctors from TICC stands talking to Kinch and Callmer. I am so happy to see Callmer that I call out 'hello' and raise my hand towards him. He's immersed in their conversation. He looks grey and seems tired. Sax lifts the material covering Karin's hips and studies the cannula in her groin. We have to correct the venous cannula, we must have a flow of about five litres, he calls out, and hurries back to the computer. I stand hidden behind the door and look out of the window through its encapsulated steel mesh. I can't see if Sax is yelling at the staff in Room 2 or into a telephone: Extraordinary doses of vasoconstrictors, acute circulatory instability, multi-organ failure, extensive bleeding from all orifices, membranes, infarcts, come on people, the patient is basically dying on us here.

Tompa, where are you? asks Stefan down the telephone. I need to find Livia but I don't know the way back. Where are you? he repeats. I went with Karin, then I got lost down here, I'm here now. Tompa, are you at TICC? Yeah,

I'm sitting here outside the section. Tompa? It's okay, I'm just tired. How are things with Karin? Not good. Wait, I'm running, I'll be there in a minute, can you remember what floor you're on, you don't have to answer, wait. I hear Stefan panting and the sound of him sprinting on gravelly tarmac. Tompa, I'll find it, just sit tight, I can see the parking now, it should be right, I'll ask the first person I see, I think this is it, yeah, Thoracic Clinic, here it is, I can hear you, Tompa, you don't have to answer, we'll talk later, damn, Tompa, just stay where you are, I'll be there in a few seconds.

The stillness in Neonatal, the slow movements of the midwives, the whispering voices, the milk replacement which they heat in microwave ovens and which smells like honey, the teddies, the dolls, the faint cooing noises from the incubators, the noticeboard by the entrance with photos of babies and parents, and the corridor decorated like a pre-school. All this space to breathe. I sink into the armchair and put my legs up on the footstool. Livia closes her eyes. Her chest moves, sometimes she curls up her fingers. I am woken up by the father of the kid in the next incubator. He pushes my arm and says: Hey, my wife needs the feeding chair. He's skinny, with a large, hard belly. The woman, who's much younger than him, stares at me. I thought it was just a normal armchair, I say, standing up. She's feeding here, take one of those, he says, pointing at two wooden chairs by the wall. It is actually a feeding chair, his wife reiterates. He drags the armchair and the footstool across the floor, the scraping sound fills the whole room. Livia starts moaning,

I go over to her. She's wearing sunglasses and lying under an ultra-violet lamp. I can't have been sleeping for more than an hour, but that lamp wasn't there when I went to sleep. I give her the dummy. The woman sits in the armchair, preparing to feed her child through the tube, the man sits on the footstool in a sort of sentry position. I ask in the reception why there's such a strong lamp over Livia. The midwife explains that she has a higher level of bilirubin, so needs light therapy a few hours per day. Okay, I say. Premature children often have that, she says, it's nothing unusual, it's what's making your daughter's skin slightly yellow, the light breaks it down, and then she passes it out in her urine. Doesn't she look cool in her shades? Yes. It's like she's on the beach, isn't it? she says.

The walk between Neonatal and TICC takes about twenty minutes with Stefan, David, and Hasse guiding me through the basement passages. Sax is tapping on his computer when I come into Room 2. He doesn't look at me. Husband? he barks. Yes? Can I have a few words with you? Okay, I answer. He leads me into the corridor and cranes his neck so I can look into his half-crazed eyes. While he intones about the risk of Karin passing away from the slightest intervention, we're joined by Helmer Lovén, the older doctor who first admitted Karin at TICC. He has a double chin, bags under his eyes, huffs and puffs in a reassuring way when he opens his mouth: Despite everything, we've seen a slight improvement since this morning, your wife's lactate levels have dropped considerably, I think the last time we checked it was at eight or something and going down, we can probably expect to begin chemotherapy as early as tomorrow. Thanks, I needed to hear some good news, I answer. Sax leans forward even more and says in a muted voice: I heard that all information should go via you first? I can't cope with any information unless it's coming directly from the doctors in charge, I say. We can fully appreciate that, answers Lovén. That was also Karin's wish before she was sedated, I say. Understood, nods Sax.

The sounds in Room 2 are difficult to get used to: the hissing membranes in the ECMO machine, the vibrating cannulas, the wheezing and gargling of the respirator, the dialysis machine, the infusion stands, while from the window you can hear slamming sounds from a construction site, a huge pit, bucket loaders, cranes, drilling machines. On large streamers it says: *Building the hospital of the future!* The intensive care bed has a high rim of plastic moulding along its sides with built-in monitors, it's cranked up so the medical staff don't have to bend down, while sitting on the stool I can't reach Karin, I can hardly even see her, which means I end up standing up, but I have to keep in constant motion so I don't get in the way. An assistant nurse pats me on the back and says: Someone from Central IC came over with this photo. It's the laminated photo of Livia. Can I keep it here somewhere? I ask. Yeah, that's fine, she answers. I reuse the old pieces of sticky tape to fix the photo on a pillar by the bed. We'll be massaging her uterus every fifteen minutes, it's to staunch the bleeding, she's bleeding heavily from her lower abdomen, she says. Okay, I answer. She's wearing latex gloves when she prises open Karin's eyelids. Her right eye is red, it looks like a fish-eye. Plasma is running from her tear ducts.

In Neonatal, at midnight, a lamp lights up the midwife's desk. I mention to her that a night nurse at TICC said it was a bad idea to put Livia's cuddly blanket on Karin's chest. Uh-huh, well I don't know anything about that, answers the midwife. Could Livia absorb something poisonous from the blanket? I ask. Do you want me to ask our doctor? Probably just as well to, if that's okay. Sure, now, or . . .? If it's not too late? No, she says, and walks over to the reception as slowly as only Neonatal staff can walk, then when she comes back murmurs: He'll be here in a minute. I jump to my feet: Is it serious? No, not at all, he said there was no problem, he just seemed to want to tell you himself. The paediatrician is short and wiry and speaks with a German accent. He looks either at the floor, or at one of my hands. I am told that, along with another paediatrician, he is responsible for everyone in the Neonatal ward. He explains that there's nothing dangerous about Livia having a blanket that's been on her mother's breast. He waits for me to respond and then, when I don't, adds: I called the Haematology Department just to be on the safe side, it's fine, you can carry on with the blankets. Thanks, I answer. He moves half a step closer. We've listened to your daughter's heart and looked at the X-rays, he says. Okay, and is everything alright? He taps a little notepad against his hip, then stops and explains that Livia has what's called patent ductus arteriosus, a prenatal blood vessel between the pulmonary artery and the aorta which, in children born after full gestation,

62

withers and disappears, but in premature babies is sometimes still there; the blood likes to take a short cut through
this duct, you can hear it like a sort of whistling in the
stethoscope. Okay, that doesn't sound so good, should I
be worrying? I don't think so, it's not all that unusual,
he answers. Okay, so what happens now then? Nothing
yet, but the heart will have to be listened to later, there
can be problems with the circulation if it doesn't disappear. Usually it does so by itself, if it doesn't we can
operate or give medication.

The night nurse at TICC is skinny, blonde, and has
a nose like a parrot's beak. She approaches me, eating
an orange: As I said, I think it's a bad idea switching
the blankets like that. I tell her I've spoken to the doctor
at Neo, and that it's not a problem. I'm her intensive
care nurse, I'm the one taking care of her, I'm telling
you it's a bad idea, they're in their own bubble over
there. The doctor at Neo had it okayed by the haematologist, I say. Obviously miffed, she answers: Do what
you like, but if it was my child I'd give it a miss. She
washes her hands and rubs disinfecting gel into them
and, when she pulls off the tape around the cannula in
Karin's hand, pieces of skin peel off.

I've learned to find my way through the basement
passages: the sign covered with a black bin bag, the
burnt-out fuse box, the oily sock that seems to have been
hanging for years on an emergency exit sign, the chipboard
at the T-junction, the hastily scribbled numbers on the
support strut of the side railings, the thick black skid-
marks of truck wheels, the cable-ladder with a broken
fixture. David falls asleep while we're lying chatting in

Family Room 1. I shave, brush my teeth, shower, and go back to the bed. I check my telephone. Almost thirty missed calls and as many texts. Three of the calls are from my father. He hasn't left a message. It feels like I've been living in Family Room 1 for months. Sometimes I think it must be even longer than that. I've grown attached to the view of the brick wall and the colourful eggs glowing in the dark. I know that I'll soon have to leave the room and go home with Livia. I've become afraid of the flat, Lundagatan 46 scares me, I want to be able to run between Livia and Karin in fifteen minutes, to change the orange blankets at any time of day or night, and I like the proximity of the Neonatal nurses and the midwives, I even like the hospital's instant coffee and the dark cement mosaic in the stairwell, the blue-green wooden cupboard above the bed where I am keeping the presents, the Italian chocolate, the drawings made for Livia by our friends' children, the clothes from Polarn O. Pyret, the books, magazines, postcards of fox cubs and angels. That first day in Karolinska I was given a map of the hospital, I folded it and put it in my jeans pocket. I turn on the reading light and get the map out. A thumb's-width corresponds to about thirty metres. I measure the distance through the air between Livia and Karin's beds.

Sax is sitting at the computer in Room 2 as usual. Is there still a shortage of beds in the ECMO Unit? I ask. I wouldn't let her go now anyway, he answers. Okay. She won't survive another move, he adds, standing up, stretching, rubbing his eyes, then goes on: Your wife has poor circulation in her right leg, her foot has gone cold, its coloration has deteriorated, so we decided last night to make an emergency addition of a distal perfusion catheter. Okay, I answer blankly. Sax presses the tip of his tongue against the corner of his mouth, his pupils are no wider than the point of a needle, he massages his temples and says: It failed. Okay. The artery is small and too deep, about five centimetres, it's not clearly visible using ultrasound, the conditions are difficult, oedema and a lot of subcutaneous tissue. I tried it myself this morning, it didn't work. What does that mean, then? We've called in the vascular unit, they will come here this afternoon, they will open up her thigh to reach the artery. If the vascular surgeon doesn't manage it we will have to amputate. Amputate? I ask. Yes, he answers, rubbing ointment from a tube onto his lips. Take her leg off? I ask. Precisely, yes, amputate her right leg.

The Day Room at TICC is minimal, a chair and a two-seater sofa, a small toilet and a window with drawn tulle curtains. There's no space for me, I stand in the doorway. Sven yawns repeatedly and Lillemor sits with her handbag on her thighs. Måns sits facing them, then stands up and leans on the table. He offers me his seat. I sit down. Her lactate is better, I say. Yes, we heard, answers Sven. His face is red, and there are pearls of sweat along his silver fringe. Lillemor fans her throat with a bus timetable from her handbag. I'm feeling optimistic, I say. That's good, Tom, Sven answers. Mum slept here on the sofa last night, says Måns. How was that? I ask. I've slept better, she answers. Don't they have a family room? There is one, but I won't put my foot in there again, it was dire, she says. Don't you get people coming in here? I ask. They leave as soon as they see me, she says. Have you been to see Karin? I ask. Yes, Måns replies. Sven clears his throat all the time, often when he hears people criticising psychoanalysis, or just generally if he disagrees with something, or if he's about to say something important. We've only seen Karin once here at Karolinska, you have been with her a lot, I can imagine you're getting used to it, he says and clears his throat. Yes, maybe I am, I answer. It wasn't an easy thing, he says, seeing one's own daughter lying there with all those machines.

The main entrance is a construction of glass and thin ribs of steel, and through the doors I can see Karolinska Vägen and the North Cemetery with mausoleums, gravestones in the shape of small obelisks, memorial groves, chapels, old bare deciduous hardwood trees, and black wrought-iron gates. Only when I take the map from my back pocket and decide on an exact route around the hospital do I find the energy to set off. I keep close to the brick walls and the ivy. Outside the Centre for Molecular Medicine I catch sight of Callmer. He's walking slowly and looks deep in thought amidst all the people rushing around him. I stare down at the concrete paving stones, I walk at a good pace but slow down by the hospital park. The branches are lashing against each other, there's the slamming of wheel loaders and diggers, Portakabins have been lined up along the tarmac-covered path. I decide to make a detour from my planned route and sit on an outcrop of rock in the park, which has a view of a pond and the back of the hospital. Wood chips are spraying from the chainsaws of the tree surgeons, chips that are tossed about in the wind and come raining down over me, there's a smell of burnt wood and oil, it is a little like the smell in the hospital basement. Rusty red and smooth branches are lowered from the pine trees into the back of a lorry.

Livia has been allowed to come with me into Family Room 1 for a few hours. She's filled out a good deal, she has round cheeks now and sleeps with her chubby arms behind her neck. I pick her up and carry her against my chest. Her umbilical cord stump looks like a little morel. One of the more dynamic midwives knocks at my door, enters and sits on the chair in front of the guest bed. She has a body and skin that remind me of a healthy Karin, her throat is smooth and pink, her body long and ample. Can I just butt in for a quick word? she asks. Okay, I say, ashamed of my sweaty feet, BO and bad breath. It's about the room, she says. What about the room? Now that Livia has perked up she doesn't need to stay here any more. I know your wife is in TICC and everything, but our departmental head takes the view that the family room is in principle for mums who need to recover after giving birth. I put Livia back into the incubator. I've already spoken to the departmental head, he said I could stay here for as long as I had to. Yes, that's what he thinks, he's in charge when he's here but he goes back and forth between Karolinska and a hospital in Germany, she explains. Who's making the decisions now, then? I ask. I don't think you've met her, she says. Okay. I know how it sounds, she looks at it in black and white: In black-and-white terms Livia is healthy and doesn't need to be kept here. In black-and-white terms Livia's mother is seriously ill, I say. You don't have to convince me, I see it totally like you do, it's just that technically she's not in the care of this ward. When do I have to leave the room? I ask. She hasn't said, it depends on how many premature babies we have coming in. Can't I stay somewhere else around here? I'll check. I think there are rooms you can rent, but at Neo there are only the family rooms, you can only use the guest accommodation for a night or two. She puts her hair up in a fluffy hairband and goes to the incubator.

On the way from Room 2 I talk to Stefan on the telephone. He tells me that he spoke to my father just as the doctors were attaching the ECMO cannula to Karin. Apparently Dad had been moaning and sobbing. Stefan was shaken because he'd never seen or heard my father break down before. He likes Karin, I mean he met Karin at the same time as he got his own diagnosis, I say. He's worried about you, Tompa, he's been trying to get hold of you. It reminds him of his own illness, I answer. Tompa, come on, he's also worried about you. I'm down in the basement, I can hardly hear you, let's talk later, I say. You're cutting out, Tompa. Let's talk later, I repeat. I can't hear you, Tompa, I'm hanging up now, I'll call you later.

Outside the lifts by the Thoracic Clinic, two men in overalls are standing by a tube from a sludge truck, it's hooked up to a suction pipe in the refuse room, people pass by with their hands covering their noses. I grab my phone and dial my father's number but hang up as soon as I hear the first signal, and instead I call Karin, I want to tell her that my dad's had a breakdown. I sit down on the floor, then quickly stand up, I squat on a step underneath an electrical cupboard, I have to keep one eye closed, I'm having problems seeing straight, I stand up, I call her again. Karin's voice is so close to me that I feel as if her mouth is against my ear, her voice is the pure opposite of mine, my blaring, loud bark, she has such resonance and fullness of tone, a vibrant, rising intonation, one voice to make you relax and one to get you moving; also she sometimes has trouble articulating the 'r' sound, it's a hangover from the operation in 2004, Karin calls it her speech defect and feels a touch self-conscious about it, but for that very reason I call her back again: Hi, this is Karin, leave a message and I'll call you back as soon as I can.

The Neonatal nurses have got involved in my project of passing blankets between Livia and Karin. They write labels: Mum's scent, Livia's scent. I leave a fresh blanket with Karin. She looks as if her skin has been burnt. Two round, reddish-yellow wounds suppurating over her chest. What's happened here? I ask. The doctor swivels round in his chair, the one Sax usually sits on. He is one of the younger specialists in the section, the day before yesterday he introduced himself as Jens Nygren, and, in the same breath, told me he was so terrified when his wife started having contractions in the bath that he called an ambulance. He explained that he'd only told me this because he couldn't imagine what it must be like, becoming a father in my current circumstances. He stands up and looks at the wounds. It looks worse than it actually is, he says, those are burns from the electrical cardioversion, we had to try to regulate her pulse. I was here for that, I say, but I didn't realise it would burn her. Her leg is better, he answers. I heard you won't need to amputate, I say. That's correct, there's circulation in the leg now. Okay, but she looks like she's turning blue, is that something to do with the oxygen? Her hands are completely blue, even her nails. Yes, she has irregular circulation and generally poor blood flow, she's having problems maintaining the required blood pressure, that was why they tried putting in methylene blue, it may have affected her colouring. Okay. He fetches the stool and puts it by the office chair. Do you have time to sit for a minute? he asks. Sure, I reply, sitting down. I gather Franz has already spoken to you about the situation? Yes, he said we should wait and see after tonight, I answer. He stares down at his crossed legs. I've heard that you're very scrupulous about the information you get from us, he says and looks up at me. You're welcome to interrupt me if I express myself unclearly. Okay, thanks. The need for inotropes has increased, your wife has serious heart problems, abnormal heartbeat, atrial fibrillation, atrial flutter, tachycardia, her lactate seems to have parked itself at twenty-eight, her pH value is now at 7.1 in spite of aggressive buffering, we've had almost industrial flows going into her to stabilise her levels. I know what a pH value is, and that's it, I say. Okay, so, normally the pH value is between 7.35 and 7.45, it's a precondition for life, the human body can't tolerate the slightest deviation from that normal value. Okay. At cellular level a body can't live under these kinds of conditions, he explains.

Okay. His pocket vibrates. He takes out his phone and looks at it, then gets up and goes over to the infusion stand. His back is towards me. Hi, no, I won't be home in time, don't expect me, yes, we'll have to talk later, no, let's talk later, he says and hangs up. He runs his hands through his hair, his gaze falls on the photograph of Livia. It's been up and down every day, I say, don't you think she could pick up? He turns to me and says: I think you should stay with your daughter, and then we'll call you as soon as anything happens, but if I were you I'd call over your loved ones and prepare them for the fact that Karin may not last out the night. I understand you've been together a long time? He presses his hands against the sides of his jaw and again goes over to one of the infusion stands, then back to the computer, where he writes something while remaining on his feet. Last time she ended up in a rehabilitation home, I say. He stops writing, sits down, and pushes his chair closer to me. I've only read the medical records, he says, and I reply: She was there a month, she was stiff after the operation, she couldn't turn her head, I had to stand in front of her when we wanted to kiss, we were actually able to laugh about it.

I decide to take a stroll back to Neonatal around the hospital. I take a short cut across the parking area, the car alarms flashing away in different colours, glowing points of light in the dark by a bus shelter, I wander along a bicycle lane, black, naked trees, there's a thumping behind my left eye, the thundering of traffic from the Essinge overpass sounds like the sea, exactly like the sea, if I close my eyes I feel as if I am walking barefoot along the beach at Vändburgsviken. I ask one of the nurses at Neonatal for a migraine tablet and I get a mixture of Ibuprofen and Paracetamol. It must be what they give the mothers for pain relief. I sit next to Livia in the armchair, I lower the incubator using the electric control. I'm so tired that I don't dare pick her up. I lay my hand over her belly, she wakes up, sucks her dummy, she tries to push me away and then goes back to sleep. I push my finger into her grip and lean back. The midwife who was there during the Caesarean comes up to me. How's that headache? she asks. Okay, thanks, I just get migraines sometimes, it must be hereditary, Mum gets them and Dad has cluster headaches. Sorry to hear that, maybe you'd better go and lie down? I will, but it's nice sitting here. Yes, well it certainly looks it – oh, I meant to ask, what's that song you sing her? Sorry, was I too loud? No, you're not disturbing anyone. 'Here Comes the Sun', I say, and then I explain: I was already singing it when she was in the womb. Oh right, well, it's just that spring is around the corner now, and, well, you often sing it, do you like the Beatles? A bit, I say. Maybe it's not the sort of music your generation listens to. The Beatles are time-less, I point out. You're right there, it's a beautiful song. George Harrison wrote it, but I prefer the Nina Simone version, have you heard it? I ask. No, she answers. You should check it out. Nina Simone? Yes. Thanks for the tip, well, you've probably noticed we've stopped using the lamp, her bilirubin level's improved and she's not as yellow any more, so you can finally take her home.

*

72

Stefan is asleep in Family Room 1, the one where I spent the first night at the Karolinska, and David and Hasse are resting on the sofa in the day room. They can't sleep. Karin's friends have been temporarily accommodated in another room on the ward, they're wrapped up in blankets and drinking tea: Caro, Ullis, Johanna. Also Edith and Jenny, but I don't know if they are staying the night. They reminisce about Karin growing up, the language courses, the parties, Karin as a twenty-year-old theatre critic for the *Entertainment Guide*, the trip to Uruguay, Ivan the dog, the house on Skyttevägen and her first flat on Norra Stationsgatan. Alex and Andy are listening to music in Family Room 1. Of all our friends, they're the two I've seen the most of these last few years. Andy sits in the armchair with his jacket over his legs, and Alex is resting on the bed though he's still wearing his outdoor clothes. Andy plays Sam Cooke on his mobile and tells us about Jupiter and Venus, and how their orbits are so close at the moment that they appear as a single celestial body. Me and Stefan thought it was a satellite or a meteorite, if we're thinking about the same thing? I say. We probably are, it's really bright, the newspapers have written about it, it's a really unusual phenomenon, answers Andy. How old is Karin's brother? asks Alex. We were at his fortieth birthday party about a month ago, why? I ask. I never met him before, what do Karin's parents do? asks Alex. Do you mean work-wise? I ask. They must be going through hell, Alex says, have they taken sick leave? I don't think so, I answer. But they're very proud of Livia, right? he says. Yes, I answer. Stefan told me Thomas has got worse, says Andy, taking off

73

his shiny leather shoes and resting his feet on the stool. He keeps calling me all the time, I say, I don't have the energy to answer. Why not? asks Alex. I don't know. You've been pretty close lately, haven't you? Alex points out and unbuttons his denim jacket. Yeah, the last few years have been good, I don't know, I guess I can't deal with thinking about his illness, I say. I get that, Tom, this is agony . . . maybe it's hard for you to talk about Karin? It's okay, I say and lie down on the guest bed. I've got such a great photo of you from David and Kristina's wedding, you still had your beard and your Wyatt Earp moustache, then you kiss her like the terrier you are, so energetically, it's like you've jumped her, I think she finds it prickly, she's both relishing it and suffering, wants to turn away from you but can't, wonderful, you terrier, he says. I haven't seen it, I say. I'll email it to you, he replies.

I run into the corridor and on towards the stairwell, I leap down, I run on the rough concrete, along the railing struts, I run through the Thoracic Clinic, I press the entry phone, I take a left, I run another thirty metres. The door of Room 2 is open. I had been expecting a closed ring of specialists around Karin. The room feels abandoned. No one is there except for Nygren and a nurse. Tom, this is not going to work for much longer, says Nygren. Okay, for how long? I ask. I've elected to continue her treatment for a little bit longer, but it's a hopeless position, hard to say, maybe an hour or so. I put my hands on Karin's cheeks, I run my fingers over her forehead, she's sweating. Can I be alone with her?

Of course, take as long as you need. The nurse lowers the intensive care bed so I can sit on the stool and at the same time hold Karin's hand, then she fetches a cup of coffee for me, the ventilation window is open, I can see the car headlights over the Essinge overpass, I daren't kiss Karin, her hair moves a little in the draught of air, I want to kiss her so much, I look at her in the half-light, the embroidered foliage winding across her nightgown, I am lying on the off-white sofa, I am drinking in small sips, I have never stayed the night with Karin before, the windows facing onto Metargatan are open, there's a slight draught running through the flat, she is making notes in a book that she hides behind the pillow, she puts in some earplugs and takes off her glasses, she says goodnight, Tom, and I answer goodnight, I can't sleep, I flick through a play by Sarah Kane that I find in the bookshelf, on some of the pages Karin has written in the margin, not a critic's annotations, more passing fancies, ideas for books, one or two lines of poetry, and in one place she's written in blue ink: *The bird skeletons wait patiently under the balls of tallow.*

Sven and Lillemor are waiting on the sofa in the day room, the air is filled with perfume, their faces are sunken, their eyeballs protruding, their eyelids swollen, they look old and decrepit, they don't even say hello, they just watch me as I sit on the chair opposite, Måns is standing next to me, he already knows what's happened, he had to come and fetch me from Room 2, he had to lead me through the corridor, I don't know how to articulate it so I just repeat what Nygren said to me: The electrical activity in Karin's heart has stopped. Lillemor presses her hands over her ears and closes her eyes. Sven shakes his head a little and asks: What are you saying? Dad, Karin's pulse is zero, says Måns. If Karin's pulse is zero that would mean she's dead, he says. It takes a few seconds before a groan is heard rising from his throat, and his head drops. Lillemor is trembling, saying something I can't quite catch. Måns sinks onto the floor in front of them.

The nurse seems to type what Nygren says into the computer while he more or less ceremoniously walks up to the machines. The patient has been in a state of asystole since 05:52, continued rising potassium, lactate steady at twenty-eight, ECMO unchanged at five thousand five hundred revolutions per minute, 5.1 litres of flow, the prospects for continued life considered to be non-existent, and I now make the decision to turn off the respirator and ECMO. Nothing makes a sound any more; the room becomes silent. Nygren checks his watch and adds: Patient is pronounced dead at 06:31.

THERE ARE NO more than ten people on the premises, not counting ourselves and a bartender who between orders plays Sly and the Family Stone on vinyl. A colourful mix of office-attired women and men in a foggy after-work session. David chuckles to himself, standing there by the table:

Stefan, remember that time in Sundsvall when Tom started having bloody *breathing difficulties* or whatever it was, and he just – stood there in the room – spluttering?

Stefan looks up at the ceiling fixtures and bursts out laughing.

Are you for real? I say.

David squeezes his thighs and Stefan hides his face in his hands. Tompa, you're just pissed because we're having a laugh about it, says Stefan.

No, I'm not pissed, I just don't think it was very funny.

It was, Tom, says David.

Yeah, that was actually quite funny, Tompa, says Stefan. We've talked about it before, Hasse, you never remember anything. Hasse flushes, and he drinks some more of his sparkling wine.

It was insanely funny, says Stefan, then settles into the story: In the middle of the night, after a particularly epic session at the pub, we were fast asleep in the hotel room, when Tompa suddenly comes charging in stark naked with his hands over his head and he's spluttering and groaning, it sounds totally messed up, we all wake up, it was all happening so fast, all you had time to think was, oh yeah, here comes Tompa and he's still partying.

By this stage, David and Stefan are absolutely weeping.

When was this? asks Hasse.

Oh I don't know, maybe we were eighteen or nineteen, I answer. The thing is, I threw up like a pig that night, I don't know if I breathed in the vomit or something, I couldn't get any air, I panicked, I ran out of the toilet and I needed help. David was just jeering at me, and Stefan kept giggling.

Tompa, it was completely off the wall – picture it, here's Tompa in the nude running around the room making weird noises, says Stefan, having trouble even saying the words because he's laughing so much.

It's not *that* funny, says Hasse.

Exactly, Hasse, thank you, I say.

You weren't there, Hasse, says David.

If he had been there he would have jumped up and given me a slap on the back, right, Hasse? I say.

Yes, I would have.

And you would have given me mouth-to-mouth.

Absolutely.

You're a true friend, I say, putting my arm round his

shoulder: Not like those two sadists. As I gesture I accidentally knock against a man at the bar. He turns around and shakes his head at me.

Sorry, I say, then I hear him say to his friend:

The guy's just come out of a coal mine. His friend gives me a disdainful look. Stefan immediately says:

Let it go, Tompa.

I take off my cap and put it on the table, then turn around. He has a navy blue, tailor-made suit. I tap him on the shoulder. They both turn around.

Excuse me, I was just wondering what you meant by 'he's just come out of a coal mine'? He looks at my gym shoes, my jeans, then at my T-shirt, and replies:

Go back and stand over there. I keep staring at him.

Ooh, kid's playing all angry, says his friend. You're gonna come a cropper, mate, I'm trying not to laugh.

Just give him a krona and he'll leave, says his friend, then pats me on the arm and adds: We're only joking.

Both have shaved heads, grey eyes, they seem heavy with muscle and fat. I eye him steadily and then, when I sense he's becoming less sure of himself, say:

You're afraid of me.

David steps in between us and exclaims: Gentlemen, there's no bloody need for this. I go back to the table and put my cap back on.

Shit, Tompa, whispers Stefan.

At half past twelve David raises his arm and shambles up to a Portakabin on Hornsgatan and starts tugging at the door. That's not a cab, Hasse yells at him. Only Stefan and I have the staying power to go on to Folkets Kebab shop. It's empty upstairs. Plastic palms with glitter

79

balls. Arabic music. Stefan grumbles about how he'll be woken up early by his son Charlie. There's garlic sauce dripping off the table. Chomping away at his food, he says: And this is what you've got to look forward to. He notices that it makes me thoughtful. Tompa, children are fun, really they are, but not always.

I'm mostly worried about our finances.

How's the book going, then?

I have to be done by May.

So that's when the kid's due.

That's right.

You're writing a real book, not a poetry collection?

A poetry collection is a real book, isn't it? But yeah, it's prose.

You think you'll manage to get it finished?

I don't have a choice, I have to, I'm out of money.

Yeah, we noticed.

I know . . .

It's fine, Tompa, you'll return the favour when you've got bread, but May, six bloody months away?

That's not very long when you're working on a book.

Shit, Tompa, you've been working on it for an insane amount of time. I only wrote one long essay at high school, I wouldn't want to do that bloody thing again, it took two months, that's long enough as far as I'm concerned.

After hugging Stefan by the taxi on the junction of Hornsgatan-Ringvägen I hurry home through the sleet and get straight in the shower. Karin is asleep.

I grab a bottle of wine from the fridge and sit at my desk. I have been working on my book for three years, twelve hours a day. It's a documentary novel about a murder in Huddinge, a suburb of Stockholm. I spread police photos of the crime scene over the table and look through the paper-clipped bundles of pages from the police investigation, two thousand in total, packed with annotations and scribbled Post-it notes. On 15 June 1991, a dog owner found a naked dead man in a cave by Lake Orlången. His chest was gouged open down to the bone, his face mutilated. As children we spoke of it as *the murder in the cave*. It took months before a pathologist was able to identify the man as twenty-nine-year-old Mikael from Huddinge. Cause of death: bleeding from exterior wounds. In the Muslim, Christian, and Jewish faiths Michael was the foremost of the Archangels, the good Angel of Death, he was sometimes called; the name comes from Hebrew and means: Who is like God?

In due course the team of investigators presented a theory: Mikael had paid twenty thousand kronor for assistance to end his life. It had been a sort of mercy killing but without any mercy. A colleague at the post office in Klara was detained but released by Huddinge District Court on the grounds of insufficient evidence. Mikael had periodically gone to the psychiatric clinic at Huddinge Hospital. He was plagued by suicidal thoughts and felt alone. He told his psychiatrists that he had entertained the idea of taking his own life but lacked the courage to carry it through. The psychiatrist wrote out a referral for supportive therapy with a welfare worker and gave him a prescription for thirty Mallorol tablets. In the welfare officer's notes it is revealed that Mikael longed to have a girlfriend. He had never had one, and he believed that his anguish would gradually disappear once he did. Mikael's mother left him when he was a child and moved to a town in Norrland. This had been traumatic for Mikael. It was difficult for him to talk about it. Mikael had a good relationship with his father but didn't like his stepmother. There was a note from the welfare officer about a telephone conversation between Mikael and his mother. She was going to visit Mikael in Stockholm, and he was looking forward to it. The train pulled into Central Station. Mikael looked for her along the platform. A week later he received a letter, in which his mother apologised for not coming. She wrote that she had had to babysit for a friend. According to the notes, Mikael had no contact with his mother between 1986 and 1989. In that period he became obsessed with the idea of finding a girlfriend. My theory was that the longing for his mother became such a source of inner anguish that Mikael transformed it into a more manageable desire for a girlfriend. The forensic technicians felt that Mikael's nudity was voluntary, there were no signs of struggle, he had undressed himself and lain down in the cave. I studied the photographs of the triangular opening in the rock and thought about the naked, blood-covered body. Mikael had apparently gone back to his mother's womb.

Are you working? asks Karin. She's standing in the hall.

Shit, you scared me.

I was just going to the loo, did you have a good time?

Yeah, it was good, but it's always double-edged meeting up with old friends like this, it's so long since you last saw them. Karin is wearing flimsy knickers and a faded black vest top. Her breasts have become heavier.

Yeah, I know what you mean, she says. On the one hand you feel safe as houses, on the other hand they see you as the person you used to be, not the person you are. Because, you know, you change.

Yeah exactly, I say, sipping some wine.

Are you really going to drink more now?

There was this guy there, bloody nasty piece of work.

Okay, but does that mean you have to drink?

Can't you just ask me what happened?

Okay, she says.

Well, ask me then.

All right. What happened?

He said something about my clothes, I confronted him.

Confronted him?

He was like an ape in a suit, but nothing happened, although I'm capable of letting myself go like I'm on fucking autopilot.

Jesus, Tom, I'm glad I've never had to see that . . . it only seems to happen when you're with the guys, though, no?

Yes, I think so, yes, that's probably right.

Don't you ever wonder why that is?

I'm still a bit shaken, to be honest. I won't be able to show my face in town for like a week, I think the bastard might have actually been some kind of criminal. I don't get it, I had a real bloody panic attack in the shower when I came home, the shakes, I was just shivering, I had to sit down and do some work.

Why, though?

So I could think about something else, I answer.

Yeah, but why did you panic in the shower?

What does that matter?

I was only asking, she says.

I happened to be standing in the shower, I suppose I relaxed a bit.

But why in the shower?

What the hell, it might just as well have happened in bed.

Okay, she says.

I've never been someone who looks for a fight, I don't just hit people, well, I mean, it did sometimes happen when I was playing ice hockey, I add, turning my chair towards Karin. Why do you never say you love me? She looks surprised. Don't look like that, it's an important question.

You're drunk, Tom.

I often tell you I love you, I point out.

I do love you.

I'm looking forward to being a father.

That's good, she says, sitting on the chair by the wall. Were you at Folkbaren the whole time?

Yeah, we ended up having quite a bit of cava, David knows the bartender, you know. David got so smashed, he wanted to go on to Riche, but he couldn't put it in words, he just pointed, and we knew what he wanted.

Was he *that* drunk?

No, I'm exaggerating, me and Stefan were most drunk, then Hasse, David was just a bit merry, and a bit tired, he had a cold as well.

Karin turns her head and says: Please, can you put away those photos, they're unpleasant. I just don't understand where you get the energy for this, no wonder you have nightmares.

This is my workplace.

We have to live here as well, she says.

I pile up the photos and put a file on top of them and say: All my friends have children, and yours too, it's strange.

What do you mean?

I don't know.

Are you going to work for much longer?

No, I'm mainly just thinking, I'm not working.

That is working, isn't it, for you anyway.

I can't go out like this any more, I don't have time. You go to bed and I'll be along in a bit.

Karin carefully scratches her thighs with her nails, then says quietly: I've been thinking.

And?

I already asked you, but I didn't get an answer at that point, she adds.

About what?

I was reading online about testing your amniotic fluid and I ended up looking at an essay by Peter Singer.

Who?

The philosopher?

Oh yeah, him, yes, yes, I know.

He's written a lot about euthanasia and children.

Oh dear, okay, but what was the question I never answered?

I want us to agree that we'll keep the child even if it's not healthy.

Yes, but we already talked about that.

So we're of one mind?

We're of one mind.

I don't want to have the amniotic test tomorrow, she says.

So let's not do it, then, just don't think Singer is someone I'm big on, I've hardly read him.

You're in favour of euthanasia, aren't you? she says.

I'm not in favour of it and not against it either, fuck it, it doesn't matter, we're of one mind when it comes to Scrunchie.

Maybe it was stupid of me to bring this up now that you're drunk, maybe you'll change your mind tomorrow.

What the hell, sometimes you talk to me as if I was a fucking idiot, seriously, why would I change my mind tomorrow?

You're right, sorry.

Hey wait, you have to listen to this, I say, and start searching on the computer.

She sits down again. As long as it isn't anything from the book, I can't handle it, she says.

No, it's not mine, this is properly good, I answer. I plug the speaker into the computer and say: Sssh, Professor Longhair, 'River's Invitation'.

Darling, it's three in the morning.

Sssh, I exclaim.

Darling, not so loud?

Properly good, sssh.

Tom, please, turn it down.

Scrunchie wants to dance, come on now.

You're such a nut, she sighs as I pull her onto her feet.

Scrunchie loves the rhythm.

No, Scrunchie's asleep, Scrunchie hasn't moved for several hours, she answers.

I put my hand against Karin's stomach and say: A good rocking motion, it's like a cradle.

Who are you? she asks.

Who do you want me to be?

Darling, we're going to the Maternity Unit tomorrow.

Seriously, feel my hips, I say as we sway.

Coach Henri and the assistant Lasse lift me out of the rink and drop me at the far end of the bench.

Shit, Malmquist, you're fifteen and you smell of piss, that's fucked, mutters Henri.

That was stupid of me, I answer.

I don't have time for this, he says and hurries back to the door by the subs' bench.

Huddinge Hockey's B-team juniors have their changing rooms in Björkängshallen's pine-green cabin. Lasse leads me to my place by the fan heater in the corner. I use a Stanley knife to cut through the adhesive tape around the chin guards. My right ankle is grotesquely swollen. Last time we played against DIF in a league game one of their heaviest players body-checked me in the middle of the hockey rink. I had to be carried off on a stretcher: Concussion. The guy was more than one metre ninety tall and forty kilos heavier than me. This time I took him out. He went crashing down by the boards but got up straight away and slashed me across my ankle with his club blade. I tossed my gloves away, got him down on the ice by grabbing his helmet cage and started feeding punches into his kidney.

Lasse sits next to me and stares at my calf. Damn it, Malmquist, we have to get that bloody swelling down, Jesus, he says and gets the freeze-spray. Put up your pins, he adds. I lie down on the floor. He grabs my ankle and sprays my calf, then wraps a compression bandage round it tightly and rests the foot on the bench. Just lie there, take twenty, then you can go home. He goes back into the ice rink. I can hear the announcer's voice through the walls, and the buzz of voices from the stands. There's snuff stuck to the ceiling, some of it has probably been there since before I was born.

Dad has waited for me. He stubs out his cigarette on the tyre and opens the car door.

Where's Mum? I ask.

She wanted to go home.

Is she cross?

She's worried you'll hurt yourself.

Thanks for waiting.

I had a suspicion you might have trouble walking.

I get into the front seat. He closes the door and says:

Off the record, you did the right thing. He won't dare injure you again, you're a tough little bastard.

We walk along a small road behind Hornsgatan. Scaffolding covered in green netting obscures the walls of the little hospital. In the same building as Eken Midwives there's a residential care home known as the Maria Rehabilitation Centre for people with substance abuse problems. There's always some flotsam of humanity in the elevator, clinging onto the handrail just so he can stay on his feet.

Our finances will work themselves out, I tell her once we're on our own.

Really? asks Karin.

My writing grant will keep us going until June.

And then?

I've told you, I'll look for a job.

Sorry, she says.

I can understand your anxiety, but it *will* sort itself out.

I hope so, I'll be on maternity leave, she says and then stops herself. Scrunchie's moving, she says, and I quickly put my hand inside her long black quilted coat. It was really strong that time, she smiles.

The little hooligan, kicking his poor mother.

No, Scrunchie doesn't kick, Scrunchie just moves. Across from the lift is a brownish red steel door with a sign on it: Eken Midwives. A strip of bright red tape across the terrazzo tiles of light-coloured cement indicates that shoes aren't to be worn inside. Bright yellow walls, furnishings in a combined style of hospital and pre-school. Our midwife Sissi has still not appeared by quarter past two. I while the time away in the waiting room by flicking through children's books. On the sofa next to us sits a woman with a baby in a car seat. On the other side of the room sits a woman who can't decide which of her stick-like thighs she should put on top of the other, or which of the women's magazines she ought to be reading. She doesn't look pregnant and she's probably no older than twenty. Much like Karin, her eyes keep gravitating to the baby.

Karin, the midwife calls out. Sorry, we're understaffed today. She shakes hands with me.

I've been here before, I say.

Oh yes, so you have. She's about fifty or so, petite, with attractive features framed by blonde hair. Her room is full of thank you cards, photos of mothers with their children. She looks out of the window and says as she sits down at her desk: We're relocating soon, for now you'll have to excuse all the commotion of the builders, it's probably more of an annoyance to me than to you. A thundering noise comes from the walls and floor. It annoys me that she only looks at Karin while she's giving us advice about our future as parents. Then she smiles at me and says: Many fathers feel a bit left out in the early stages. She emphasises the importance of being there for the mother all the same.

And also for the child, I hope, Karin interjects.

The midwife laughs and answers: Of course.

She puts on her reading glasses and glances between her computer and a sort of revolving cardboard calendar.

We don't want to do the amniotic fluid test, says Karin.

The midwife takes off her glasses and answers: Well, it's not mandatory, it's up to you.

Good, so we're agreed, then, I say.

The midwife creases her nose at me and says: As I said, it's not obligatory.

We don't want to do it, repeats Karin.

Okay, so we'll skip it then, says the midwife as she replaces her reading glasses and peers at the computer screen. Karin, you started taking Niferex because of your iron deficiency, do you feel less tired now? she asks.

Maybe a bit.

And your itchy palms?

That's gone, Lergigan is helping, says Karin.

Oh that's good, well, so we'll just do the ultrasound scan now, she says and stands up.

Karin lies down on a PVC-covered bench and pulls her jumper up over her stomach. The hands that touch her have done this many times before, there's an instrument panel with lit-up reddish yellow buttons, the midwife squeezes out a mint-blue lubricant. She moves the nozzle over Karin's stomach while turning a lever with her left hand. A little womb figure appears on a monitor next to Karin's feet. The midwife takes a long time over her business without saying anything.

Is it all looking okay? I ask.

There's a little bit too much amniotic fluid, but that's normal, she answers and informs us that this could be the reason for the abnormal growth curve of the foetus. Karin has grown dizzy from lying down. She wants to sit up.

Is it a boy or a girl? I ask.

That's hard to say now, I better not guess, she answers and tries to catch Karin's eye.

It's easier to come up with a name if you know the sex, I point out. She grimaces a little at me and hands over a strip of ultrasound photos.

Thanks, says Karin, looking at them, smiling, holding them up to me, and then tucking them into my shoulder bag.

I stand in front of a fishtank in the corridor while Karin sets up the next appointment with the midwife. I tap the thick glass, the fish seek their way towards the sound with wide open mouths. On the wall by the exit is a poster with educational photographs of babies sleeping in a variety of positions; a caption reads: Sudden Infant Death Syndrome and Preventive Advice. Karin has sat down on an ottoman made of black-and-white sheepskin to take off her shoe covers. I read the poster.

What does it say? asks Karin.

It says that Sudden Infant Death Syndrome happens before the baby's six months old, it's rare, only affects one in six thousand, the best advice is to let the child sleep on its back. Shit, one in six thousand isn't actually that uncommon.

Don't talk like that, says Karin.

On Hornsgatan, drivers accelerate through the traffic lights, there's a number 4 bus, some cyclists. People are hidden inside their quilted jackets, hats, and scarves. Just as it always is in winter, apart from the roadworks. Diggers have turned the tarmac upside down. In the right-hand lane is a long, two-metre deep trench filled with snow, sand, and steaming pipes. The roadworks have narrowed the pavement. It's so cramped between the house wall and the pedestrian barriers that Karin and I can't walk next to each other. I have to shuffle behind her, with one arm holding hers. The December sun is strong. I can't see Karin for a few minutes. Every time I try I get dazzled and I have to look away or close my eyes. But I feel her.

A bull mastiff lifts its nose and sniffs when we walk into the video shop. It's the shop owner's dog.

Hi, I say.

The owner is drinking cola from a half-litre bottle. Hi there, he answers. Karin stumbles along between the shelves. I help her to a stool by the cash counter. At first she smiles at the dog, but all of a sudden it seems to make her anxious. No film is entirely to her taste.

What about Wenders, then, a documentary about Pina Bausch? I ask.

Fine, she says.

How are you feeling?

Tired, she answers.

Darling?

Yes, I'm just tired, she says.

I pay forty kronor for the films, and the shop owner asks: Will that be all?

Yeah, thanks, I answer.

You want a bag?

No, thanks.

He burps, apologises, and says: The run-up to New Year's Eve is a good time for a film day.

Okay, thanks a lot, I say.

He calls out: Have a nice weekend. About ten metres away from the video shop Karin has to sit down on the window ledge of a ladies' clothes boutique. The next pit stop is a bench underneath a frozen cherry tree. The air is cold and illuminated.

How about now, darling? I ask.

Pelvic girdle pain, I think, it hurts like crazy when I walk, she says.

Before the hill on Lundagatan I find Karin another bench outside a closed ice cream kiosk. We can see the brick steeple of Högalid Church just beyond. I lead Karin up the stairs to our inside courtyard and then into the stairwell.

The bedroom is only just wide enough for our

double bed. At night we have to clamber onto the foot end and crawl up to the pillows. As a bedside table, Karin has a narrow oak plank fixed crosswise to the bedframe. On it she keeps a tin containing earplugs, a little glass bowl of hairbands, a bag of throat lozenges, her mobile phone, iPod, headphones, a leather-bound notepad, a couple of fine-pointed felt-tip pens, and novels standing upright. I rub the arch of her foot. Her feet are swollen and vaguely purple. The thought of giving birth makes Karin nervous, she frets about having opted for a vaginal delivery. She stares at me, as if attempting to make me understand how it's going to feel, but I can't possibly imagine. And Karin can't either.

Caro and Julian have gone to pregnancy yoga, she says.

Is that like tantric sex?

Are you at all interested in what I'm saying?

'Pregnancy yoga'?

You learn to breathe the right way.

Do you have to go to pregnancy yoga for that?

Tom?

Karin?

Please?

Okay, okay, pregnancy yoga, sure, I say.

You know it's not just about that.

I do?

Yes.

What is this?

You know what I mean, she says.

Look, I want to be involved, if that's what you're

driving at, but I do have my book to get on with; hope-fully it will lead to an advance so I can look for a job without too much stress after that—

Or you'll just start writing another book, she inter-jects.

What do you want, you want me to stop writing?

No, of course I don't want that, she says, staring towards the kitchen.

You need to say what you actually think.

I don't always know what I think right away, all right, I'm slow, I need time, can you just wait a moment?

Okay, I say, before adding: Are you slow or reserved?

The moment I don't have the same opinion as you, you start saying I'm reserved.

No, you're not reserved, sorry, you have integrity. I'll think about it, try to sleep a bit now, I'll wake you in an hour.

Uh-huh, okay, she says and puts in the earplugs, then takes them out again and says despondently: I'm afraid you're going to disappear.

Disappear? Oh *please*, Karin!

Not physically, of course, but all you've done these last few years is read and write, I don't want things to be like that, she says.

Karin, how many times have we talked about this?

And why have we talked about it?

And what have I said?

I know you have to hand in the manuscript in April, she says.

Before we become parents, yes, after that I won't have time. You're not being fair now, I work hard, but at the same time I try to be a support to you, I mean, I came to the midwife, didn't I?

You say that like it's some sort of achievement; this is our child.

I did *not* say it like it was an achievement.

Tom, do you really want this, for real?

I get out of the bed, stand up, and answer: Darling, it's an absurd question, no, you know what, it's an insult, we have to do this together, you'll have to trust me. I'm going to finish this book, then I can put the writing aside if that's what you want.

That's not what I want, I also want to be able to write, I want to publish my own book. I don't have the energy for anything any more, I don't want to be some housewife, sorry, I'm just so damned tired.

It'll work itself out, darling, I promise. In a year's time everything will get easier, you're going to be a fantastic mother, and you'll publish many books, I promise, try to sleep now.

I feel like a lump of dough full of hormones.

Love you, I say, hugging her.

So you're not having doubts, then? she asks and extricates herself from my arms.

Stop it now, please, I say.

You said before you were having doubts.

Uh-huh, yeah, well forget about it, it was a while ago, maybe it's normal to feel a bit unsure about such a big life change? I answer.

I just feel so weird.

I'm not having doubts any more.

Love you, she says and puts in her earplugs. She looks

up at some pictures that I have stuck to the wall with Blu-Tack next to the reading lamp. One is a postcard from her parents of the painting, *Marine bleue, Effet de vagues*, by Georges Lacombe, depicting a sea rolling in and a sky with heavy clouds. The other is one of the square ultrasound photos from Eken Midwives. Apparently you can see the profile of our child in it. The photo is blurred and if I hadn't known it was an ultrasound image I wouldn't have guessed there was a child there. It looks more like a cluster of fluorescent plankton in a deep, dark sea.

In the oven is a Frödinge curd cake. In the last two days Karin has eaten four of them. I read the lid of the packaging.

Hey, this might be irrelevant, but curd cake contains bitter almond, isn't that fairly toxic? I say. Karin gets up from the sofa and I add: I figured there wouldn't be enough of it in a curd cake to harm Scrunchie? She presses the palms of her hands against her temples.

I'm so clueless, she groans.

I call the Nutrition Information Helpline, the woman who picks up at the other end has never had that question before. Karin is relieved to hear that she can go on eating curd cakes, but she loses her appetite for them. Instead she wolfs down a whole jar of pickled gherkins and says: I read online that it takes eight bitter almonds to kill a child, God, I'm wincing just saying that. She lifts out a basket from the wardrobe. Inside she has some orange wool and a pair of knitting needles. Ullis called, she says.

How is she?

We were going to go for coffee one day, she answers.

Nice.

I don't have the energy for it, I don't have the energy for anything.

That's to be expected.

I feel isolated, she says.

Can't you invite her here, then? I ask.

Yes, I suppose I could do that. It'll have to be after New Year in that case, I just don't feel up to it at the moment.

I sit on the floor beneath the sofa and I ask: What are you knitting?

An umbilical cord hat.

What's that?

It's just like a normal hat, but tied at the top, we'll see if I manage it – I'm not a great knitter but it's so small it shouldn't take too long.

I stretch towards the DVD case of the Wim Wenders documentary lying on the window sill and read the sleeve notes.

Who would you say is your closest friend? she asks.

Haven't got a clue, I don't think that way.

Stefan? she asks.

Maybe, no, not any more, I don't know, though I've known him the longest.

David, Alex, Hasse?

They're lovely, all of them.

Andy?

I don't think they'd see me as one of their closest friends. I don't know actually, why are you asking, are you planning a surprise party?

I don't know who I'd consider to be my closest friend

any more. Johanna has her own life in Uppsala, she has her children, and Caro and Ullis turn into right ladettes when they're with Elin, it feels like we've grown apart, I mean I love them, but it's a bit sad, she says.

How would you define 'ladette'?

You know, she says, wobbling her head from side to side.

No.

Well how would you describe someone who's a bit of a lad?

Someone who burps and farts and talks about sport and cunt.

I shouldn't have asked.

No, but really, you've got other friends, there's Caroline, Edith, Josefine, Helena.

Yeah, I know, but I hardly see them.

Friends come and go, maybe in a few years you'll find your way back to them, or if not you'll get other friends. You could try to stay in touch as well, couldn't you, maybe that's not your strongest suit. Are you feeling bad, darling?

I'm just tired, she says.

In the evening light I can see tiny particles floating through the air.

Shit, it's so dusty, I say, waving my hand in front of me. You said earlier you feel isolated.

I was just thinking out loud.

Which makes it even more important, but what did you actually mean by it?

I think it's got something to do with the pregnancy, I'm just worn out, she answers and puts away her wool and knitting needles. Can I say something without you getting angry?

That sounds worrying.

No, no, it's just that we've never gone abroad together, we go to Gotland in the summers, sure, it's nice, but it's just to my mum and dad's, and then sometimes we go to your parents' summer house.

Okay.

I know travelling makes you anxious, I do, and I know you want to be with your father because he's ill and everything, but all the same, I don't know, I don't just want to get stuck here.

If we book a trip for next summer, would that make you feel better, a honeymoon?

Darling, sorry, I'm just so fed up with being tired all the time, she says, sipping some steaming hot tea from her spoon. Karin's upper lip, the full, fine line of it and the faint clinking sound when her teeth skim against the curved steel, and the careful slurping and the heavy swallowing, makes me remember why I wanted to touch her that first time.

What if Scrunchie ends up being really hard work, a nasty kid, God, one that's so horrible the other kids are afraid of her? she says.

I laugh and answer: Shall we watch this now before we have to take it back? I hold up the cover of *Pina*.

Do you feel like watching it? she asks.

Pina Bausch seems cool.

It feels like I picked it, she says.

What do you mean, feels like? – you *did* pick it, I've never liked Wenders much.

Have you seen everything he's done?

Do I have to have seen everything to have an opinion?

It would be more modest.

What I've seen of his has been so bloody stylized, same thing with Tarantino's stuff, it's bloody infantile, I hate that shit.

Tom? says Karin with a look in her eye that makes me drop the DVD case.

I pick it up, wave it in the air, and say: But I don't mind watching this one. I hide behind the DVD cover, pretend to read the blurb, and say: I think this one's good, I'm curious about it, a lot of dance, dance is good.

Okay, she says.

Did you get grumpy there for a bit?

No, but you get so pissed off. Anyway, you're the one who said to me I have to listen to everything by this or that artist so I can have an opinion, why should it be any different for you?

True.

Do you want to watch something else? she asks.

No, I want to watch this with you, but do I get a red card if I have a glass of wine?

Does it make any difference if I say yes or no?

The thermometer outside my parents' kitchen window indicates that it's ten degrees below zero. The park, Tantolunden, lies hidden under snow, and people on Jägaregatan shuffle backwards into the wind. Harriet leans towards Karin who's sitting at the table, folding napkins.

I didn't quite catch what you said earlier, Karin, did

you say that the baby doesn't kick very much? she asks.

Yeah, I don't think it does, mainly it just moves about.

Boy or girl, if I may be so bold? says Ammi.

We don't know yet, they couldn't tell.

She's in the sixth month, says Mum, pouring some more wine into my glass.

Round about now it develops a sense of smell, says Karin, it can recognise what you're eating, apparently.

Gosh, says Mum.

I heard that babies recognise their mother's smell immediately, as soon as they're born, says Harriet.

It's kind of strange, isn't it? I have two hearts inside me, says Karin.

Yes, I guess you do, answers Ammi.

Harriet stands next to me. She holds the cutting board for me and asks: Tom, you're very busy, what is this, is it a seafood cocktail?

Yeah, sort of, prawns, lobster, mint instead of dill, a bit of mayonnaise, crème fraîche, sea salt, a dash of white wine, an obscene amount of vendace roe, silver onions just because they sound more upmarket than red onions, and then I dole out the whole caboodle on warm buckwheat pancakes.

Ammi laughs. I hear my father's voice from the sofa: How are things, Karin?

Oh, fine thanks, Thomas, actually it just occurred to me I only said hello to you but I forgot to ask how things are with you?

Not too bad, he says, then adds: The other day I woke up and I was in such a state that I was hallucinating, I thought I was on a spaceship, I thought I'd been abducted by aliens. Your poor mum was an absolute poppet about it, she told me she wasn't an alien although she did feel like one. I kiss Karin's neck while they're all laughing.

Is there wine in the starter? she asks.

Don't fret, I boiled it, I tell her, then sit down next to Börje on the sofa and find myself in the middle of a conversation. Börje stretches his two-metre-long body and gets out a business card from his wallet, hands it over to my father, and says:

Now that he doesn't have to smuggle little plastic bottles of booze into restaurants any more, he finally feels important.

Dad peers at the card and says: He's a role model for anyone in the loony bin.

Who are you talking about? I ask.

Can't you just sit tight for one minute and wait when we're talking? says Dad.

I stand up and answer: Sure I can. Then I lean my head against Karin's shoulder and mix a drink. Börje waves at me.

Yes, I say to him as I go back to standing by the sofa.

He looks at me and says: Tom, you have a father who's Superman – operations and medication, and here he sits, fitter than ever. He nods towards Dad and says: Cheers, Malmen.

You're classic, Börje, how long have you been saying that? asks Dad.

A long time, says Börje.

Must be fifty years, says Hans.

Hans, if anyone here is Superman it's you, Dad replies.

He works with his body unlike the rest of us, we're just a bunch of weaklings, he's wrestling rams to the ground and tossing bales of hay while the likes of us are solving crosswords with the help of a magnifying glass, says Börje. Hans, aren't you getting tired? You're almost seventy.

Early dinner, early to bed, he answers.

Every day? asks my dad.

Hans pulls his fingers through his big grey moustache. Livestock don't take holidays, he replies.

Dad leans his head back and says: As usual, Junior has picked a decent set of tunes.

And as usual there's a maddening lack of Elvis and George Jones, adds Börje.

I sit on the sofa and drink my grog. Dad presses his hand against his forehead and concentrates on the music.

This song is good, but damn it, I don't know, he says. Börje seems to be filled with divided loyalties when he says:

It's old gospel, you know, a lot of people have recorded it over the years, well, I suppose it's had its day.

'Lonesome Valley', I say.

I recognise the voices, says Hans.

Fred Neil and Vince Martin. I recorded it for Karin when we met, I was sure I'd be allowed to snog to that, but I wasn't, I say.

Possibly not an appropriate song lyric for a date, says Hans.

Sharpen up, Tom, says Börje, raising his index finger like an old schoolmaster.

Well, things worked out anyway, adds Hans.

What the hell were you thinking? asks Dad, shaking his head at me.

If a song makes you too happy all you want to do is dance by yourself, I answer.

You dance by yourself when you're happy? he asks.

Malmen, we're all outmoded, says Hans.

The last time I danced with you, old man, was at your sixtieth birthday party because Mum wasn't strong enough to pick you up, I say, and Börje quickly interjects:

Tom, it's great that you like older music, but it's on CD, it's unacceptable, it's got to be vinyl, you know. He stands in front of my father's record collection: several metres of country from the sixties and seventies in a sooty black upright bookcase made of solid wood. There's something inimitable in the way Börje, with his big hands, lifts out an EP by George Jones, blows off the dust and puts it on the turntable.

It doesn't get a whole lot better than this, he says and straightens his back.

Hans wipes the peanut salt on his jeans and answers: Rubbish, it really does get better, and let's raise our glasses to that.

Ammi calls out from the kitchen: Bisse said food's ready so can you put on Piaf or Baez, none of us want to listen to that screeching.

With the main course Harriet puts out two carafes of Spanish red wine, and on the other side of the table Ammi laughs so loud that Börje hollers at her: Ammi, you can't see and you can't hear either, but you can be *heard* half a mile away. She blows him a kiss. He shakes his head and turns to me: How can you let Karin keep such bad company?

All right everyone, my mother interrupts: You have to help me now, the beef is ready, the salad's there, the dauphinoise potatoes are done, I'm working on the gravy now, I think we're there but is there anything I've forgotten?

Hans rolls up his shirt sleeves and says: I don't want to be disruptive while the hostess is getting everything ready, but is it a good idea to make the béarnaise sauce in a little cup?

But Hans, is that a cup? answers Mum and he says:

You never make less than three litres of béarnaise sauce for a party.

Even for a party of eight? asks Börje, who in the midst of his conversation with Harriet has picked up on Hans's comment.

Yeah, anything else is just silly, says Hans.

That would be almost half a litre of béarnaise each, says Mum.

Exactly, says Hans.

You're classic, Hans, Börje points out, raising his glass and booming: You over there, the loudmouths in the corner, Ammi, yes, you, silence! I'll keep this short and sweet, I just want to propose a toast for our hosts, and to Hans, the lawyer, who in his autumnal days has become a cattle breeder, and Harriet, our very own fine artist, you've made your way to Stockholm and soon you have to get back to Mellösa and your animals, and in a blizzard to boot, world class, five stars, yes, and then to Tom and Karin who wanted to take part in this pensioners' get-together.

Speak for yourself, Ammi calls out.

Börje lets his gaze sweep across everyone around the table. Karin, he asks, you won't let Ammi bring you down to her lamentable level, will you?

Karin looks at me when she answers: I think Tom and I reduce the average age, which I suppose makes this a meeting of middle-aged folk.

Jesus, what a lot of nattering, can I ever finish this toast? says Börje.

Harriet calls out: Carry on, Börje.

Thanks, Harriet, yes, so this is going to be a heck of a year with countless luxurious parties and millions won on the lottery, no really, he says then stops himself. His eyes are wide open and red-rimmed. I forgot to mention Tom's starter. He sighs and goes on: Tom, four stars, if you hadn't boiled away the alcohol in that seafood cocktail you'd have got five of them. He turns to Dad and Mum: Malmen, Superman, and Bisse-bean, always six stars.

I was the first *Expressen* journo to ever give anyone six stars, that was to Glenn Hysén, says Dad.

Malmen, you're wrong about that, I've been giving your wife six stars my whole life, answers Börje.

Thanks, Börje, says Mum.

What about that toast? asks Hans.

Nicely put, Hans, this is the most confused speech I've heard since Lindfors went public about how he used to console himself as a child by stuffing his face with cake, says Dad, and when Mum sits down a moment later and says 'Please start,' a spasm rolls through Dad's body, beginning in his heels and disappearing in his white, close-cropped hair.

How are you feeling, Thomas? asks Karin.

Bloody awful, he answers.

Thomas, do you want to lie down for a moment? asks Mum and is about to stand up.

No, fuck it, I'm fine now, he says, taking a mouthful of water.

Tom, says Hans.

Yes, Hans, anything missing, apart from three litres of béarnaise sauce?

Hans dabs his moustache with his napkin then puts it back on the table. I was thinking, you're interested in literature, aren't you, 'The New Year's Bells', who wrote that?

Tennyson.

I see, he says, and looks as if he's thinking about it.

I was actually asked the same thing last New Year. I answered as confidently then as I have now, except my answer was incorrect, I don't know who came up with the Swedish version of it.

What was the original version called? he asks.

'Ring Out, Wild Bells', I answer.

It's a better title, he says.

Ring out, wild bells, to the wild sky, The flying cloud, the frosty light; The year is dying in the night, I recite. He pats me on the shoulder on his way to the toilet.

Karin slices through the filet and makes a concerned face at me. I fetch her plate and fry the meat through.

Sorry, Karin, sometimes I'm such an idiot, says Mum.

No, Bisse, beef filet is really not a problem, says Karin.

Better safe than sorry, says Harriet.

Yes, I think so too, answers Karin.

Mum reaches for the bowl of cocktail tomatoes and olives. She watches me giving Karin her food and, when I sit down again, says in a low voice: Karin is so sweet, I said so earlier to Ammi and Harriet, she has that sort of old-school elegance about her, you were really lucky to meet such a fantastic girl.

I hope there was a bit of skill to it as well? I reply.

I've been thinking about names, what do you think of Idun, the goddess of love and knowledge? asks Mum.

Idun?

Yes, Idun, do you like it?

The daughter of a dwarf, raped by a giant?

No, Mum exclaims, you're making that up!

It's a lovely name, thanks, Mum, but we don't even know if it's going to be a girl.

Karin thinks so, you should listen to her.

I chew for a moment and say: Mum, you're my favourite cook.

Do you mean that? she asks.

Your casseroles are the best.

Should I have made an ossobuco instead?

I move my chair a little closer to her and ask: How are things going, Mum?

She seems to have been expecting that question, and she answers: This morning Dad said he wanted to live a bit longer, he wants to meet his grandchild so much.

Mum, believe me, he'll outlast us all.

Darling, you're like Börje, so optimistic, no, I really must stop being feeble now.

The dog has tucked his nose under his tail. He's lying there trembling on the sofa. Mum and Karin sit on either side of him, stroking his brush-like coat. It was Tom who picked him, says Mum.

Yes, I know, answers Karin.

You know, one starts repeating oneself when one gets older, says Mum, then looks at me and adds: Do you remember how jealous you were of the cat?

I thought you were talking about the dog, I reply.

Wasn't Bosse the only puppy that didn't come up to say hello? asks Karin, although she knows the answer perfectly well.

Yes, we went to a woman in Flemingsberg, didn't we, and, well, the flat was perfectly clean and nice, it was the top flat in a high-rise, a striking lady although she did look as if she'd been wearing the same clothes for the last six months, she cared more about her dogs than herself and recommended that we take the Cairn terrier that came up to greet us, otherwise there could be something wrong with it, oh right, we thought, all the puppies came up to us, several of them had already been promised to others, oh how they jumped and yapped, they were so sweet, but then there was one miscoloured little wretch who stayed under a chair, chewing the table leg, that was Bosse, there was no way of reasoning with Tom, he was absolutely decided on the dog no one else wanted.

I would have picked Bosse too, says Karin, taking my hand and pulling it towards her.

Mum kisses the dog on the nose and says: Every New Year you get like this, well, you don't like bangers and rockets, no you don't, oh how horrible New Year's Eve is and it's not improved by being an old fellow who wants a bit of peace and quiet.

Are you tired, my darling? asks Karin, looking at me.

You want some more cider? I reply.

I've already had four glasses, she says.

There's a ludicrously small amount of alcohol in it, it's not worth thinking about; you want an orange juice instead? I ask.

Yes, please, she answers, and when I come back with the juice she says:

Mum and Dad send their best, I had a text message from them.

Oh right, okay, that's nice, send them my best back, I answer.

They're with some friends, you said? asks Mum and looks at Karin.

Yes, they go to the same place every year.

Oh I know all about it, one tends to get repetitious, says Mum.

Börje lumbers out of the kitchen with a bottle of Rotari and calls out: The music isn't loud enough, there aren't enough scandals brewing, and we're nowhere near midnight yet. Karin stands up and smooths out the wrinkles on her body-hugging dress, the black one with the foliage pattern. She puts her hands on her stomach.

How are you, Karin? asks Mum.

I'm fine.

I turn up the music, switch on the TV showing the live

broadcast from Skansen, and go to fetch Karin's jacket. Dad is sitting in one of the plastic chairs on the balcony, swept up in a thick woollen blanket, and smoking a Marlboro Original with Ammi. Mum folds one more blanket over Dad's legs and hurries back to the dog.

Aren't you cold, Karin? asks Dad.

No.

Dad gives me a shove and says: Go and get a scarf for Karin.

I don't have time to answer before Karin says: Thanks, Thomas, it's actually nice, I got so hot in there with all the candles.

Like the bloody Ice Age out here, Dad answers.

You'll only have to put up with it for a little longer, Malmen, says Ammi.

On Jägaregatan people are clustered in groups, holding champagne glasses, and at the party next door they are throwing streamers from the windows.

Did Hans and Harriet get back alright? asks Dad.

Mum got a text, they're back at the farm, apparently it was tough going on the smaller roads, I tell him.

They shouldn't have a farm at their age, says Dad.

I agree with you, Malmen, says Ammi.

It sounds like a wonderful life, says Karin.

They're not youngsters any more, says Dad.

Hans works too hard, and then there's Harriet's rheumatism to deal with, no, they ought to sell up and move into town, says Ammi.

They seem happy enough, Karin points out.

Of course you're quite right about that, says Ammi and stubs out her cigarette on the balcony railing. I press myself against Karin and place my mouth behind her ear. In the low, leaden sky there's already a blaze of colours. A smell of gunpowder in the air. Börje steps out, swears about the cold, and then tops up the glasses on the snow-covered fold-down table.

ON THE DOORMAT lie two letters. One is junk mail from Enskede Grave Maintenance which offers a twenty-five-year guarantee on all stone materials. The brochure that comes with it features photos and prices of head-stones. Black granite: 18,050 kronor. Blue labrador: 19,500 kronor. The other letter from the Department of Social Services demands that I should account for the liabilities and assets of *infant girl Unknown Lagerlöf*.

I place the envelope on the desk and sit on the bed alongside Livia, who's lying in her basket gazing up at a mobile of soft frogs holding mirrors. They glitter in the afternoon light that streams in through five windows facing onto Lundagatan, one floor above Fahlcrantz Luggage Service and the studio of the ceramicist Eva Sjögren. The bed was moved to the living room by friends of Karin and mine before I even came home from Karolinska with Livia. Karin used to sleep on the left side of the bed. The clear white of the headboard has been worn down only on my side. I have always been a nervous sleeper. What used to be the bedroom has become a guest room for Lillemor and Mum, who are taking it in turns to help me with Livia at night.

Between the desks, Karin and I have a bookcase made of ash. The books are in disarray. Much of Karin's and my time together has been spent here, opposite one another, separated by the shelf, working on our books. At the end of every month I would read out the account numbers of the bills, Karin would enter them on the screen, and we'd agonise so much about the next month's finances that we'd end up regretting past choices and blaming ourselves for how we lived. What encouraged us to keep writing was the dream of becoming a financially independent poet couple, a sort of happier version of Sylvia Plath and Ted Hughes.

Under Karin's desk are two cardboard boxes of rejected manuscripts. She stopped writing entirely a few months into her pregnancy after a combination of pelvic girdle pain and sheer exhaustion soured her mood and sapped her inspiration. Until February she'd been working at the Stockholm Art Centre, getting paid by the hour to help children cut and glue, paint, write, sing, and play instruments. Before she was put on sick leave she worked every shift she could get. She was worn out in the evenings. During her morning shifts I missed her desperately; I even missed her when she was sitting on the sofa in the other room, watching television series. The creak of the office chair when she moved, the crunch of her chewing on sesame biscuits, drawers being opened and closed again, the ink jet printer starting up without prior warning, her little high-pitched snorts while she was pondering something, her pencil grating in the sharpener, her tentatively typing fingers and her similarly tentative sighs.

Livia falls asleep while I'm watching her. I roll her basket into the kitchen, climb the little stepladder below the cupboards, and continue clearing. At the bottom of the spice shelf I find a small key no larger than the nail of a little finger, it's so small that it gets caught in the Wettex cloth. I've never seen it before. It's too small to fit into the padlocks that Karin used to take with her to the gym. I put it in a metal tin containing paper clips and rubber bands at the back of my desk drawer. I throw most of the contents of the kitchen cabinets into black bin bags: pumpkin seeds, black quinoa, apple and cinnamon muesli, raisins, tins of tomato pulp and white beans, cocoa, vanilla sugar, cartons of green tea, toasted linseed, spelt flour, walnuts, dried apricots, some of the expiry dates go back as far as 2003. Next to the pepper mill is a tube of Herbamare herb salt, it's almost empty. I preferred flaked salt or smoked cod roe on my breakfast eggs, but not Karin, there wasn't a morning when she didn't portion out some Herbamare herb salt by tapping her finger against the tub. It sounded more or less like: tap, tap-tap-tap. Or like a 'B' in the Morse Code alphabet: one long and three short. There's a white, eroded patch on the green label, from Karin's finger. I put the tube in a transparent bag, seal it with freezer tape and put it in a plastic container in which I keep everything that matters to me.

The number for the Social Services is at the top of the letter. The case officer, a man with a cool and slightly nasal voice, listens to what I have to say, then interrupts

117

me: What is the child's social security number? His tone makes me hesitate, I have to rifle through the pile of papers not to give him the wrong serial digits and birth date number. Let's see, then, he says. I have the impression that he's reading and familiarising himself with the case. She's a baby, she doesn't have any liabilities or assets, I say. Wait, he says. He starts humming. The infant girl Unknown Lagerlöf, it says here, doesn't the child have a name yet? Of course she has a name, I answer, she's my child, her name is Livia. Is that name registered with the Tax Department? he asks. Yes, I think so. You think so? Well, clearly it hasn't been registered, I say. It's not that I doubt what you are saying, but we have to proceed on the basis of available information, what I can see here is that the child's mother is deceased. He stops abruptly and continues in a muted voice: The child has a care of address of Lundagatan 46, nothing else, so I have to refer you to the Tax Department. But why do I have to clarify her liabilities and assets? I ask. Well, she's registered as being in your care, yes? Are you serious? I have to provide information on the liabilities and assets of a four-week-old child who obviously has neither? Will she inherit something? he asks. We haven't even started thinking about the division of joint property, I point out. Well, you'll have to inform us of your decision in due course, as I said, we base our enquiries on the information we have. This is absurd, I mean, really, can't you hear how this comes across? It's the information we have, he says. So, what, I have to provide accounts of the liabilities and assets of the girl child Unknown Lagerlöf to the Department of Social Services? Yes, that is how it's done, he answers. Our task is to secure the child's interests, and that's what we try to do. Is it? Yes, he answers. You *are* talking about my child now? I understand that it may sound quite formal, but what I see here is that the child is registered at the same address as you, Lundagatan 46, that's the information we have, our task is to make sure that the child based on available details is not disadvantaged financially or legally, and for this reason you have to specify her liabilities and assets. The situation now, I say, is that I can't pay the rent, I don't receive any parental allowance because I apparently don't have a child, and I can't work because in actual fact I do have a child. I can't comment on that, he says. What I'm getting at is, do you honestly think that the Social Services is helping my child in this difficult situation? I can't answer that, he answers. You can't answer that? I'm basing what I say on the information we have, he says. So Livia has no parents, then? What is it you don't understand, no one is claiming that, look, all you have to do is specify the child's liabilities and assets, just that. Do you have any children yourself? I ask. I'm not going to answer that question. Have you read Kafka? I think you should call the Tax Department, I can't do anything else for you, he says.

In the photo on my Toshiba, Karin is standing with another student from the creative writing course she was attending at the time, she seems to be listening to a conversation. It's the first photo of her I ever took. If I right-click the photo and press 'Properties' I can read for myself: Created on 13 October 2002, 13:04:38. It's ten years ago, almost a third of my life. Karin has a slight curve at the base of her spine, her arms hang down along her sides, her posture is soft, not a hint of coldness or hardness. The jumper she's wearing is kaolin white, with a pattern of cadmium-red carnations. I'm sure of the colours. Already that winter I had found them with the help of a sales assistant at Kreatima, the art shop on Sveavägen. I liked the names colours went by: Cyprian umbra, caput mortuum, terra di sienna. If I quickly glanced at Karin's jumper when she passed me on campus or sat in front of me in the lecture hall, it seemed to be plain-coloured. The same colour I felt I could see when I closed my eyes and sort of stared through my eyelids at the turned-on overhead light in my flat in Huddinge. In my diary I called it 'Karin red'.

Karin walks in front of me in one of the connecting passages between the wings of the university. On one side: noticeboards and doors leading into lecture theatres. On the other: windows looking out over the north side of Djurgården. She has a piece of chocolate in her hand. Her chewing is as calm as her steps. She stops by a bin and clears her shoulder bag of receipts, folded flyers, and pastry cases. I stand next to her and ask if she's on her way to the underground.

Yeah, I am, Tom, she admonishes. Are you in a hurry or something? Karin apparently has to stop every time she gets something out of her bag. Throat lozenges, her phone, lip balm, a diary.

No. Sorry, I answer. As we go down the long, steep escalator to the platform I ask Karin about an assignment, a translation of a Sylvia Plath poem. The deafening screech of a train pulling in forces me to repeat the question. She answers that she lives on the other side of Blecktornsparken. It's a confused conversation which leads up to our deciding or at least thinking we're deciding to call each other that evening. Back home on Edsvägen I have some quick-cook macaroni with curry ketchup while reading through the list of course participants. Names, telephone numbers, addresses, and the first six digits of their social security numbers. Karin is twenty-five. I call her three times that evening. She doesn't answer. The following morning I get a text from her: *Hi Tom, did you try to call me, not quite sure what we decided?* Karin has a friend with her when we meet that weekend in a bar on Odengatan. Helena is as tall as Karin, but slender. A blonde, younger version of Joyce Carol Oates. Apparently she's had a few poems published in *oo-tal*, the magazine. Karin introduces me and explains that we're on the same creative writing course. Helena is surprised to discover that Karin writes poems.

Secretive Karin, she says.

Helena dresses fashionably, a short pleated skirt, a discreet overcoat, a thin-as-thread necklace in white silver, a designer handbag. Her tights have a serpentine pattern. Karin tells me that Helena lives with a hairless cat on Rehnsgatan. Karin and I drink draught beer. Helena drinks white wine and throws darting glances at tall, dark men in expensive suits who are at least twenty years older than me. She is introspective, buttoned up, as if enveloped in ponderous thoughts. She wrinkles her nose when I talk and stings me with her replies. Karin is unremarkable in comparison, and when they stand next to each other at the horseshoe-shaped bar and I can see their hips, Karin looks ungainly. Helena is mundanely desirable, she has a body that I want on top of me. I am disappointed when she feels nauseous and takes a taxi home. Karin and I are left there, by the stand-up table. Karin is sensible and considerate just as in the lessons, but I don't have any particular desire to stay with her. And yet it's Karin who takes her handbag off the hook and says: Now I've yawned one time too many, but we'll see each other at school on Monday, won't we?

Karin lives at Metargatan 9. The flat has a surface area no larger than my bedsit in Huddinge. A decent flat, cosier than mine, cleaner, a more appealing fragrance about it, higher ceilings, more tasteful furniture. Karin has promised to critique my poems, to give a more personal reading than one can in a seminar room: I have invited myself. Karin sits on the bed, she's leaning against the wall. I shove aside a big decorative cushion and sit on the sofa, the same Stockholm white denim sofa that is now in Lundagatan. Between us is a kitchen table with a Marimekko tablecloth and a cheap, Californian red wine that I brought with me. I am the only one who drinks it, Karin prefers green tea. First she reads the poems slowly, then more rapidly, but not left to right but right to left and in an upward direction. She holds her breath, puts the sheet she has just read at the bottom of the pile and picks up another. Karin doesn't say much in the writing classes, but the few comments she does offer about my own and other people's texts are always insightful. She makes me realise I am not as good a poet as I had thought, which fires me up, provokes me.

Lovely, she says, gathering up the papers and gazing into the air.

Lovely? I blurt out.

Yes, lovely.

I hate lovely.

Okay, how about good, then?

You don't look like you found them particularly good.

How am I supposed to look?

It's a pretty easy thing to notice, I answer.

Oh right, she says in a muted voice and looks down at the floor.

I mean, quite honestly you look like you're sitting on a piece of fermented herring and telling me it smells good – I'm not blind, you know, I say. She chuckles and answers:

They're good, Tom, I've just underlined a few sentences I'd say you should think about, just minor things. She hands me the pile and I sit down. How long had you been with the girl in the poems?

Ellie, almost five years, why?

I was only asking.

Karin's pencilled marks, suggested cuts, are crinkled and thin like burned-out filaments. I put the poems back in my rucksack.

That thing you wrote about her dead father was powerful, she says.

Okay, thanks. She wriggles her toes in her ankle-length socks. Why did it finish? she asks.

We grew apart, or I don't know, I moved to Stockholm and she stayed on in Uppsala.

Is that where you studied?

Yeah, that's right, I answer.

So . . . is it her long eyelashes you miss most of all?

No, I don't know.

That's definitely the impression you give your reader, she says.

Okay.

I'm thinking there could be more specific details about your relationship that might be more personal?

Aren't eyelashes personal? I ask, and I can feel my jaw jutting out and my eyes becoming heavier.

It can become . . . clichéd, is that the right word? she asks. I take my rucksack into the hall, then stand there facing her. She looks at me and says: I haven't upset you, I hope?

Sod it, never mind about the bloody poems.

Already in the first week of the writing course there was gossip going around that Karin was related to Selma Lagerlöf, and that in the nineties she'd been the chief editor and theatre critic at the *Entertainment Guide*. I mention the rumour. She answers that she grew tired of the newspaper world and finds it silly that I'm interested in her being related to Selma. She even looks offended by my questions. I pursue my line of enquiry. What was her salary? Her influence? I want to know why at the age of twenty-one she decided to abandon journalism. She puts her hand over her mouth to cover a yawn, stands up, and smiles with genuine kindness, sincerity, and self-confidence, even though she's screwing up her eyes. I put my empty glass in the sink. She checks the clock on the bedside table.

So, were you up all night discussing the Lumière brothers? I ask.

Sorry, I don't follow . . .?

I heard you're dating a film critic.

Really.

That was just what I heard, someone on the course told me, I say.

Is that so?

Swedish National Television, tall, famous, dark hair, wrinkles around his eyes, somewhere between forty and ninety, pointed nose like a garfish?

God, she exclaims.

Does he bust out of the care home so he can see you? I ask.

Tom . . .

Sensitive subject, is it?

No.

So you are seeing him, then?

You really are a live wire, she says, staring at me with owlish eyes.

Sorry, I couldn't resist it, it's nothing to do with me, sorry, I say, twisting my heels into my shoes and putting on my gloves, before adding: Okay, see you on Tuesday. She stops me:

Tom, thanks for letting me read the poems, they were good.

I'm the one who should be thanking you, and no, I

know you didn't think they were any good. I should become a film critic on TV instead, I'll get older anyway whatever I do, well, okay, see you.

Okay, bye, Tom, she answers and smiles as she closes the door.

Metargatan, Ringvägen, I continue down Götgatan, across Medborgarplatsen, past Bofill's Arch, down towards the railway lines. I can't stop thinking about how Karin pronounced my name in the hall. She even managed to incorporate a little snap of the tongue on the consonant and she drew out the vowel so it sounded like a sigh. The last train to Södertälje, fifteen minutes through a landscape that always makes me feel gloomy. Apartment blocks, terraced and detached houses, motorways. The track runs parallel to the main road and on both sides of the cutting are kilometres of graffiti-sprayed noise barriers. Not even the passing seasons change this view from the train windows. There's always an atmosphere out there that empties me without making me feel any lighter. The tallest building in Huddinge has a gigantic H on the roof, the crossbar is a blue heart that shines in the dark, it can be seen from miles and miles away. I yearn to go back to Södermalm whenever I see this sixteen-storey monstrosity, I long for the small artists' flats around Vita Bergen, Tantolunden, Brännkyrkagatan, anchor plates on the façades, Mickes CD & Vinyl on Långholmsgatan, the cobbles, Pelikan Beer Hall, the kiosks open all night, the busker in a Soviet soldier's cap by Björn's Garden, the smoky second-hand bookshops by Mariatorget. Huddinge is a proper suburb, everything is empty and silent after ten at night, apart from that constant thundering from the dual carriageway.

The nurse is from AHACHC, the Advanced Hospital-Affiliated Children's Home Care, and she comes every week. How are things here, then? she asks, placing her shoulder bag in the hall. She asked me that the last time she stood there in my doorway. She has short wavy hair, square glasses, and darting eyes. The man behind her makes little jerking movements with his head before he takes off his gym shoes. This is Andreas Huhne, our senior physician, she says. He shakes my hand and says: We met briefly at Neonatal. Yes, I remember, I say, even though I don't. He looks down at Livia, who's sleeping in the sling. And here we have the little girl, he says, then walks in with his rucksack in his hand. His high forehead and shaved skull emphasise how much his ears stick out, I find it difficult not to stare at them. Are you moving? he asks, looking at the black bin bags in the hall. No, just clearing up, I answer. Can we sit down for a moment and talk? Sure, absolutely, take a seat, I say, and point at the sofa. The nurse and Huhne sit down. They rub disinfectant into their hands. I bring over a kitchen chair. Livia wakes up when I sit down. Huhne explains that he has come along to listen to her heart and then holds forth, gives me a minor lecture on the importance of vitamin D in what he calls the Nordic darkness. Five drops per day up to the age of two, but I think you could carry on for longer than that; in Finland they recommend an additional intake of vitamin D up to the age of eighteen, he says. I'm giving her five drops every day, I answer. He nods, and looks at my fingers, which are playing with Livia's hands. You've got used to it, I see, at Neonatal you weren't as confident in your paternal role, he says. Maybe that's to be expected, the nurse cuts in. I haven't had much of a choice either, I answer. Huhne turns to the nurse and says: I had one patient in his thirties, he had a tough start, that's the way he put it more or less, a year later he would have stood in front of a train for his kid. I mean I've got used to it because I'm on my own, I say. Life never turns out the way you expect it to, he replies and stretches his arms out towards Livia: Shall we have a listen to this little girl now before she falls asleep again? He sits Livia on his lap while clicking his tongue against the roof of his mouth. He prods her stomach, checks her throat, then without warning slaps the palms of his hands together. She screams. Did you see that! he bursts out. Yes, you managed to scare the living daylights out of her. That's the Moro reflex, it's from the time we lived in the trees when infants clung to their mothers to avoid falling and getting killed, he says. Okay, that sounds like useful information, I answer. He slides his finger over the sole of Livia's right foot. And there we have the cutaneous reflex, he says, observing Livia's eyes. He moves his finger through the air in front of her. Do you have a dummy? he asks. Yes, I answer. Can you get it? I bend over Livia's basket, pick up the dummy, and hand it over. He gives it to Livia and starts laughing. You could practically fix a couple of these to the wall, then if you didn't know what to do with your little one, you could just hang her up, she'd stay there because of the

sucking reflex, he muses. The nurse finds him funny.
Isn't that just amazing? We retract our hand instantly
if we touch a hot ring on the stove, and we blink if
something suddenly comes towards us, it's absolutely
amazing; if a neurological command such as the auton-
omous reflex is not working it's an indication that
something is not right, but this little girl is fully func-
tional, she's developing exactly as she should be. He
glances at the nurse and she stands up at once. He gets
out the stethoscope and adjusts the earpieces. The nurse
steadies Livia's head. Slowly he moves the metal disc
across Livia's naked body. Yes, it sounds good, he says
at last and hands her over to the nurse. He puts the
stethoscope back in his rucksack and adjusts his glasses.
I gather you've been worried about your daughter's heart,
the doctor at Neo did tell you about ductus, right? Yes,
he did, I answer. I can't hear any abnormalities there
now, but you'll be called into Karolinska in due course
so they can have a proper listen to it, ductus usually
goes away by itself, he adds, before interrupting himself
mid-sentence and turning his ear towards the window.
The bells of Högalid Church are ringing. I also live near
a church, he says. In town? I ask. Lidingö, he answers.
Lidingö Church? I ask. You know it? It's where Livia's
mother is going to be buried. Oh right, it's a beautiful
old church, he answers, then raises his eyebrows at the
nurse and says: I'm done. On the chest in the hall stand
the table-scales, lent to me by AHACHC. They look like
meat scales you'd find in a market. The general idea is
that I should weigh Livia every other day and make a
note on a yellow health card. I've done it reluctantly. The

nurse takes off Livia's nappy and lowers her into the bowl. She screams. It'll soon be over, little one, says the nurse, one hand holding Livia's legs, then she lets go and reads the display. Just over three and a half, she says. Huhne looks up from his mobile and asks: What was her birth weight? Two and a half, I answer. He puts the phone back in his jeans pocket and says: She had an age correction of five–six weeks, isn't that right? Seven weeks, answers the nurse. It's a good weight gain, how much milk replacement are you giving her now? he asks. Eighty millilitres, maybe I should increase it, I'm told she's been quite unsettled at night; I've been getting some help with her, I answer. If I were you I'd go up to ninety or a hundred, what they don't want they just leave, he says. I hold Livia's legs while the nurse checks her length. Fifty-three, she says, and sits on the sofa with Livia. She makes a note on my health card and then measures Livia's head. Is there anything you're wondering about, or do you have any special needs looking ahead? asks the nurse as I put a new nappy on Livia. Don't think so, I answer. Nothing? I guess I'm a bit stressed about taking her outside, I'd probably like a bit of support there, maybe if someone could come out with me for a walk, I haven't taken the pram out yet. I'm sure I can help you with that, she answers. I clip Livia into the sling and accompany them to the door. The funeral is quite soon, I'll have to take her out then, I say. When is the funeral? asks Huhne. Next Friday, I answer. You're going to notice that children have an unsentimental relationship to death, my children dance on my mother's grave, literally, he says. The nurse tries to catch his eye, then squats down and gets out a light blue plastic bag from her shoulder bag, one of those bags they had for used nappies and wet wipes at Neonatal. Tom, she says, these are things we think you left at Karolinska, could that be right? They may well be, thanks, I answer, not daring to look into the bag, instead quickly shoving it up onto the hat shelf, accidentally knocking down a bicycle light and a pile of junk mail. I get down on my knees. Among free newspapers and advertising from Pizza Express is an information sheet from Eken Midwives printed on 23 February 2012. At the top of it is written: Parents' Meeting, 2 April. The nurse and Huhne have gone outside onto the landing. Okay, Tom, if something comes up just give us a ring, she says. Thanks very much, I answer. And we'll be in touch about that walk, she adds. That would be fantastic, thanks. Huhne smiles broadly at me and adds: Walks might be something for your mother or mother-in-law to help you with; at AHACHC we conduct hospital-affiliated childcare in the home, but I'd say start on a modest scale, take a walk around the house.

Nils Jardesten has a Norwegian accent. I've spoken to him on several occasions but never registered it before. He's called to say that my request to kiss Karin goodbye in church cannot be accommodated. I only ever met him once, at Ignis Undertakers on Sveavägen, with Sven and Lillemor. A face carved in wood, age indeterminate, fifty, may just as well be over sixty. Why not? I ask. It's just not possible, Tom. Why? Tom, I'm only the messenger here, you have to ask the people at Karolinska, at

Pathology. Pathology? Yes, the morgue is in the Pathology Department. I thought it was you and the officiating priest who decided? Tom, I've spoken to Pathology, they've said no, I can't do any more than that, if you want an explanation you have to ask them, I don't know why they declined. Surely it's not up to Karolinska to decide? Hold on a minute, Tom, I'll get you their telephone number.

Lillemor looks like an uninvited guest, she can't decide whether to stand still or move about, speak or hold her silence. She's wearing baggy trousers, a glittering shawl, and a plush jumper from Vamlingbolaget. She smells heavily of perfume. Sven comes in half a minute later and almost trips on the threshold. He holds out his hands in the air in front of him and says: I'll keep my distance, I can't shake hands, I've got a cold, I don't want you to catch it. He strides in wearing his walking boots and almost falls over the shoe shelf. Sven, hisses Lillemor. He stops abruptly and looks around. Lillemor shakes her head and points at his boots. He looks down at them, then at me. I'm so sorry, he says. No harm done, Sven, I reply. He unlaces his boots and makes another attempt to enter the flat, mumbling something, opens the first door on the left in the hall and steps into the cleaning cupboard, turns around, clears his throat and opens the next door, peers inside, and says: Oh right, here's the toilet. Lillemor sits on the sofa. For the third time since she came in she rubs Alco-Gel into her hands, she's brought her own little bottle in her handbag. Where's Livia? she asks. Here, I say, pulling the basket closer to the sofa. As Lillemor cranes her neck and peers down, her stone-pale face seems to relax and acquire a touch of colour. I put coffee and some Marie biscuits out on a tray in the kitchen. Sven emerges from the toilet and stands by the sofa with his arms behind his back. He observes Livia for a while and then sits as far from her as he can. I'll keep my distance, he says, probably best. Lillemor has brought some baby clothes in two paper bags. Most of this was given to us, not least from Jonna, she says, taking out the garments one by one and holding them up for inspection. I can give them back if you don't want them, that's not a problem, but they are quite sweet, she adds. Thanks, it's just that I have such an insane amount of clothes. I have three sacks here, everyone sends me clothes. I haven't even had time to look at them, and then I get messages asking whether I got the clothes. Yes, of course, she says. Extra clothes are always handy, just put them there, thanks Lillemor, I say. It's Jonna you should thank, she says and continues: I was thinking it it might be good if she had an overall when she's out in the pram. Absolutely, thank you, I say. Do you want milk, darling? asks Sven, who's leaning over the little sofa table. Lillemor purses her lips, sighs deeply, and asks: How long have we been married? Sven starts laughing and answers: Darling. Lillemor looks at me and says: I've never taken milk in my coffee but Sven has always taken milk in his. I know, I say, either way I don't have any milk at home, but I could offer you some formula. Sven inhales, fills his chest, blows on his coffee, and answers: Thanks, but I'll say no to that. I was only joking, Sven, I say. Uh-huh, well, he says. Lillemor puts the clothes back in the paper bags. She has brought a copy of *Dagens Nyheter*. She opens the newspaper at a page marked with a Post-it note and asks: Did you see this, well I expect you did, of course, but did you get an actual copy of the newspaper? I didn't, but Mum saved it for me, I can't look at it now, I answer. That's quite understandable, she says. We agreed on the formatting of the death notice last week at the undertaker's. At the top we decided on the silhouette of a flying swift. In the summers, last year's swifts used to return to the same spots under the roof-tiles of Sven and Lillemor's house on Gotland to build new nests. Karin and I had spent our summers there since 2004. The association between Karin and swifts was nothing more elaborate than that she liked the chirping of their chicks and was fascinated by the ability of adult swifts to sleep in the air, borne by the winds.

Lillemor picks up a notepad, puts it on the sofa table and, without looking up, asks: Can we agree on plot 64 on block 5? Sven brushes biscuit crumbs from his shirt, apologises, and tries to collect every crumb from the floor, his hands scuttling along like crab claws. Leave it, Sven, I'll go over it with the hoover later, I say, and turn to Lillemor. But haven't we already decided that? I say. I just wanted to make sure, she says. Fine, says Sven. The headstone will be made of limestone from Gotland, it will be placed in an upright position towards the fields and the bay, Kyrkviken. At first, Lillemor and I decided on block 4 and plot 350 next to a woman artist with a millstone as her memorial mark, just next to the gravel path. But the following day we changed our minds and

I wandered down to the churchyard reception and explained that in fact we'd rather have block 5 and plot number 64, explaining that there were a lot of ostentatious stones around plot 350, and that the family of the woman artist had laid claim to more than the regulatory 120 centimetres, and we had no desire to engage in conflict about their ferns. Plot 64 on block 5 is positioned in the central row of discreet gravestones on a slope. The spot gets sun from morning to evening. Lime trees and oaks line the raked gravel paths, also Reeves spiraea, cotoneaster, and various cherry trees, and the masts from the small harbour are visible from there. For the time being there'll be a wooden board, says Sven. When will the stone be ready? I ask. Towards the summer, they thought, they have to break the stone first and then cut it to size, he answers. I suppose there's no rush about it, I say. No, I don't suppose there is, he says and looks at Lillemor. It'll be a relief if it's done by the summer, I have a feeling this may be fairly prolonged, I want the stone finished before we go to Gotland, she says. Yes, darling, answers Sven. That wooden board is horrible, she adds. I don't know if I agree with you there, answers Sven. Lillemor slides the tip of the pen over her pad and says: Well, anyway, can we all agree that we don't want a coffin shroud? The coffin is beautiful just as it is, answers Sven. I was asking Tom, she says. Oh, sorry. We've already had time to talk through this, she points out. Yes, darling, he says. She coughs and splutters into the crook of her arm, and then says at last: Sorry, I got something stuck in my throat, well, maybe I'm odd or something, I couldn't stop thinking about how maybe it would get so hot in the coffin if there was a thick shroud on top of it. No shroud, I say. Very good, and what do you think about the music in the church? she asks. I have no particular wishes, the psalms and songs you emailed me look fine, but I have been looking in Karin's computer, this year she's been listening a lot to *Bist du bei mir*. Oh really, Lillemor bursts out. Can you see that from her computer? asks Sven. Yes, there are statistics, I mean she had music on the computer, it would be nice to include a piece that she liked while she was pregnant, I say. Could I just have a listen to it, not that I'm opposing the idea? says Sven. Absolutely, I'll just get it, I answer, and then I connect Karin's computer to the speakers: I read that it's popular both for weddings and funerals, I say. It's Aafje Heynis singing, *Bist du bei mir, geh ich mit Freuden zum Sterben und zu meiner Ruh*. Sven pats Lillemor on her lower arm, she stands up and shakes her head, then goes into the hall and stands with her back to us, her arms held as if she's pressing her wrists over her mouth. Sven is about to get up and rush over to her, when she says: I have been thinking a lot about Karin's jewellery. Sven leans back. She takes a scrunched-up tissue from her pocket and sits down on the sofa again. Some of her jewellery we gave to her, and some of it came from her grandmother, my mother, she says and peers at one of the speakers while adding: It's beautiful, Karin had such lovely taste. She presses the tissue against her upper lip. I know that Karin got a silver ring set with a malachite from her grandmother, she says. Wouldn't it be nice if Livia could have that when she grows up, though? I think Lillemor just means that she'd like to borrow them, says Sven, and Lillemor interjects: Yes, I don't want to take them, they belong to Livia, I just thought it could be good if I wrote down where they come from, it's something that might be interesting to know, jewellery is lost so easily, a few of the pieces are quite valuable. Karin's jewellery case is in the corner, I haven't even had time to look at it, I mean some of the jewellery I bought her myself, I answer. I was mainly thinking about the jewellery she inherited, says Lillemor. You want me to go and get it now, or . . .? I ask. Tom, what was the name again of the song you just played? Sven interrupts and looks at both me and Lillemor with a sense of calm that I recognise from Karin. *Bist du bei mir*, Karin particularly liked Heynis's voice, I answer. It's a lovely piece of music, says Sven.

The woman from the Tax Department has a piercing voice. The line hisses and crunches between each sentence. I can't answer for what the Social Services sent you, it must have been done before the name was registered, she says. They're calling my daughter 'infant girl Unknown Lagerlöf', I point out. I am not familiar with their procedures, in the national register she's listed as Livia Karin Lagerlöf, she replies. But Social Security say they're acting on the basis of information obtained from you? Yes, I suppose they are. I want my wife's first name and surname to be my daughter's middle names, Karin Lagerlöf should be a part of my daughter's name, Livia Karin Lagerlöf Malmquist. Well, you were only turned down for Malmquist, she says. But why? It says 'FC' here. Okay, and what does that mean? I ask. Placed in care with someone else, she answers. I don't understand, I say. It means she's in foster care. I am Livia's father. You weren't married, though, as I understand it? Every time I have contact with an official body or a bank they notice that my daughter has a different surname from my own, and I have to explain, and I can't deal with that. You weren't married, that's the only explanation I can give, if people aren't married this is how it ends up, unless one can provide a fatherhood certificate, didn't you get one of those? Isn't it usually done after the child is born? I ask. One can also fill out the form before the birth, she explains. I took a DNA test at Karolinska, I am the father, Karin and I lived together for ten years, I have been taking care of Livia since the moment she was born, what more do you want? There has to be a court decision that you are in fact the father of the child, she answers. So, I've been sitting here in a phone queue for the best part of an hour and this is what the Tax Department has to say? Young man, I can't turn back the clock and help you with your fatherhood certificate. What did you say? No, hold on a second, let me finish, the hospital reports to us that a child has been born, we register the child and give it a social security number, then we send out name forms to the child's mother, if the mother is unmarried the child automatically takes the mother's surname, this information is saved on our national register, and this is the information with which other authorities comply, in other words I can't sit here and answer questions about the Swedish statute book, or questions of right and wrong. What we need now is a court decision, how this should be achieved in a practical sense I wouldn't pretend to know. Have you spoken to someone at the City Court?

All the books I have not read or have read and do not want to read again I put in removals boxes. In the flyleaves of some of them are little Christmas greetings or congratulations from friends or old boyfriends of Karin's. Two of the books she has borrowed from Hornstull Library. Doris Lessing's *The Fifth Child* and Nina Bouraoui's *Our Kisses are Farewells*. They must be at least a month overdue. The library card has to be shredded, I'll need to do that, after the funeral I have to go to Hornsbruksgatan 25 and say: Karin Lagerlöf won't be borrowing any more books. I fetch a scouring cloth from the cupboard under the sink. The door of the guest room is closed. It sounds as if Lillemor is turning on the bed inside and leafing through a newspaper. I don't hear Livia. I go back and clean up the mess around an over-watered and leaking *Monstera* plant, or Adam's rib as it is also called, and in the process I almost wipe away a couple of coffee stains under Karin's desk. She avoided caffeine during the pregnancy. So the coffee stains must be older than 26 August 2011, Karin's thirty-fifth birthday, the same morning that she put aside the champagne from Reims and came back with a Clearblue digital pregnancy test indicating that she was pregnant, in her second or third week. I save the stains, photograph them, then go and get Karin's coffee cup from the corner cabinet, in fact it's an antique teacup from Gefle porcelain factory with a gold rim and a crinkled surface. I sit on Karin's chair and try to imagine her writing on her laptop and spilling the coffee. She must have been bringing a full-to-the-brim cup towards her while at the same time twisting towards the bookshelf. On the edge of the shelf I see an A4 sheet with transparent tape on it. Karin's slightly slanted handwriting in green felt-tip:

To Be Purchased Before May
Pram
Changing table
Cot
Sheets
Pillow
Duvet
Raincover or parasol for pram?
Nappy bag
Sling?
Babybjörn
Car seat
Bathing oil
Hat
Comfy trousers
Cardigan
Jumper, warm
Overall
Socks
Babygrows

At the top of the bag the nurse from AHACHC brought is a black cotton slip from H&M. It can't be Karin's, they cut up her slip in Room B at CIC. I don't even recognise the scent. Karin's used slips and jumpers smell a bit of cedar from her Palmolive deodorant, now and then they smell of one of her perfumes, DKNY, Carolina Herrera, Yves Saint Laurent, Elizabeth Arden, Clean Fresh Laundry, sometimes a bit of lavender, but above all a smell of Karin, her skin, her sweat. The slip isn't hers. I fold it up and put it in a bin bag. Also inside are two laminated sheets, fifteen by fifteen centimetres. Livia's nameplate with a guardian angel on it, and a cast of Livia's right foot and hand, in a corner it says '25th March'. Both used to hang on the side panel of the incubator. I go to bed and turn out the lights, but turn them back on after half an hour of brooding. On Karin's desk is a framed postcard, under glass. She's had it a long time, since Metargatan. A copperplate in Romantic style. An angel with a young woman in his arms is rising into a blaze of heavenly light. It resembles Wilhelm von Kaulbach's painting *Schutzengel* but it is darker, more wistful. In the background is an ocean reaching to the horizon. Foaming, breaking waves. On a black rock lies a curled-up man.

Not until early spring 2003 does Karin tell me she has been collecting angels. Angels in porcelain, wood, plaster, and filigree. Angels on stamps and mugs. She sits on her bed, and I on the sofa opposite, we have sat like this so many times that I recognise every knot in the floorboards between us. I have never seen Karin intoxicated before. Only her earlobes seem different, they're flushed, and she peers into her cleavage every now and then when she isn't speaking. She pokes her finger into her wine glass and removes a little speck.

Have you seen *Angels in America*? she asks, pressing her weight against the wall.

The one about the gay couple?

Have you seen the play? she asks.

I didn't know there was a play, the series was bloody brilliant.

I saw it performed here in Stockholm, they had an angel flying over the audience on some kind of cable, it was really dramatic.

Is that what made you collect them?

No, I only just remembered when you asked about the angel in the bathroom.

Are you religious?

I just collected them.

I had a period when I was collecting porcelain pigs.

Really?

I'm not collecting them any more, I add.

She laughs without making a sound. I was totally potty about angels, my friends must have thought I was ridiculous, I had an angel made of papier mâché hanging from the ceiling up there, she says, pointing to a hook above me, and then goes on: I always got angel stuff when people gave me presents, that one for instance. She looks over at the bedside table. There's an angel on the tin I keep my earplugs in, she explains.

Okay.

I got rid of most of them. Angels are fascinating, they're beautiful and they have something wistful about them, but actually it was quite hard work surrounding yourself with them. I had a double-edged relationship to them, I grew up in an atheist home, my mother is a philosophy teacher, my father's a psychoanalyst, basically just a psychiatrist.

Must you be an atheist if you're a philosophy teacher and a psychoanalyst-psychiatrist? I ask.

That's mad, why did I tell you that?

Maybe they had good arguments against the existence of angels?

I'm an atheist myself, she emphasises.

You sound more like an agnostic, I say.

No, I'm an atheist, or I don't know, or no, I am an atheist, at least I think so.

An atheist believer?

Yes, that's mad, I feel drunk, she says.

My mother went to evening classes, Dad started working when he was sixteen, I think both have some kind of faith. Dad wears a crucifix around his neck, Mum gave it to him on his thirtieth birthday, anyway, I think I got my academic hang-ups from them, I have a difficult time with academics, I hate them.

But aren't you an academic yourself? she asks.

No, I'm not.

You're such a loon, she says.

I was all over the place at school, I went to special needs classes, I didn't give a shit about school, I still feel like a hockey player even though I stopped playing when I was sixteen.

Oh, you played hockey? she exclaims.

Yeah, I was a so-called hockey prospect.

Uh-huh, well I didn't know that. God, I have a hard time imagining that, did you just stop?

Yeah, more or less, I answer. Porcelain pig collecting took over, did it? Absolutely, but actually no, I didn't have the grades to get into university, I nagged my way

143

onto a course and lied a bit. Karin laughs and before she has time to ask me about it, I say: So why did you stop collecting the angels? She thinks for a moment, stands up, and goes to get a glass of water.

That mural of the angel in the bathroom, the earplug tin, and the picture there on the desk, they're the only ones I have left, collecting things is so pathetic, isn't it? she says. I walk up to Karin's desk and take a closer look at the angel.

Is it a famous picture? I ask.

I don't know, I've asked around, no one seems to know. A friend of my father's is a professor at the Academy of Fine Arts, I showed him the postcard, he thought it had been done by an unknown jobbing illustrator, some passage from the Bible, anyway the postcard is from the fifties, it says so on the back. I like it, it makes me feel calm when I look at it. She leans forward, picks up the wine glass, takes a mouthful and puts it back. I sit down once more. Karin disappears into the hall. It sounds as if she's looking for something in a case or carrier bag. I get restless and nervous and can't tell whether we've spent an hour together or talked through the night. It takes a while before she comes back. She polishes her glasses with a silk cloth and puts them on and starts blearily examining her fingernails. I had a brain haemorrhage, she says, adding immediately: When I was twenty-one. I've not been given the all-clear. I don't know how to reply, but she doesn't wait for my answer or any reaction, instead she says: I saw an angel at the hospital. She gets a paper tissue from the bedside table, dabs it against her tongue, and starts rubbing at a stain on one of her trouser legs.

Karin, I had no idea.

She clears the glasses and side plates. I want to help but she tells me to stay where I am and asks if I'd like green or black tea. I tell her I'm quite all right as I am. Once she's done, she sits down on the bed again.

A real angel, you mean? I ask.

What's a real angel?

Yeah, stupid question.

She describes the angel, it had a strong light around it yet it was still corporeal, with colossal swan-like wings, a solar being, it came at night, reminding her of those bookmark angels she had loved as a child. Karin suggests that the angel was a neurological phenomenon. A projection of her need for consolation. She goes back to the kitchen cubicle.

But still, there it was right in front of me, I saw it, she says and turns off the tap. She comes to a halt just in front of me. Her grey-black cardigan reaches down over her thighs, her jeans are also grey-black, but her blouse is white with light-coloured wooden buttons.

You should write about this, I say.

But I do, she says.

Yeah, I suppose so.

Or what did you mean, exactly?

I didn't mean anything in particular, I say.

You said there's a noticeable depth in my poems, that made me happy.

Yes, there is, I felt you had been through something, you had separated from someone, I say.

Do you have to describe things in exact detail, or should you keep them secret?

You're a poet, I say.

No one has ever called me a poet before, she answers after thinking about it.

You are. I look up at a poster of a colourful sculpture which Karin has above her bed. I like that, I point out.

It's Niki de Saint Phalle, she says.

Is that what it's called?

No, she's the artist, she answers.

I know that Karin is not seeing the film critic any more, and I'm too tired to be polite: Is it okay if I stay over on the sofa? Karin seems uncomfortable. I explain that the last train has gone, I'd have to wait two hours for the night bus. I can't afford a taxi, I add. She drinks her tea in quick gulps.

Yeah, sure, I guess that's okay, she says.

Shit, that's really decent of you.

She traipses into the bathroom. The door closes. I hear the shower. It sounds as if she has toothpaste in her mouth when she calls out: There's a stain on the sofa, it's only red wine, nothing else.

Karin goes to sleep before I do. The only thing I can hear is a slight rumbling from the cast-iron radiator. It takes me a while to find the light switch in the bathroom. On the handbasin is a bottle of perfume. Apple fragrance. I open the bathroom cabinet over the handbasin. Arranged over four glass shelves is contact lens fluid, perfumed talcum powder, tampons, deodorant, cotton tips, a foot file, nasal spray, mouth ulcer cream. I sit on the toilet lid. I see the angel on the wall to the left above the handbasin. I noticed it the first time I was in her flat. Karin just chuckled at the time and said,

I haven't had time to paint over it yet. It's been painted using a fine brush. Open wings in gaudy yellow. Flowing hair and a bright red breast in the form of a heart. Two fangs protrude from its upper lip. I study it for a long time. Then I turn my head towards the bathtub, an orange plastic mat inside it. Karin's half-metre long hairs snagged in the floor drain.

Karin's flat suddenly feels like a collection space for silence, a process that has only been underway for an hour, yet the extent of the silence already exceeds everything. The dusty mullions, the cracked white paint, the thirties bathtub with claw feet, the hob with its sooty cast-iron pan support, the little coffee percolator on the shelf of flared grey limestone. I sit on the floor with my mobile and make a call, I leave a message:

Hi, Karin, it's me again, can you get back to me, please, okay, bye, hope everything is fine, okay, bye.

I insert one of her favourite albums into the CD player, Joni Mitchell's *Song to a Seagull* and the song 'Night in the City'. I stand in the kitchenette by the window. Karin answers at last:

Hi, sorry, I need to think, really sorry.

Shoots of the jasmine bush push through when I open the window.

Where are you?

In Djurgården, I'm taking a walk with Caro, it's not about you, Tom, I know it sounds like a bit of a cliché putting it like that.

I jump up and sit on the broad window seat. There's a droning of bumblebees and hoverflies.

I think I'm mainly just surprised, I say.

Look, I'm so sorry, Tom, I just don't think I'm ready for a new relationship, I've got too much baggage, I need to think.

I don't know what to say because you're not saying anything, I respond.

Sorry, she answers.

Okay, but I'm sitting in your flat now, maybe it's not a good time to be waiting for you here, then, or what?

Sorry, but I really need to think. There's a spare key in a cup in the kitchen just next to the coffee percolator, the one with a key ring like a lightbulb.

Okay, I'm sure I'll find it.

If you could just lock the top lock and throw the key in through the letter box, she says.

Okay, yeah yeah, but can we be in touch later?

Sorry for just leaving like that, I haven't been feeling right lately, sorry, you're great, Tom, but it's all gone too fast for me.

On the way to the train I call Karin again, she doesn't answer, I leave yet another message:

Hi, Karin, I put the keys through the letter box like you said, I drank all the milk, I bought you some more, I cleaned a bit as well, or tidied, I vacuumed the hall and picked up my own crap, I listened to your Joni Mitchell albums, I understand what you mean, I agree, more interesting than Dylan, I think my favourite is 'Amelia' from *Hejira*, okay, sure, maybe it's a bit weird but I couldn't stop myself buying you another album, I was passing by the Vinyl Window anyway, *Two Steps from the Blues*, Bobby Bland, don't think you've listened to him, start with track five, 'Lead Me On', good soul, no, better just listen through, well anyway, this is an idiotically long message, sorry, take care of yourself, and call me if you like.

I find the telephone number for Stockholm City Court on the Internet. I am passed between different departments and every time I speak to someone new I have to explain about my being the single parent of a child and how Karin has suddenly passed away. Every time they respond with something along the lines of: Okay, what's your case number? Finally when a district court clerk says I've come to the right person she asks if she can call me back. Her voice sounds young, no older than twenty-five, she's precise and pleasant. Half an hour later she calls on my landline. I answer at my desk and make a note of her name: Najma. I've brought myself up to speed now, she says, there doesn't seem to be any simple or quick way for you to become the father in a legal sense. Okay, I answer. The city of Stockholm has to apply for a summons through Södermalm City Council, she continues. What does that mean? Your daughter has to take legal action against you, she can't do that herself, of course, she's a baby, the city of Stockholm has to do it on her behalf. Legal action against me? It's not as bad as it sounds, that's just the terminology we use, your daughter will be the petitioner and you'll be the plaintiff. The city of Stockholm? Yes, you have to call a case officer at Södermalm City Council, we have to receive a summons, the local council administration must, in accordance with the sixth chapter and ninth paragraph section two of Parental Law, report to the city court that your daughter does not have a custodian, I think it's the Social Services Department that must then nominate you as the custodian, the only thing you have to do is accept the plaintiff's case. Well, I am her father, aren't I? For you to be able to act for your daughter you must first have custody of her, this is the quickest way, a court decision on your paternity will take time, a paternity investigation will have to be done, and it will require an ombudsman who can represent your daughter in the case, and it will need materials on which to base a decision. Okay, okay. In other words it's quicker to make a decision on a custodian than a decision on paternity, she says. I really don't understand, I'm saying yes, I'm not denying it, am I? That doesn't matter a bit, that's how the law is. Is this crap written in the nineteenth century or something? I don't know, she answers. Barons had it away with the milkmaids and denied paternity so they wouldn't have to pay maintenance? There are some laws today that leave a certain amount to be desired, she says. So if Karin had told some bureaucrat old bag at the Social Services office that I was the father of the child then this whole crock of shit would never have happened? Exactly, she answers. A woman's word is considered more trustworthy than a DNA analysis from the National Board of Forensic Medicine, and my voice, the voice of the father, doesn't mean shit? The best thing you can do now is to make sure we get a summons in so that a decision can be made on a specially designated custodian. This is diabolical, I say. I understand your frustration, really. Even if I become the father in a legal sense, the Social

Services will require that there has to be a trustee to say yes or no to my financial decisions until Livia's an adult. I can understand your concerns, she says, but I interrupt her: They'll supervise me as a father. Supervise may be a slightly strong word to use here. They'll clip my wings as a father. I understand what you mean. What hurts me most of all about this bullshit is that a simple marriage certificate that you can sign after getting to know each other for fifteen minutes in a bar seems to count for more than living together for ten years. Is a marriage licence worth more than a family's history? The telephone line hisses. Hello, I exclaim. Yes, I can hear you, I am listening, unfortunately I'm not allowed to give legal advice in my position. I never asked for it. In my opinion you should contact an experienced lawyer who can help you, as for the Social Services there isn't much you can do, that's how heavily the marriage licence counts. I cough, down a mouthful of my Coca-Cola, and say: Karin was sick before, she got a cyst on her brain that almost did away with her, she came home after a month at the hospital, I proposed, it was Christmas 2004, she said yes. I really am very sorry, she murmurs. Okay, what did you say I had to do to get custody?

I have four banana boxes with me and two plastic bags when I move in with Karin on Metargatan one Sunday in the winter of 2003. The rest of my stuff I have thrown away or dumped in my parents' attic in Huddinge. Only when moving do I actually touch all my belongings. A point of contact with the past is established, which goes beyond memory. Even an eraser or a couple of bent

151

picture hooks in the hand can feel irreplaceable. Before I go to bed that night I slip into a hot bath. I look around. Something in the bathroom is different. I can't say what it is and don't understand why it makes me feel ill at ease. I guess I'm tired after the move and disoriented after a difference of opinion with Karin about a mirror I've brought, a Baroque plaster copy. There's a seraph at the top of the frame and, at the bottom, a demon from hell. Whenever I looked into that mirror, in my old flat in Huddinge, my pale and malleable face seemed to peer back at me, squeezed in between those two eternal figures. Karin finds the mirror kitsch and depressing. I don't like it much either, but as far as I'm concerned it's a matter of principle; I don't want everything in the flat to chime with Karin's parents' homely and bourgeois taste in interior design. Karin's mural ought to be visible from the bathtub. I lean forward. She has painted over the angel. And not with a roller either. She has carefully filled in the red and yellow lines with a fine brush, using a white covering paint that is shinier than the rest of the wall. I pick at the glass fibre weave. Karin must have done it this morning while I was cleaning my empty flat on Edsvägen, but I can still see the angel; from certain angles it's lit up by the ceiling light.

Livia touches my mouth and nose with hands that remind me of Karin's testing a piece of fruit for ripeness. I kiss her, she doesn't like that. Her nails are thin as paper, the Neonatal nurses advised me to keep them short by simply tearing them off, apparently you can do that with newborns' nails. But I can't, I'm worried I might pull off the whole nail. I trim them with clippers, so carefully that I can only do it when she's fast asleep.

Livia's clothes are kept behind the door of the guest room. In the drawers are some small cloth bags of dried lavender that Karin made. She took the lavender from the flowerbeds at her parents' summer house. Quite apart from the protection they give against moths, she liked the scent of lavender, she kept one of the cloth bags tied to the bedpost, and she used to rub her fingers against it before she fell back on the pillow with her hand over her nose. I dress Livia: dove-grey baby trousers with knee pads and a striped cardigan in the same colour, size fifty-six. Also a cap, tights, and socks. The clothes smell of lavender but mainly of pine, the wood the drawer is made of. Karin bought the clothes two weeks before we went in to the maternity ward of the Söder Hospital. That afternoon she was caught out when I appeared in the doorway, bags in my hands from the supermarket. She was resting her neck against the back of the sofa. Her black singlet was drawn up over her navel. I got the idea she had been whispering secrets to her belly and listening for answers. The clothes were on the kitchen table. Karin had arranged them so that they looked like a perfect outline of an infant child. She kept her eyes on me when I touched them, and told me that she had bought them with her mother the other day.

Do you like them? she asked.

And what did I do then? What was I doing while Karin was picking out clothes for our child?

*

153

It takes me an hour to come up with the idea of some cut flowers, and another hour to find a florist who has carnations in the right colours. The flower hall on Birger Jarlsgatan. The florist, a man roughly my age, claims that the carnations are red and white. This is a simplification, they are the same colour as the jumper Karin was wearing that first time I saw her at Stockholm University. I pay 1,560 kronor for just over one hundred carnations. I can't afford any more, that's all the money I have in my account. It's Thursday, 26 August 2004, and I catch the number 59 bus on Rådmansgatan. I press the bouquet so hard against my chest that the water seeps out of the wrapping paper, the crotch of my jeans gets wet, I look as if I have peed myself. The bus stops outside the entrance to the Karolinska University Hospital in Solna. I want to charge about and run. I daren't. I don't want people staring at me. On the lower level of the Neurocentrum is the Bistro Amika, it looks like a road-side café, I go inside and get rid of the wrapping paper. Patients with turban-like bandages around their heads, by mobile drip stands, in wheelchairs, leaning on walking frames. A nurse stops me in one of the corridors on floor six. She's wearing white clogs and carrying a tray, on it a small plate with a half-eaten cheese sandwich and a stainless steel jug.

It's not visiting hours now, she says, and tries to establish eye contact.

I have to get to R16, I answer, hiding my crotch behind the bouquet.

This is R16, who are you visiting? she asks.

My partner, she came in this morning.

Who is your partner?

Karin, I answer.

Karin who?

Karin Lagerlöf, she came in from Karolinska in Huddinge this morning, she's having emergency surgery. She surveys the corridor and says:

Room 604, it's on the left after the food trolley there, she just got some sedatives, she's sleeping. Then she glances down at my offering and adds: But this is the Neurology ward, no flowers.

It's her birthday today, I answer.

Lovely, but you have to leave them outside, we have to think of the patients, some of them have allergies.

Can't I just quickly show them to her? I ask.

No one's allowed to bring flowers, she answers, pressing down with her elbow on the door handle of what seems to be the entrance to the staff room. I stand there dithering for a while before I go back the same way I came, there's a trash can in the elevator hall. It looks like a composting bin and it's overflowing with wilted bouquets with handwritten cards. I bin the carnations.

On top of the bathroom cabinet is an old jam jar half-filled with sand. Karin cycled off on her own to fetch the sand before we went back from Gotland in the summer of 2009. She explained that sand with soap is good for the body, it exfoliates, clears dead skin. The jar was left where it was. I know that Karin used to look at it while brushing her teeth, especially in the winter-half of the year. It stinks when I open the lid, as if something has decomposed in there. I strain and boil the white sand, then pour it into a glass jam jar, which I put on the bookshelf so I can see it from the bed. I continue throwing away rusty hairpins, old tubes of ointments and deodorants, half-empty toothpastes and dirty earplugs. In a plastic bag under the basin I find an unopened carton of contact lenses, contact lens fluid, and a tube of lens drops. There's a receipt at the bottom; Karin paid 738 kronor for it all at Östermalms Optik. She was out that whole day, tracking down the right lenses. I want to save the contact lenses as a memento for Livia but I change my mind and throw the whole bag in the bin bag. On the middle shelf in the bathroom cabinet lies Karin's hairbrush. Her hairs are still snagged in its plastic teeth. She didn't have time to prise them out and throw them away as she usually did. The brush is thick with hair, I smell it, I press it to my mouth.

Livia continues emptying her bowels into my hand, I can't let go of her with my other hand, in case she rolls round and falls off the changing table, there's another ring at the door, I have to shunt the changing table against the sink with my body while I rinse the excrement off under running water, all without letting go of her.

The vicar has a motorcycle jacket and Ray-Bans, heavy black boots, close-cropped hair, a short beard shot through with grey streaks. Tom? he asks and takes off his sunglasses. Yeah, that's right, and this is Livia, I answer. Oh yes, Livia, yes, hello there. He takes her hand then offers me his. Totta, he says. Yes, I worked that one out, I answer. We did say eleven o'clock, didn't we? Yes, we did, I was changing a nappy, there was shit everywhere, I answer. He chuckles, steps out of his boots, stares with curiosity into the hall, and says: I was a bit early so I had a wander around the area, it's nice, how long have you been living here? He has bright red socks, he moves along gingerly, carefully lowering his head as he goes through every doorway. We moved here in 2008, I answer. It's a one-bedroom flat? Yes, it's all studios and one-beds here, when we moved here we found out that all the flats here used to be accommodation for widows, it was a charitable thing run by the Association of Burghers on Högalidsgatan. Really? Yes, at least that's what I heard, it's the sort of thing I commit to memory these days. Tom, I am very sorry about what has happened, what's happened to your family is truly tragic. Thanks, you want anything, coffee? I ask. Thanks, I'm fine, I already had a meeting here earlier about a christening, I've had enough coffee, a bit of water would be welcome, thank you. I open the fridge and bring the water jug. It's one of the good things about being a clergyman, one can play a part in the big events in people's lives, he says and takes the glass from me, immediately putting it down on the table without drinking from it. He looks at the sofa and asks: Is that reserved? Sit, please, I say and pull out a kitchen chair for Livia and myself. One doesn't get any younger, he says, stretching his legs and adding: As I said on the telephone, I like to do it like this, home visits are by far the pleasantest way of handling things, church premises often seem too formal, an open-hearted chat, nothing else. I say, Sven and Lillemor told me about you, they told me you confirmed Karin. Yes, I remember Karin very well, and her brother. Karin was very receptive, good at discussion and speaking, a person who liked to write even back then. She was honest, on one occasion she apologised, she wanted to confess something, she was properly ashamed, and then she admitted to me that maybe she was only getting confirmed because she wanted to rebel against her parents. She described them as atheists, she had an admirable ability to empathise, she was a person who waited for the other children, if you can appreciate what I mean? Yes, Karin was kind, but not a walkover, I answer. He picks up a notepad bound with black leather and makes notes. Is that an attribute that you could see most easily in Karin, kindness? he asks. Maybe, I answer. Kindness can be a bit of a walkover but kindness without being a walkover is obviously something quite different, he says. I'm allergic to summing people up like that, whether it's about being kind or nasty; she was in many ways the diametrical opposite of nasty, she complemented me, my weak areas, my volatile temper, my small-mindedness, my inability to let things go, the list is bloody long, believe me, but she cleared my system of all that shit, she got me to take responsibility, she was the only one I listened to, she got me to like myself, kind was one of the finest words she knew, I mean the significance of it, anyone could have died but not Karin, it should have been me, it should have been Karin and Livia here now, she was worthy of a long and happy life. Tom, I can understand it all seems black as night, because it is black as night, he says, but I interrupt him and ask: The ways of God are mysterious, or what? I was going to say that it's in this very darkroom that we humans are developed. Uh-huh, okay, I answer, with a little laugh. I think those were the words of Nils Ferlin, the poet, he adds and then leans forward and caresses Livia's head. I heard that you're working on the funeral oration, he asks. Yes, I haven't finished it yet, I answer. I imagine it must be a relief for someone who has an ability to write, that you can get it off your chest a bit? he says. Well, I would never let anyone else take care of the oration, I say. Have you ever written a speech before? What does that matter? No, of course, it has no particular importance, this is just a bit of a chat, I mean Karin was someone who wrote, that's what I've understood from everyone I've spoken to, maybe you are too? Karin loved to write, I answer. Are you going to give the speech yourself? No, a friend of Måns is an actress, she'll read it, I answer. Is there anything in particular that you intend to bring up in your speech? I won't swear in church, I answer. If that's what you want to do it's okay with me, that's not why I was asking, he responds. You can read the speech when it's ready, but I can tell you right off that I will not be paraphrasing Ferlin's *Gethsemane*. He's confounded by that, and rubs around his mouth. I was mostly asking because I don't want to say anything that you may also be saying, repetitions like that are a bit boring, he says. I realised that, that's why I said I won't be paraphrasing *Gethsemane*. Tom, I don't doubt for a moment that there are things you want to say in the oration, important things, but I usually double-check a bit with the speechwriter before the ceremony, how long will it be, do you think? I don't know, what do you think? I usually say five to ten minutes is about right, but obviously it varies. I'm basing it on the five senses, I say. He leans back in the sofa and touches his chin, leans forward, turns his head. You were asking if there was anything special I was going to bring up, and there is, I add. The senses? The five senses, I answer. It sounds like a bold concept, I mean I almost want to ask how it might be done? I don't know if it's so bold, it starts at Söder Hospital when we first got the leukaemia diagnosis and Karin gave Livia her name, I don't know, I can't explain it any better than that, but at least it's a sort of answer. He reaches out and caresses Livia's head again, and says: Tom, once you have met Karin you cannot lose her, that's the sort of person she was. You're speaking of memory, maybe it's true you don't lose that, except in cases of dementia or death, but at the same time you can hardly lie there with your arms around a memory. Were you thinking of some particular sense? he asks. No, the oration will be divided into five parts, one for each sense, it's a mix. A mix? I can't explain it better than that, I answer. He drinks his water and looks down at his socks. I also lost someone close to me, he says. I wasn't aware of that, I'm sorry. He interrupts me: I didn't tell you because I wanted your empathy, it happened a long time ago. He writes something in his notepad, then closes it and puts it back in his rucksack. Obviously you don't have to answer this, but did you doubt your faith when it happened? I ask. The way I usually put it is, prayer is doubt, why else would anyone pray? He tries to look me in the eye. I feel uncomfortable, and keep my gaze on Livia and her blueberry-coloured fleece blanket with Moomintrolls on it. My son lived till he was twelve, I hit the wall, one of my best friends moved in with us, he saw how bad I was feeling, he realised I didn't have the strength to come back, and so he asked me: Totta, the grief you're feeling now, would you exchange it for never having known Johannes at all?

Metargatan doesn't want me here without Karin. I can't get to rest in the one metre twenty-wide bed. Just the sight of it makes me angry and jealous. The day I moved in with Karin I immediately asked how many men she'd had in that bed. I remember she stared at me as she answered:

It's only a bed. It's another twelve hours until Karin's operation. I haven't got rid of my leasehold flat in Huddinge and I feel I have to sleep there. At a quarter to three I take the night bus from Skanstull and get off by the old bus station in Huddinge. My migraine has come back. I have to rest against an electrical box below the high-rises by Kvarnbergsplan. In a flat nine floors up I see a globe in the window. Its stand is the shape of a foot and it has a built-in light. Apart from the streetlamps, that globe is the only thing that's illuminated, it's so real. For a few moments I imagine that it *is* the Earth, and that I'm staring at it from an immense distance.

The morning after two nurses come out with Karin from the post-op section. She's lying in the hospital bed. Confused with all the drugs she's on, she complains about the pain in the back of her head and tries to scratch herself under the dressing. I spread the council-issue blanket over her feet. Two doctors are waiting in R16, one of them the brain surgeon who operated on

Karin, Taavi Marsala, he's never had time to answer my questions. The other is the anaesthetist, an elderly man with bags under his eyes and a half-circle of grey hair on his head. I've never seen him before. The nurse reads out the social security number written on Karin's wristband. The anaesthetist leans over the bed and checks the drip stand.

There's no need for more morphine, he says.

Karin puts her hand on her oxygen mask. It's as if the light is harming her. The brain surgeon exchanges a few words with the anaesthetist before he hurries out of the ward with rapid steps, a phone pressed to his ear. Karin is rolled down the corridor. She is left by a large, semi-open window. She has a support collar around her neck. There's dried blood in her hair by one of her temples. Her cheeks are swollen, her lips dry and cracked. She's fallen asleep again. Below the brick building the Eugenia Care Home can be seen, and beyond that I can make out the neighbourhood of Vasastan through the mist. So much late summer hanging over it all, so much everyday darkness. I ask the anaesthetist if it's wise to keep the window open. He backs away from me. I point out that dirt might make its way in and infect Karin's wound. He answers:

Fresh air never hurt anyone.

I fall asleep in the armchair next to Karin until voices in the corridor wake me. The blinds have been lowered. The morning light can be seen on the polished plastic floor in a striated, trapeze-shaped pattern.

Hey, I exclaim when I notice that Karin is looking at me. I stand up and take her hand in mine. How are you feeling?

162

You're still here, she answers.

I'm a bit drowsy.

You're still here, she says again.

Yes, I slept here. She turns her head away. Are you in pain?

I've been awake for a while.

How are you feeling?

I have to ask you about something, she says.

Of course, anything. Karin's support collar is gone and someone has washed that blood off her temple.

I just want you to be here, she says.

How do you mean? Of course I'm here, obviously I'll stay, whatever you want. She turns to me again and says:

I can't deal with having my parents around.

You're cool with each other, aren't you?

Promise me that? she says in a slightly louder voice.

What's the problem, I don't quite understand . . .

I've been ill before, she answers.

Yes, I know, did something go wrong last time?

Will you stay with me? she asks.

But darling, I love you so much.

Do you promise? she says.

Please, you're starting to scare me, the operation has gone well, everything is fine, or has something happened, is there something you haven't told me? She puts her hands on her stomach and says:

You moved away from home when you were a teenager, you separated, you had your fights, you didn't have contact with your parents for a long time, I could never have done that.

You've had your flat for many years, I point out.

I didn't mean like that, I just can't deal with having my parents here, I only want you to be here, please, understand me, she says.

Well I *am* here, or do you want me to keep your family out of the room?

You don't get it, she sighs.

Well explain it to me, then, I say. She looks at me and snorts:

What, my family?

Yeah, I mean obviously I can tell them you need rest, no problem, I can say you're sleeping.

You are my family, aren't you? she points out. I sit on her bed and answer:

Yes, of course, darling, we are a family.

Only you, she says.

Okay.

Promise?

I promise, I answer tenderly. You're really serious, you don't want them here at all? I ask. Karin looks away when she answers:

I can't bear feeling that I'm unfair, but I don't want to be a child any more.

I have never seen a death certificate before. It's a white A4 sheet from the Tax Authority which, in terms of its content, is similar to a birth certificate apart from the date of death and the sub-heading: *Children of Deceased*. Next to it is Livia's social security number, but no name, only three long dashes. According to the Tax Authority database I have never existed in Livia's life, so if some genealogist in let's say two hundred years should be wondering about Karin Lagerlöf, they would see nothing but an unmarried woman from Stockholm who gave birth to a nameless girl. I add the death certificate to my pile of letters from government authorities, banks, and insurance companies. I bring Karin's handbag to bed with me and inhale the smell of tanned leather. Throat pastilles, sanitary towels, keys, and her red calf-skin wallet. Bank card, ID card, cash machine receipts, throat pastille wrappers, a twenty-kronor note. Also inside is a little bag of lavender, tied with a silk band. The glasses in the case are by Giorgio Armani, oval frames, dark brown with a hint of red. I put them on. The calibrated lenses are so strong that everything I look at becomes hazy, almost dreamlike.

After a week at Neurocentrum Karin is moved to Erstagården, a rehabilitation home in Nacka which from the outside resembles a pre-school. In the mornings she sits waiting for me on the same two-seater teak bench in the blinding white corridor. Her hands are clasped together on her lap. Her head is bandaged. She wears her pale blue cotton dress that I brought. The walker is in front of her. She opens her mouth when she sees me, not very much, just so that her teeth can be partly seen. She says:

Hi.

Karin is discharged on a Wednesday. She refuses to cut the patient band around her wrist and declines the offer of hospital transport to get home. She grabs the sleeve of my jacket and says: I want to take the bus. It's autumn, a slightly chilly day. We get on to bus 401 at

Nacka Kvarn and pass Järla Lake. I have been going past the lake twice a day for a month without paying it any notice. But there it is: an absolutely still body of water. From Slussen we continue home to Metargatan by taxi.

Karin stops in the hall and peers into the flat. The loft bed is white-tinted, without support struts against the floor, which would impede free movement. It's suspended from the ceiling with two sturdy planks. On the edge I have hung a flower-box with geraniums, so that the overall effect is like a balcony overlooking the sea. Karin approaches the construction. She holds out the palm of her hand as if to push it, but changes her mind.

Did you build it? she asks.

Yes, we have space for two desks now.

How did you have time for this?

I had time, I answer.

Did you throw my bed away? she asks, squeezing her lips together with her fingers.

No, it's in the attic, I've wrapped it in plastic. She removes her hand from her mouth and says:

Tom, it's really lovely, but you're a funny one, maybe you could have asked me first?

I'm asking now, what do you think about having a loft bed?

Yes, but what if I say no?

Then I'll demolish it, I say. Karin wants to try lying down on it but can't get up the ladder, which is bolted to the wall. She scrutinises the screws fixing the planks and retires to the sofa. I show her how easy it is to climb the ladder. Karin takes off her red duffel coat and asks

166

me to fetch the one twenty-wide bed. She goes into the hall.

Just for now, she calls out.

But we have space for two desks now, I say.

Just for now, she calls out again.

We can sit next to each other and write, that's something you've been wanting, isn't it? She comes back into the room and leans against the bed.

Please, she says.

There is no lift in the house. I have to drag the bed down in the same way that I dragged it up – on a piece of rag rug. I push the bed in under the loft bed, that's the only space there is for it.

The patient band turns out to be a sensitive issue. Eczema flares up underneath, but still Karin won't take it off. Sometimes her scratching wakes me up at night. One night I ask her to throw it away. She turns her back on me and mumbles something about how she gets stressed when she thinks about Midsummer.

It's half a year until Midsummer, I point out.

I know it's been tough for you as well, Tom, she responds.

Don't say my name like that, it sounds so bloody formal.

Okay.

Are you in pain? I ask.

It felt important to be able to say that, she says.

The most important thing is that you're home, I answer.

Ludvig left me when I had the brain haemorrhage.

Ludvig?

Yes.

Your ex?

It was too much hard work, she adds.

Okay, so there you are, and hard work is a euphemism, I take it?

He's just a human being.

Is that what your therapist said, or what?

Stop it.

Are you in pain, shall I get you a tablet?

No, she says, and goes on: The cyst came because of the laser knife, that's what the doctors said. She stares up at the bottom of the loft bed but snatches up the duvet over her head when I turn on the bedside lamp. Turn it off, she groans, and I turn it off.

The laser knife? She scratches at the patient band and answers: I got the headache the day before Midsummer's Eve.

But hold on, you said the laser knife?

Ludvig drove me to Karolinska.

Okay, okay, you never told me, but I don't have a bloody clue what a laser knife is.

Can't you just listen?

Okay, I'm sorry.

I'll get to that, she says.

Okay, I'll be quiet.

I had a job on the side as a nanny, it just hit me on the way home, I didn't even dare cry, I was worried that my tear ducts would widen somehow and make the headache even worse, I called Ludvig, he drove me to Karolinska, they admitted me right away, they said I had bleeding on my cerebellum, they said it was an arteriovenous malformation which had developed into an aneurysm, they decided to inject an adhesive . . .

An adhesive? I interrupt.

Yes, in the brain, don't ask me how or why, I don't remember, it was going to plug it somehow.

Okay.

The risk was there might be disruptions to my sense of balance, worst case scenario was death, I had two rounds of that treatment, neither worked. I interrupt her again and ask:

Had this Ludvig cleared off by then?

Why are you asking about him?

Okay, I'll let it go.

Yes, he had, I had Mum living with me at the hospital.

Bloody disgrace, Karin.

I didn't care, she says.

You didn't care about what?

I had other things on my mind, or, yeah, sure, I was upset that he left, but I was feeling so bad, I was so sick.

You asked me to keep your parents out of your room at the Neurology Ward; you don't see a connection there, do you? I ask.

Please, I'm too tired to get angry now.

Were you about the same age?

He was two years older, but I don't want to talk about that any more, it's not important.

Not important? I burst out.

Please, Tom.

Okay, okay.

I feel tight here at the back, she says and carefully runs her hand over her neck.

Are you sure I shouldn't get you a tablet?

Is it difficult for you when I talk about it? she wonders.

No, not at all, or I mean of course it is, but not like that, you didn't seem to want to talk about it any more, but shall I get a tablet?

I just don't want to talk about Ludvig, he's not important.

I find it hard to imagine that it's unimportant, someone leaving you when you're most in need of closeness and support, I say, and look for her hand to hold. She nods her head a little. Okay, but the laser knife, it sounds like the sort of thing Darth Vader would have under his mantle, I say, placing my hands on my chest.

That's what it's called, she says.

And it caused the cyst?

The doctors said it did, yes, she answers, and asks for a sip of water, and I reach for the glass on the bedside table. She drinks and I put it back.

Which doctors said that?

The ones who operated on me, the brain surgeons who removed the cyst, she answers.

Okay, but why did they do that shit in the first place?

I was dying, she says.

Jesus, Karin!

It was considered the least risky treatment, obviously they didn't know it would cause cysts.

Is it some kind of laser cutter, or . . .?

No, a machine, she answers.

A machine?

Yeah, I was screwed into a head frame, are you all right to listen to this?

Yeah, yeah, but what sort of head frame do you mean?

It was screwed to my cranium, I had to lie completely

still for several hours in the machine while a load of radioactive rays incinerated those sick blood vessels.

Bloody hell, I say and I want to caress Karin's hand. She pulls her arm away before I get anywhere near her. She puts a pillow on her stomach. It must have hurt like hell, I say.

The brain can't feel pain, she answers.

I didn't know that, I say.

I didn't feel anything, but it was hard work lying still for so long, the machine made a crackling sound, the laser knife, the sound was a bit like tyres on gravel, so I just lay there and remembered about when I learned to ride a bike. She goes quiet, angles her head, and says: Thanks, Tom.

Darling?

For listening, she adds.

It's not so bloody weird if I react a bit, is it?

No, it's beautiful that you react, it actually reminds me that it's sad, and I find it touching that you care, thanks.

No need to thank me, that's perverse.

Perverse?

Actually, yes.

You're so rhetorical sometimes; I'm perverse for thanking you? she asks.

Yes, you don't thank me when I kiss you, do you, so why thank me for caring? It's just so curious that you never told me this, I've asked so many bloody times, shit, I wish I could have been there, just think if we'd met a few years earlier, you know what, your ex, give me the address of that fucker, I'll go over to him tomorrow.

Stop, please, I don't have the strength for this.

Okay, forget I said that.

I don't have the strength to deal with you taking over my feelings, she says.

Okay.

It's beautiful that you listen, it's beautiful that you feel things so strongly, but I've already gone through what you're feeling except a hundred times stronger. Yes, it's true he ran off, but it's not important, he's not important.

Okay, I say again.

Okay?

Yes, okay. She sits up in the bed and puts the pillow against the curve of her back. She looks at me in the dark.

Are you afraid you'll turn into Ludvig? she asks. At first I laugh but I stop when she seems to get irritated and then I say:

I'm listening.

And?

I'm still here, aren't I?

Yes.

Go on, tell me more now, I say.

I've forgotten what I was saying.

You're at the hospital, the machine is crackling, it reminds you of bicycle wheels. She remains silent, and just as I'm about to ask her how she's feeling, she says:

I was a late learner when it came to cycling.

Uh-huh.

I had been given my first bicycle when I was six, a yellow, shiny thing, white saddle and support wheels, but something felt blocked inside me when I got on it, everything was wobbly, spinning, it was that giddy feeling like when I stood by a steep slope, the other children in our road teased me a bit about it, I felt excluded and angry, in actual fact I thought it was quite enjoyable sitting on the bicycle and slowly pushing myself along with my feet on the ground, trying it at my own speed, but the other children were always there to take the mickey out of me, our flat was in a line of high-rise blocks, Källängsvägen, as soon as one did anything the others came out, they wanted to be with you or watch, I wanted to be left in peace, then suddenly one day I wanted to do it, middle of July, baking hot, most of the others in our houses seemed to be away on holiday, for several days I had been playing on my own down in the courtyard, many of the children who'd been teasing me the most about the cycling weren't there, I asked my dad to get the bicycle out of the bicycle shed and take off the support wheels, for some time Mum and Dad had been keeping the bicycle out of sight so I wouldn't get stressed by it, beside the long gravel path a hedge grew with white flowers that smelled of dust and something sweet, at first my feet couldn't keep up, I yelled, I laughed, Dad pushed me from behind, he ran as fast as he could to keep up, he held onto the bicycle with one hand, and then in the middle of the gravel track he let go.

The pathologist at Karolinska introduces himself as Gunnar Cronberg. His voice is as drawling as the undertaker's. I explain why I am calling, and he answers: I know what it's about and as I said to the undertaker earlier it would not be something I'd recommend. That's what I was told, but why? Your wife is in very bad condition, he answers. I know Karin is blue, I saw her at TICC, I was there when she died. The body is in a considerably worse state than what you saw at TICC. That doesn't worry me, I answer. Tom, was it? Yes. Tom, I'm going to put this to you plainly, large sections of skin have come away from the body, there's blood seeping out and bad-smelling fluids, all in all it's a sanitary problem once you cut the plastic open. You're keeping her wrapped in plastic? That's the normal procedure, he answers. Is she not refrigerated? She is refrigerated, but the microbes have nonetheless gone quite far in the process of decomposition, it's not a pretty sight, not the sort of thing you want to remember. I don't give a shit if it's a beautiful sight or not, I want to kiss my wife goodbye. Tom, she doesn't have any lips any more, and it's not only that, there's also a risk of contagion if the plastic is removed in church, there'll be a terrible stink. In my experience, the microbes seem to get along rather well with patients who have died in ECMO. But she's only just died. Yes, it's all gone very fast. Okay, okay, I understand, I won't disturb you again, thanks for your time.

I take off my T-shirt and let Livia sit against my skin in the sling. I tear down all the photographs of Karin in the flat. Even the enlargement that was going to be used at the funeral, taken on the afterdeck of the Gotland ferry the summer Livia was conceived. I have decorated every wall with pictures of Karin, but I can no longer look into her eyes. I leave just one, on the fridge, the only one where she isn't looking into the camera. I was sitting behind her when I took it, it's an old photo, her hair is held up by hairpins, I can see a bit of her right ear, her back is smooth, her bikini top is tied around her neck. She's looking out over Vändburgsviken. She is sitting in the sand, which is covered in shadows and sun-dried seaweed.

Even in dense darkness I can distinguish Karin's footstep. At least when she's barefoot on the floor in Metargatan. The toilet door closes. I hear her stream hitting the water. Once back in bed she covers her head with the duvet. I feel inadequate, it's an inadequacy I don't want to admit to myself, but I understand it, I hate it. By the time Karin wakes me up by sitting up in the bed I have already started dreaming again. I fall back into a slumber, but wake when she starts rummaging about in the hall. I haul myself out of bed and see her by the front door. She's putting her duffel coat on over her nightie. She's wearing her blue wellies.

What are you doing? I ask.

Going out.

It's the middle of the night, it's bloody winter.

I didn't mean to wake you.

Where are you going?

Do you really care so much? She tugs at her sleeves.

What's that supposed to mean?

Tom, your moods, I can't take it.

Moods, are you serious?

Why are you so dead set against going to a psychologist?

Actually, I want to tell you something.

Go on, do it, tell me I'm a basket case.

175

This is so bloody stupid, darling, come on, now . . .
– but she backs away when I take a step towards her.

That's what you always do.

Drop it, I say.

I'm a cunt. I'm retarded. Right?

Okay, Karin, if you want to stir up the shit then please
go ahead, but honestly, I may have said that once or
twice, but if so I've apologised.

What an honourable man you are, Tom, such a fine
person, really.

Hello? Where are you? Are you with me here and now,
or with that fucking swine who left you in 1998?

You're out of your mind, she yells.

You don't have to be much of a psychologist to see
that somewhere deep inside you miss that him. She sighs.
If you like I can turn myself into him.

Stop it!

Seriously, I'll be like him, I'll make myself twenty
centimetres taller, I'll be all cool and bourgeois, I'll trim
my eyebrows and take cocaine, I'll become an editor,
I'll quote Thomas-fucking-Bernhard, exactly like him,
and then I'll leave you, just like that fucking swine.

Are you done?

No, believe me, I could go on.

Tom, you've got so much to work through.

You know what, go home and eat snacks with your
father.

Why don't you go home and have a booze-up with
yours?

Seriously, wait, that was a psychologically relevant
question, what fucking year are you in?

You're actually not well, she says and closes the front door in such a calm, composed manner that I convince myself she has carefully thought things through and decided never to come back again. I feel so enervated that I don't even chase after her. I am so tired that I have to sit down on the floor. I call her up several times. It takes me a while to stand up and go to the window. I open the espagnolette lock and peer into the whirling snow. It's very cold. After almost an hour Karin calls me back.

I didn't hear, I had the phone on silent, she says.

Where are you?

In the stairwell.

What stairwell?

Ours.

Here?

I stayed here.

Before lunch the next day Karin cuts off her patient bands. She does it hastily, almost nonchalantly, as if she has forgotten why she ever wore them. A snow plough drives up and down Metargatan. Karin takes a closer look at the window pane and says it needs to be polished.

That's the sort of thing you do in spring, I tell her.

She walks out of the kitchenette, walks into the hall, gets out her Filofax from her rucksack, looks through it, and asks: Can you take off the bandage? It's time to do it now.

Don't they have to do that at the hospital?

It's only a bandage, she says, and sits on the bed. I wash my hands and loosen the surgical tape, layer upon layer of gauze. The compress is exposed. Beneath it is a ten-centimetre long cleft in the back of her head, the stitches are black and coarse like cooking string.

Does it look disgusting? she asks.

No.

It looks disgusting, she sighs.

No, do you want to see? I can get a mirror.

No, I don't want to see, she answers.

By the time Christmas comes round Karin wants to be able to climb into the loft bed. It's been about four months since she last tried. She makes it up the stool ladder and slides over. She surveys the flat for a long time. She rolls onto her back, gets out of her clothes, and climbs down. She is naked, and moves slowly. She gets out a scented oxblood-red candle from a cupboard in the kitchenette. She puts it on a side plate and lights it.

Can you hold me? she asks.

Mum sits on the sofa blinking at Livia. She lowers her voice: Your father is on the last medicine. What do the doctors say? I ask, drinking my coffee. They don't say anything, what are they supposed to say? she answers. I don't know, hopefully something about how he is, if it's a question of weeks or years, I say. It's as if she doesn't want to look at me, her eyes dart about, she presses her elbows hard against her sides and, in an almost accusatory tone of voice, says: He has lived with his cancer for almost ten years now, no one has survived GIST for as long as that. I know, Mum, I answer and go into the kitchen, pour the coffee into the sink and add: This coffee tastes like fucking aquarium water. You're the one who made it, she points out, and then goes on in a milder voice: You

178

got an aquarium from me and your father on your twelfth birthday, do you remember that? Yes, I answer. You loved your fish, she says. I pull up the strainer plug, tap off the bits of food into the refuse basket, and press it back. Ten years, I say. Yes, she answers. I had just started seeing Karin when we got the confirmation, she came out to me in Huddinge, I say. Yes, Karin was so lovely to you, she says and kisses Livia on the arm. No, she adds, and looks at me. There is something desperate about her when she goes on: Sweetheart, I'm helping you as much as I can now, you know that, but I have to think a bit about Dad and Bosse too, Dad can't cope with taking him out any more, he has to have a last walk at ten, the poor thing is deaf and barks at his own shadow, he can hardly walk, I have to carry him between the bushes, he's been shitting and peeing indoors while I've been spending days and nights here with you. Mum, seriously, I can't believe you're even bringing up the damned dog in the same breath as Dad and Karin. I'm not making any comparisons between Bosse and anyone else, but while the wretched thing's still alive someone has to take care of him. Mum, whatever you're trying to say, just say it. Can't you let me keep her with me during the nights, she says. Mum, if you can't be here then so be it. Of course I want to help you. I want Livia here, I say. Tom, I can fetch her in the evening and bring her back early in the morning? I want her here, I answer, and stand by Livia's basket just as Dad opens the front door. It's certainly not getting any warmer out there as yet, he says. He's got a Marlboro butt in the corner of his mouth. He shuffles into the toilet. He doesn't close the door and there's a patch of urine on his chinos when he comes out, he hasn't even noticed. Mum has started looking through her diary. Do you have any ideas for the floral message? Haven't got a clue, I answer. You leave wreaths by the coffin, usually you write something. It doesn't matter, I say. We were thinking we'd put something simple, like, *You will live on in our memories*, and then our names, she says with a look at Dad, and then another at me. That sounds fine, I answer. We'll go for that, then, she says, and writes something in her little book and then puts it back in her handbag. Dad tickles Livia's foot and says: Granddad's little football. He's pale, his hair has turned white in an unnatural way, brownish sores are spreading across his arms, and his upper neck is scrofulous with little boils. They stay no longer than thirty minutes, and when it's time for them to leave I have to lift Dad out of the sofa. Mum helps him put on his quilted jacket and hat. She caresses Livia's forehead and says: What would we do without you? I ask, When are you coming back? Tonight, I have to take Bosse out before I leave, she answers. Ten? I ask. Yes, expect me then, and I may as well say it now so you don't forget, tomorrow you have to ask Lillemor for help, we're going to the Cancer Research Institute, and he gets so tired after that. Will you text me from the hospital? I ask. Yes, we will, she answers. Dad turns around in the hall to say something but in the end nothing comes out. Instead he just lifts his hand over his shoulder and waves at me as if I were standing very, very far away.

When I'm tidying up around the desk I notice something under the bookshelf, it casts a glint of reflected light from the table lamp. I reach inside and pull out a statuette of an owl. It looks like a tourist souvenir. Five centimetres high, two and a half centimetres wide, heavy, most likely made of iron or lead. The talons grip onto a branch inscribed with the letters AΘE. I have a vague sense that Karin used it as a paperweight, but I haven't seen it for years, and I've never held it in my hand. Its eyes are disproportionately large. I can't remember if Karin bought it at a flea market or if she got it as a present while on holiday on Aegina with her parents and brother when she was a child. I search on the Internet and find images of similar owls. AΘE seems to be an abbreviation of AΘENAION and means something along the lines of: of the Athenians. The owl is also found on antique Greek coins. It's Athena's owl. Or Minerva's, as she was known in Latin. It embodies the goddess herself, with eyes that shine in the darkness. There's a raft of folders and scattered untitled documents in Karin's laptop. I search the hard drive. Search words: *Athena, Minerva, owl, wings, night vision, hunters, battle, wisdom, Hegel*. There's nothing to explain the statuette.

Livia sleeps beside me in the bed. She drank one hundred millilitres of formula before she fell asleep. I'm worried that she'll throw up and choke on the vomit. I hold off with my Lergigan tablets until Mum comes, she's late. New search term: *Livia*. Maybe somewhere Karin has written about the name and why she chose it. Nothing, anywhere. On the other hand I do find a stand-alone diary item when I search on the word *pregnant*:

One week before Christmas 2010. Friday. A tough week. Had a miscarriage the night between

Monday and Tuesday. Was in week six, so early, but more upset about it than expected. Maybe all the changes. Had known about it for probably a week, but had already had masses of symptoms, so I really felt pregnant. Felt nauseous every day. Tom and I were at the A&E when it happened, the rest of the week has been mainly hard work. Stayed home from work Thursday to Friday, mostly I just watched TV series. Actually had panic attacks on Wednesday. Haven't slept at night, plus, was so physically tired that I could hardly walk. Still just HAD to go to H&M to get myself a top. So typical me. When I was on Mariatorget I got so tired that I called Tom in tears. He came to get me. He has been a fantastic support. I think I've taken up all the room for grieving. He's written a poem about the miscarriage, or maybe something for some novel. The text was right there by his computer, just where I walk past, it was difficult avoiding it. Should I be ashamed about reading it? He calls the blood in my pants the waste product of a possible different future. That was good, but it made me so angry.

The welfare officer calls me on Tuesdays at 14:00 and says: Hi, Tom, this is Liselotte, is this a bad time? At Karolinska I used to see her a couple of times a week in a little conference room at Neonatal. She felt familiar right away, her soft posture reminiscent of Karin, and her silvery pageboy hairstyle and rotund figure just like my mother's. It was easy confiding in her. The telephone calls are a recent development. After that time in

Karolinska I just could not breathe in the smell of hospital any more but at the same time I didn't want to stop having those conversations.

So how have you been since last time, Tom? asks Liselotte. Okay, I answer. And how are things with Livia? Fine, she's lying here next to me prattling away. That's lovely to hear. She's started smiling, she clutches at my finger, and she can direct her head, she looks right into me. That's lovely, fantastic. Karin is going to miss so much, Livia was a black-and-white ultrasound photo, Karin only knew her as something that moved inside her. Tom, eventually it will feel a little easier, naturally you'll never stop grieving for Karin, but the intervals between the really hard days will grow longer. Liselotte waits for me to answer and then, when I don't, she says: Are you thinking about something? I went to get a new ID card yesterday after my old one expired. Right, a new ID, yeah. I walked to the offices of the Tax Department, it's probably a couple of kilometres from Lundagatan to Södermalms allé. If I can just ask, did you bring Livia? No, Mum was taking care of her, I still get stressed about taking her out in the pram. What are you worried about, if you don't mind my asking? One day I will obviously have to take her out in the pram, I just don't want to pass on my own fears to her. Okay, and what do you mean by not wanting to pass on your fears to Livia? Is it okay if I first tell you about the Tax Department? Yes, of course. I showed them the receipt for my payment, and then I was pointed to a photo booth, there was only space for one clerk and a small desk with an adjustable camera, she measured me, I was a hundred and seventy-eight, in my old ID I was a hundred and seventy-six, she didn't believe me so I showed her my old ID, she took my measurement again, I was a hundred and seventy-eight. That's pretty strange, isn't it? Karin and I were the same height, she was a hundred and seventy-six as well, it became a thing for us, a physical togetherness, I don't know, it feels weird. They must have made a mistake when they measured you earlier, don't you think? I've been a hundred and seventy-six centimetres tall since I was eighteen, everyone can't have been mistaken all those times, I identify with being a hundred and seventy-six centimetres tall, now suddenly I'm two centimetres taller than Karin. Yeah, you know they say the only thing you can't lie about is how tall you are. My weight's just tumbled, seventeen kilos in a couple of weeks, I weigh fifty-nine kilos. Tom, it's not so surprising that you've lost your appetite. I think the woman at the Tax Department was afraid of me, I say, interrupting Liselotte. Okay, what makes you think that? I felt vulnerable when she started taking the photos and people were walking past, looking in, I wanted her to close the door, all the other photo booths had their doors closed, she didn't want to, she was looking at me as if she thought I'd rob her if we closed the door. Did you ask her why you couldn't close the door? She said they never close the doors. Did you not point out that the other photo booths had their doors closed? She ignored that. She didn't answer? No, 'look into the circle' was all she said, then she pointed the camera. That was a bit strange, wasn't it? I didn't recognise myself in the photos, I asked her if she could take another one, which turned out just the same, after the fourth attempt she got irritated, but it still felt wrong, I mean that's supposed to be my identifying photo, the thing that convinces people that I am who I am, my eyes were completely blank as if everything I'd ever seen had bled out of them, it was horrible, I wanted to take another picture, she wouldn't let me, I've become so servile, I just said okay, thanks, if I'd been my old self I would have asked for another photo booth and I wouldn't have left until I was satisfied. Tom, you were here at Karolinska for almost a month, just stepping into the daily grind like this is not an easy thing, not after everything you've been through, and I'd like to point out, after our last conversation when you told me about all the problems you've been having with bureaucracy, I really had the impression that you know how to put your foot down. I'd say I've never been afraid of conflict, I'm rather confrontational, Karin used to call me a little terrier, my friends as well, totally unable to see how small I am. Oh, is that right, and, well, were you offended by that? No, not at all, that was just funny. Tom, a great deal is happening inside you right now. I suppose that's it, sometimes it does feel as if I'm about to go mad, yesterday I found a statuette that was Karin's, an owl, Minerva's owl, it was under the bookshelf, it feels as if Karin is communicating with me, as if she wants to tell me something. You knew her so well, I can tell you, it's quite a common thing to have that feeling, as if those you have lost are communicating with you, especially when you're deep in the grieving process, it's not mad at all, because in a way they are communicating. May I ask, was there something special about this particular owl? Minerva's owl only

185

spreads her wings once dusk has fallen. Okay, right, sorry, I must ask, is that Livia in the background? She's trying to devour the sleeve of my jumper, chewing away at it. Liselotte laughs. Just think, isn't it amazing, she's developing her senses, obviously she recognises your smell, she says. Or taste, I'd like to have her with me at night, but I'm not quite ready. Why is that, then? I'm taking sleeping tablets and Lergigan. Oh yes, of course, but Tom, you need your sleep, and there's no hurry, you should take the time you need. Thanks, Liselotte, I needed to hear that. Tom, there's no need to thank me. Am I servile? She coughs, or laughs. Excuse me, she says, adding: It was nice of you to thank me. This morning I read my diary, I write a diary, have I told you that? Yes, you have. Okay, this morning I read through what I wrote this week, last Wednesday I was obsessing about how I'm going to be older than Karin, she was born towards the end of the summer of seventy-six, I was born in spring seventy-eight, page after page about how on 23 October 2013 I'll become older than Karin. Ah yes, well Tom, there's a before and an after. I often think about when Karin was ill last time. What in particular do you think about? Or I don't know, maybe think is wrong, it's more like images popping up, I don't analyse them, her light blue dress for instance, she wore it at the rehabilitation home. Was that after her operation? Yeah, exactly, that dress often came to mind when she was at the Thoracic Clinic. Why do you think that was, if you could make yourself analyse it? She woke up that time, she survived. Yes, and then she wore that blue dress. Light blue. Yes, that's right. Or to be exact, cerulean blue. Is that a light blue shade? Yes, like the sky.

Are you interested in colours? When I had the four-year-old check-up I didn't pass the colour test, my mother said I had a highly developed sense of colour as a child, I painted a lot, her theory was that I didn't, like other children, see red as one colour but as many different colours, or blue, or green, she meant that I didn't understand the difference between colour and shade, but she's my mother, she almost always defended me, now I lost what I was trying to say, what were we talking about? Oh, now I'm insecure about it myself, no wait, that's right, we were talking about the dress. That's right. Do you associate Karin with that dress? she asks. Not always, she was wearing it when I thought about her at Karolinska, she was pretty in it, it was made of a soft velour fabric, it was more like a nightie, she often slept in it, but at the rehabilitation home she wore it the whole time, I just thought of something else, can I tell you? Yes, of course you can, you can bring up anything and tell me about it. When Karin got the fever it was early in the morning, she had gone to bed early the night before, at eight, I was up working. Can I just ask, when was this? It was in March. Uh-huh, you mean this year, then I'm with you. It's only six weeks ago. Well, you know, Tom, it really *is* only six weeks ago, okay, you said you were up working? Yes, I went to bed late as usual, Karin had left me a note on the kitchen table, she often did that. You've told me about that, how you often wrote each other notes, yes. She had drawn herself as a heart with big eyes and long, curled eyelashes, and inside the heart she had drawn another small heart. Uh-huh, I see. The little heart was the child in her belly. Yes, I see, yes. In a speech bubble she'd written that she loved me infinitely with a lot of exclamation marks, now that I tell you about it, it sounds silly. Not at all, Tom. Well, it was silly, but that's what was nice about it. I see what you mean, yes. I brought that note with me to the bedroom, but I didn't get across the threshold, I sort of got stuck there. Liselotte waits quite a long time for me to continue, and then she says: Right, so, you stood there looking at Karin and Livia while they were sleeping? There was no Livia then, we called her Scrunchie or Little Lizard. Liselotte laughs. She apologises. Oh don't worry, it *is* funny, isn't it, we used to laugh about it as well, that's what she was to us. You said you didn't get across the threshold. Yes, I just stood there, Karin had put in her orange earplugs, she'd propped up her back and belly with cushions . . . Tom? I felt so strongly that we had a then, a now, and a future. I was at my happiest in 2008. Sorry if I interrupt, when you stood there on the threshold, that was the evening when Karin had the first signs of her illness, so to speak, or am I misunderstanding you now? Was that when you went into Söder Hospital? No, that was a few days later, she threw up and had cold shivers that night, we thought it was the flu, I think I called Söder Hospital twenty times that week, they said it was flu, we just had to wait it out, in actual fact they were afraid of admitting Karin to the Maternity Ward, they were worried she might infect the other pregnant women. How could they know it was flu? They couldn't know, I suppose I was worried it might be something serious so I just swallowed their line of reasoning without questioning it, and, in fact, the symptoms were like normal flu, high temperature, vomiting, coughing, and then she was pregnant of course, she had an iron deficiency, PGP, she was tired. Sure, sure. It was only the day before we went in to Maternity that she started having breathing difficulties, it went really fast, every hour her breathing got worse, in the end I was certain she had come down with pneumonia, but still they didn't want us in the Maternity Ward, they probably thought we were being paranoid about it, typical first-time parents, I was in despair, at the same time I didn't want to worry Karin, I tried to keep calm, I demanded that the midwives talk to Karin on the phone so they could hear her breathing. And when they heard her they got it? she asks. No, not right away, they wanted to talk to the doctors first and they asked to get back to us, for a while I thought we'd have to go to A&E, but Karin was in the late stages of her pregnancy, we wanted to get to Maternity, we were so worried about Scrunchie. Tom, it's useful for me to hear it in context, and I now understand much better why you're standing there on the threshold looking at Karin, who's asleep, you're waiting for your first child, I'm thinking that it's a bit symbolic with that threshold as well, if you see what I mean? Yes, I do, absolutely. Maybe you think of it in a different way, but I'm thinking that the threshold is like a dividing line between what is and what's been, would you agree with that? Yes, sure, that's how it feels when I look back on it, but I didn't feel it when I was standing there. No, obviously, you didn't know then. Your thoughts of a shared future were at the fore-front at that point. Well, Tom, you said it earlier, a then, a now, and a future, could I ask, in what way were your thoughts of the future the strongest? At that moment,

189

you mean? Yes, she answers. I don't know, we often talked about growing old together, it made us feel calm when we were worrying about our finances, and something else, somewhere far ahead of us we imagined a glassed-in veranda with a view of the sea, in our fantasies that scene varied, usually we just saw ourselves sitting next to each other with novels in our hands and grown-up grandchildren on their way to visit us from Stockholm, no demands, nothing to be achieved, peace. Well, Tom, do you think you might say you felt secure when you looked at Karin there among all those cushions? Yes, ironically enough. Yes, of course you did, if I could just go back a little in our conversation, before I interrupted you, you said you were at your happiest in 2008. That's right. What did you mean there? I can't remember what I was going to say about it. I shouldn't interrupt like that, I'm sorry, but if I could ask anyway, why do you think you were at your happiest in 2008? It was just a year that I like going back to. It can be like that, yes. Karin had been given a clean bill of health, we both felt young, or, actually I don't really know, we also moved to Lundagatan in 2008. Uh-huh, so it was your first flat you got together? Yes, exactly. This may be a difficult question, but was 2008 also the happiest time to you *before* Karin got sick this last time? Good question, I don't know, I think so, we'd been through so much, in 2008 we were probably as relaxed as you can be in a relationship, we trusted each other, Karin was there for me during my father's illness, I was there for her while she was ill, when I think back on 2008 I mainly just remember our quiet walks around Zinkensdamm. Uh-huh, right. We used to go past Konsum, there are a couple of elms there where Ringvägen and Hornsgatan cross, they're as tall as the houses, probably hundreds of years old, Karin liked to sit beneath them on the benches, elms flower in early June, it was Karin who taught me that their seeds are known as winged samara, drifts of them lie on the pavements, or they fly about in the wind, it's like it's raining helicopter fruit, it patters like rain, Karin missed it in the winters, she liked talking about it in the mornings while we were having breakfast, and whenever she felt the winter glooms I might say: Think about the winged samara.

I stand in front of the mirror with the corroded quick-silver glass, Livia in my arms. David's wife has helped me with her funeral dress: antique-white tights and a butter-yellow cardigan from NK department store. I didn't dare venture out alone to buy my own clothes. Alex offered to go with me. He met me by the stairs on Hötorget. H&M's black suit and white tie: 1,797 kronor. Black leather shoes with extra insoles from Nilson: 909 kronor. A black waistcoat, handkerchief, and a white tie from MQ: 947 kronor. Before, I used to borrow my ties from my father, I can count the occasions on my fingers. This is the first tie I have bought myself. On the under-ground between Hötorget and T-Centralen I take it out of the bag. Why does it have to be white? I ask. It's just what close family usually wear, answers Alex. I know, but why? Why do I have to wear a black suit? It's inter-national, white tie is a Swedish tradition. Anyway, you'll look like a million dollars in that tie, he said.

I was already aware at that point of the tie having

evolved from the cravat in the seventeenth century, which, in turn, had been inspired by Croatian soldiers who made a habit of tying the ends of their pointed shirt collars before going into battle. I searched on the Internet when I got home but I didn't find anything about the background to the tradition of the white tie. I did discover that black became the colour of mourning in Sweden in the sixteenth century, in accordance with Spanish fashion. In the nineteenth century the white-tipped collars first appeared in black mourning clothes, but only in the following century did white collars become something for kith and kin. The ceremonial white scarf has existed for a long time in Sweden, there was nothing about it in essays on funereal ceremonies, but I found old photographs and romantic paintings from the old Swedish agricultural society. In a couple of the depicted funeral trains the odd mourner wore a white ceremonial scarf. My tie is as white as bone, it is also as white as the wedding dress Karin pointed out in the vintage boutique by Mariatorget, it is not actually a wedding garment at all, just a simple party confection from the forties.

Livia starts whimpering and I step away from the mirror. I take off our clothes and hang them up in the wardrobe. The bottles have to be sterilised in boiling water every day, it feels as if it's the only thing I ever do. PreNAN Discharge in cold water. I heat the mixture in a saucepan and pour it into a feeding bottle. I put a blanket over us and drip the milk over my wrist. It's a touch too warm. I wait. Livia's head is pink and downy. The sound of her drinking makes me drowsy. She falls asleep with her mouth open. I'm woken by the sound of the home telephone and I snatch up the receiver. Hello, I'm looking for Karin. I don't recognise the voice. A young woman's voice. She sounds so earnestly cheerful that I assume she's some childhood friend or colleague who's unaware of what's happened. Livia is still sleeping. I sandwich the receiver between my shoulder and ear and lift Livia off my chest and put her down beside me on the sofa. I didn't hear, who did you say you were? I ask. Is Karin home? she answers. Karin is the one whose name is on the telephone subscription so I'd like to talk to her, she says in the same cheerful voice. Where are you calling from? I ask. I'd rather talk to Karin about that. Karin is dead, I answer. Okay, well have a good day, then.

I've been given the name of Silverdals Crematorium in Sollentuna by Lidingö's Churchyard Administration. I introduce myself to one of the technicians. I explain that my wife is going to be cremated, and I wonder how it works. Oh right, he answers. Is there anyone there I can talk to if I have questions? I ask. You can talk to me, but actually we closed hours ago, I don't know why I picked up the telephone, he says. I get the impression I'm the first person ever to call the crematorium to ask some questions. He breathes heavily like a corpulent person. Okay, I say. Why do you want to know? he asks. I just want to know. Uh-huh, so what are your questions, then? I'm just wondering what happens to my wife when she comes to you. There's not so much to tell, he says. It sounds as if he's sitting himself down. I don't know anything, I point out. The corpses come here from the mortuary and then we transfer them to the refrigerated room, he explains. How many degrees is it in there? Are you a journalist? No, I just want to know. He laughs and says: It's a normal cool-room, the same sort of thing you get at the supermarket. Ten degrees? More like five degrees. Okay, and then? Well, then we assign each of the bodies a ceramic number badge, to avoid any mix-ups. Has that ever happened? Not on my watch, but of course it has been known to happen. So it may be the case that the ashes in an urn are actually from a different body? No, he answers. I thought you said it could happen? I once heard about a doctor who removed the appendix of some bloke who'd come in to fix his knee, of course things can go wrong, we're just people manning the controls here. Ceramic badges, okay, and then what happens? I ask. The brick oven, the body stays in there for about ninety minutes, we use oil-powered burners, what's left is a heap of glowing embers. And that's what you put in the urn? No, you rake out the ashes and let the ash grinder pulverise it into a fine dust, then it's poured into the urn and sealed. How hot do the ovens get? Hot as hell, eight hundred degrees or something like that, he replies. Do you keep the smoke? That goes up through the chimney, it's fifteen metres tall, none of the neighbours have complained as yet. Smoke is a waste product of the incineration, it becomes soot, doesn't it? We continuously check the emissions, mercury and carbon dioxide and things like that, it's regulated. Aren't the waste products of the fire considered a part of the cremated body? I've never really thought of it like that, he answers. So a certain measurable part of the body flies up through the chimney and out over Sollentuna's industrial areas? I honestly don't have a clue. Don't you need some certificate from the deceased in order to do the cremation? God no, it's been ages since that was abolished, some time in the sixties – changed your mind, have you, don't you want your grandmother to be cremated? My wife, I point out, and go on: I don't know what she wanted, my mother-in-law was convinced she wanted to be cremated, are cremations common? In Sweden, yes, there's a long tradition of it, we burned our dead before Christendom, though for all I know you may not be Nordic? In Qafzeh they've found graves that are a hundred thousand years old, they put seashells by their dead, I answer. You know what, I have to knock off now, if you want you can come in and look around, or just call when we're open . . .? Okay, thanks for taking the time. Or did you have something else you wanted to ask? No, I just find it odd that so many people I have never met have been taking care of Karin since she died. It wouldn't work otherwise, just think if folks just kept their stiffs at home, no, we should be damned thankful for that.

Sven is just about to give Livia a pat when Lillemor barks at him to disinfect his hands. He looks at me while apologising. He strides up to the pump bottle of disinfectant gel on the chest of drawers under the hat shelf, rubs some into his hands but then forgets to pat Livia and instead starts bringing in the carrier bags of children's clothes, which they've been given by neighbours and friends on Lidingö. I suppose I should get going, then, says Sven. Don't you want coffee? I ask. He looks over at Lillemor who's wilting on the sofa. Her woollen cardigan is chrome yellow, her hair is dark grey. No, I have a few errands to run in town, thanks all the same, says Sven. I've bought milk, I say. Oh really, well, no, thanks all the same, he answers, then calls out: I'm off now, darling. Lillemor answers: Drive carefully. I follow him onto the landing. Livia thought you were going to give her a pat, I say. He stops and turns around. His cheeks are sunken, his furrows longer and deeper than before, and his laugh doesn't have the same warm resonance that I'm used to. Little sweetie, how could I forget that? he says and runs his hand over Livia's cheek. He takes her hand between his fingers. Yes, there is no pity in the insistence of death, he says in a low voice. I don't know how to reply to that, so I just say: Drive carefully. Yeah, thanks, bye, Tom. He turns around and waves at Livia before he disappears down the stairs. I'm almost falling asleep when Lillemor holds up another set of children's clothes and then starts going through the programme for the memorial service in detail. Fine, I say. Yes, I do think Karin would have liked it. I stand up: I think I have to go to bed, I say, I'm so bloody tired, but I've got the formula ready, there's a jug in the fridge, all you have to do if she wakes up is heat it up. Lillemor stands up and goes to the fridge. She opens it and looks inside. Yes, I can see, she says, and turns to the plates, glasses, and feeding bottles in the sink. I don't mind washing up Livia's things here, if I'm allowed to? You don't need to do that, Lillemor, I'll do it tomorrow. I'm quite happy to do it, I can't sleep anyway. Okay, thanks, but I'd like to wash up our things in the morning.

Lillemor picks up Livia abruptly and turns her back on me. I brush my teeth and wash my face. When I come in to say goodnight Lillemor has sat down on the guest bed with her feet on the floor. That was Sven calling, she says. Really, has something happened? He just wanted to say that we left one of the bags of clothes in the car. He's not coming back here now, I hope? He wanted to, but I said we should deal with it another day. He seemed tired, I say. I don't know about that, she says. Maybe it's not so surprising. He seems to be taking it all philosophically, he's continuing with his practice. I expect he needs the routine, I say. I still can't understand it, sitting there for days on end listening to people's troubles when he just lost a daughter himself . . . Simpler than having to think about his own issues, maybe? Yes, possibly . . . did you hear about when Karin got Ivan? she asks. Yes, or actually no, please tell me. She wanted a dog so much, Sven ran his practice from home in those days in the house on Skyttevägen. Yes, I know about that, I say, leaning against the doorpost. The patients came in through the front door and we had to use the kitchen entrance. Yes, I smile, Karin told me about it, it's really funny. Karin wanted a dog so much, but Sven argued that his patients might get scared out of their wits if some dog was barking. Me and Karin argued against him, Freud had a dog, didn't he, a big white spitz I think it was, but no, the patients might feel so terrified, so Karin got Totte instead, the cat. Uh-huh, Totte, yeah. Which didn't satisfy Karin's desire for a dog, so when she found a piece of white school chalk in my room, she wrote on the steps by the front door, she did it in a fairly sophisticated way, she didn't write on the actual step, she wrote on the edge, the patients had to be observant to notice it, she wrote: *Bloody patients*. Fantastic, how old was she then? Eleven, twelve, I'm not sure, but Karin was a very sweet-natured child, there were rarely any antics like that from her, but it had an effect, we understood that it was important. Wasn't Ivan a King Charles spaniel? Yes, a Cavalier King Charles spaniel, she answers, laughing a little with her mouth shut and adding: Later on Ivan peed on the fan heater in Sven's consultation room, Karin and I felt it was his revenge, he'd made his way through the forbidden sliding doors that were there, and then one morning Sven turned on the fan heater to warm up his blessed patients, well, you could hear them groaning in there, I'll tell you that. That's damned funny, incredibly funny, God, it's lovely to laugh, I say and sit on the wooden chair alongside the guest bed. I think it's a bit hot in here, isn't it? asks Lillemor, pulling the blanket off Livia. You think so? I ask. I dreamed about Karin last night, she says. Right. Sven had a dream the other day, oddly enough a similar dream. What happened in it? I ask. She was scolding us, it was a perfectly normal situation, she was an adult, we had eaten at Åkervägen, and she was angry about something – I don't know what she was angry about. Yes, I know, Lillemor, I lived with her. Isn't it a bit hot in here? No, I don't think so. Maybe it's about right for Karin? she says. I almost correct her but decide to let it go. I lean towards the thermostat and say: It's on three, but I could turn it down, that will cool it. Can't you open the window? she asks. The problem is there'll be so much damned noise from the street, I reply. What's that, then? she asks, pointing at the air vent set into the window frame. It's open, anyway the radiator is turned off now, I say, leaning against the window sill. That should be fine, she says. I haven't dreamed about Karin yet, it's the tablets, I sleep too deeply; I think about her before I go to sleep because I want to dream about her, I say, going over to Livia in the basket. And then you wake up anyway, answers Lillemor. That's true, but at least you had the dream, I say. She stretches out one leg, squeezes her kneecap as if she's in pain, then leans against the edge of the bed and looks at me. Tom, I've been doing a lot of thinking these last weeks, a lot about Karin, but also about the conflicts we had at Karolinska, she says. Conflicts? Wrong choice of word, I take it back, but I still want to say this, I need to unburden myself, it does feel as if you kicked us when we were already down. I kicked you? I was already on the ground myself, how could I have been kicking you? Look, it's important to me that I bring this up. Lillemor, please, put it in plain language. I can understand that Karin wanted to be on her own with you when she wasn't under sedation at Söder Hospital, but to separate us from Karin at Karolinska, that was hard for us, you have to understand that, it was actually horrific. You saw her, didn't you? After many ifs and buts, and it was only a few times, we don't have to talk about it, I can understand you, it was an unbearable situation, I just wanted to say it, I just felt I needed to say it. It was Karin's wish, but I think it's more complex than that, I answer. Possibly, but it felt more like it was you who didn't want us there. Can I speak openly? Tom, I don't mean to hurt your feelings. Can I speak? Please, she replies, pulling at the sleeves of her jumper. Thanks. The way I see it, Karin never had a proper separation from you, she was twenty-one when she had just begun building a life of her own, chief editor at the *Entertainment Guide*, a career, a very handsome and smart boyfriend, then everything fell apart with the AVM, that piece of shit boyfriend of hers cleared off and Karin didn't have the strength to do the job, her friends were too young and inexperienced to understand what she was going through, only you were there for her, not that I'm saying it didn't count, of course, but she needed some separation from you, she needed to start her own life, she needed to feel she had her own family, one that was not her birth family, it was impossible, she said herself she regressed. I know all that, if anything I've looked up to Karin because she's so insightful, I have not treated her like a child, none of us ever treated Karin like a child if that's what you mean. You worshipped Karin, Sven worshipped Karin, that's really how it is, the only times I have seen you happy were when you were in the same room as Karin, I've known you now for ten years, Lillemor. What about you, Tom, do you think Karin was like a child? She was like an old woman on one level, on another level she reluctantly liked it when Sven called her his little darling, and when you constantly remarked on how wise and clever she was, to my mind that's how you talk to a child, not a grown woman. You're not being fair now, Tom, see for yourself when Livia gets older, I mean I agree with you in many respects, I do, but in our case, when Karin got ill I lay next to her in the hospital, I lay next to her when she was home between operations and tests, she was twenty-one years old, adult, child, it has no importance, to see Karin suffering like that, hear her pleading with me that I have to help her take her own life if she becomes an invalid, not to be able to give consolation to our own child because there was none to be had. Lillemor, Karin loved you, you know that, but for her it was important to feel she had a family that was not you, she needed me beside her, not you, not Sven, it wasn't an easy decision for her, she wanted to be an adult, that's what exploded for her at the hospital. Tom, I didn't mean to hurt your feelings, she says, and puts her hands on her thighs. You didn't hurt my feelings at all, Lillemor, and I hope I haven't hurt yours either, but I don't think it's a coincidence that Karin chose me, for a lot of reasons of course, I was younger, admittedly just two years younger but still, I looked up to her as a mature woman, an adult. Maybe we should keep our voices down, she says, staring over towards Livia's basket. Well, I suppose we've finished talking for today, but she doesn't seem to be bothered by us, I say, walking up to the basket. I kiss Livia goodnight. Lillemor makes a face. What is it, Lillemor? Won't she wake up when you do that? What, this? Yes, she answers. You have a problem with me kissing my daughter goodnight? She waves with her whole arm and I ask: Am I talking too loud or what? She smiles nervously and says: No, it's just an old habit of mine, I didn't do it on purpose. Okay, goodnight, I say. Yes, goodnight, Tom, she answers and closes the door behind me.

Once I am tucked into bed I feel remorseful about it, I turn on the lights, put on my jeans, and hurry back into the guest room. I knock, open the door, and keep my eyes slanted towards the floor. The beam of the bedside light throws rounded patterns over the floorboards. I'm sorry, Lillemor, I want to start having Livia at nights. I hear her moving but she isn't answering. The floorboards creak, I have to back away when she grips the door handle. She whispers when she answers: I didn't want to call out, I was lying down writing up a few memories, what Karin used to do when she was a child, I thought it could be fun for Livia when she grows up. I feel ready to take Livia at nights now, I say. That's good, but can't this wait until tomorrow? I can't wait, Lillemor, I want Livia with me now. Don't you need your sleep? You need to have the energy to take care of her in the daytime. Is it okay, or . . .? Of course, she answers. Thanks, I say, squeezing past her and releasing the wheel lock of the basket with the tips of my toes. I can't help but feel a little disap-pointed now I've come all the way here, she says. Sorry, I can pay for your taxi, sorry, Lillemor, I want to take Livia now. How about you take her until you've fallen asleep, then I'll come and get her in a few hours? I'll come in quietly so you don't wake up. Please, I want to have my daughter with me now at night, thanks. Yes, you're very good with Livia, you're such a good daddy, she says, following me. She stops in the hall outside the living room. I can't bring myself to look up at her.

In the middle of the night I am woken up by Livia kicking and whimpering. I get her out of the basket and put her on my stomach. She burrows her nose into my throat and falls asleep again. I start running with sweat and I worry that she's too hot. I put her back in the basket and pull it towards the bed. I blow on her forehead and count her toes like my mother used to count my toes, and I feel her rapid exhalation. She has the same Cupid's bow as Karin. My eyelashes. Dad's ears. She moves her middle finger, slowly, like anemone, and she makes a suckling motion in her sleep, lying there wrapped in soft, blue blankets.

I sweep up the fragments of the landline phone that I smashed this morning. Although it looked like an Ericofon it was just a copy. Karin had it since her student days. I try to fix it and then carry on tidying up. The wallpaper. Skirting boards. Under the bed. The chandelier. Chest of drawers. Drawers. In a box under Karin's desk I find a pocket diary among some receipts in a carrier bag. Pink binding decorated with little drawings of brimstone butterflies, a bumblebee, in the middle a duckling carrying a parcel. The diary seems to have been bought in a toyshop. The clasp is fixed with a flimsy padlock. I break it open with a simple twist of the hand and sit down on Karin's chair. The diary is empty apart from five pages with two dates:

Hi Duckface, 15 March 2004.
All the fears, all the risks feel endless. Or? You also have to dare to take a risk, isn't that so? There are so many risks, it's hard to know which of them are of the good sort. I've been feeling so good with Tom. He's exactly the kind of man I want. I even

see myself having children with him. Really! So what is it that's disturbing the peace now? Well, a discussion came up about alcohol. Tom has no problems with it now, but his father has alcohol problems. For this reason it's impossible to talk about it. Which has meant I can't. For a while now I've been giving him the odd barb about alcohol, which has not exactly yielded decent results in terms of being able to talk about it.

Dear little travel diary, 14 May 2004.

Nothing is more important to me than writing down what I am thinking. Maybe that is why I write? Tom and I were at the cinema this week, we saw Tim Burton's Big Fish. *Tom liked it, I was more ambivalent. On the way home Tom got upset. He grew so small, hid in my duffel coat. He didn't want anyone to see him crying. Tom's father has cancer, most likely he doesn't have much time left to him. In the film was a scene when the son said farewell to his father on his deathbed, I think the scene really hit him. I'm lying in the bath now at Tom's place in Huddinge, I have a nasty cold and strange feelings from having stopped taking my anti-depressants yesterday. Maybe it's just as well that it's come at the same time, at least I have cast-iron reasons for being physically and psychologically knocked out.*

I keep Karin's hairbrush next to me while I work on the funeral oration. I rub her hair between my fingers whenever I get stuck on the text, and I hear the neighbour's cat in the stairwell, the whine of the kitchen fan, the whistling of the air vents, snatches of conversations as people pass under the window on Lundagatan, just as it always used to be, like any other normal day, Karin's long hair drying naturally and hanging down her back. Söder Hospital is possibly a thousand metres from the window, I can hear the ambulance sirens. I've grown used to them. The first weeks in Lundagatan, when Karin and I had first moved here, we were sometimes woken by them. Livia opens her eyes, I give her the dummy, I can't cope with having to pick her up, not right now, she spits out the dummy, I manoeuvre it back in, she doesn't want it, she won't stop crying, she thrashes her body and throws out her arms, her yelling intensifies, I go into another room.

In the garage on Björkängsvägen I keep my BMX. I pump up the tyres. Tighten the spoke nuts and oil the chain. Clean the frame with a sponge and lace up my gym shoes. The air is close and my dust mite allergy is aggravated by it. I make my way along the small paths, down into a dip between two rocky knolls, passing a jogging track. Spruce, pine trees, silver birches. Overhead the high-tension cables sway from side to side. From the opening in the trees I see the mirror-smooth waters of Orlången. Beyond the inlet, on the south side, is one of Huddinge's many housing projects. I cycle on towards the sewage plant by Lake Trehörningen. It's thirty degrees, midday, the halfway point between two nights. I drop the bicycle behind a container and crawl in under the fence. Monitoring towers. Concrete cisterns with large, rotating blades. A couple of tanks lowered into the ground containing all the detritus from the sewers. I don't like Trehörningen. Not any other lakes either, not small lakes, meaning the kind you get in Huddinge. Lakes are enclosed by rocks, stones, mud, roots. Only in the winter can I appreciate lakes. When everything is covered in ice and snow and I no longer know if I'm standing on water or land. I've always liked the sewage works and often cycle here. It calms me seeing how all the waste is turned back into water.

Dad doesn't ask where I've been, he just holds out a box for me and says: For pros. It's the first time in ages that he's sat down on the floor with me. It feels embarrassing, too intimate, but I like it. I bring his present with me wherever I go. To hockey training, Konsum in the town centre, Solfagra School, IKEA on Kungens kurva. Even when I accompany Dad abroad on one of his assignments I bring my present. To the hotels, sports arenas, conferences. I don't have the same interview technique as Dad. I'm a laughter collector. I get so proficient at collecting laughter that no one notices I have a Dictaphone up my sleeve. I must have put together about fifty of them, which I listen to when I am on my own. At the top of the Dictaphone is a mint-green button for rewinding. If I get it into the right position I can listen to people laughing backwards at natural speed. It sounds like they're crying.

At three in the afternoon I can't think of anything to do except call Sven. Hi, Sven, it's Tom, I say. He clears his throat and has trouble saying anything back. Sven?

I go on. Are you calling on your landline? he asks. Yes, can I bother you with something? It says on my telephone here that it's Karin calling, he says. Uh-huh, right. I haven't had time to change that yet, it says Karin Home, he says, sounding like he's just woken up. Did you think it was Karin calling? I ask. Sorry, it just threw me a bit, how are things with you and Livia? Not good, I answer. Not good? No. Is Livia with you? Yes, Livia's asleep, she's fine, but I don't know what to do with myself, I don't feel well, it's just getting worse and worse. Yeah, Tom, it's like one of your father's friends said to us: This one's not on the map. Lots of Dad's friends have gone silent, I don't know, maybe they couldn't handle their own worries about dying, I don't know, everything has gone so quiet. Well, would you like us to come over and pick you and Livia up? I don't know, I answer. You can stay here on Lidingö, and we'll give you a hand with Livia. I don't know. In what way are you feeling bad? I miss Karin. Of course you miss Karin, dear Tom . . . death is abstract, it can't be rationally understood. Yes, I know. We have a picture of you and Karin here on the mantelpiece, and now and then we forget, we think you're on your way over for dinner, then the second we remember what's happened, the contrasts are so exhausting. I called Karin's mobile by accident, I say, she's the first person I call when I'm feeling bad. He clears his throat and says: Tom, wouldn't it be a good idea if Lillemor and I picked you both up, you can have dinner here with us? I spoke to Måns yesterday. Our Måns? asks Sven. Yeah, we must have spoken for a couple of hours, he reminds me a bit of Karin, I never thought of it before, that sense of calm, empathy, sorry, Sven, I think I should be committed. Tom, I'm not sure what you mean by 'committed'? I mean taken into care, psychiatric care or something, I don't know how it works, I'm not feeling well at all, I answer. You think it's that bad? Yes, I do, I say. What I'm hearing is that you miss Karin so much. Yeah, but I can't do this any more, I'm so tired. Tom, you're in full command of your faculties, but deep in sorrow, it's better that we come and help you rather than your ending up doing something ill-conceived, don't you think? Yes, maybe, I don't know, maybe I have to call a friend, Hasse is good in situations like this, he's helped me out before when I was in a bad way. That sounds wise, Hasse seems a steady young man, call Hasse, but get in touch with us so we know everything is all right, otherwise we don't mind coming and picking you up, all you have to do is call or send us a text. Yes, thanks, but I don't know.

I imagine the voice at Södermalm's city office as belonging to a woman in her sixties with red-tinted hair and compassionate eyes. She says that in her twenty years at the Social Services office she's never experienced anything quite like this. She seems genuinely upset. It sounds as if she's switching the telephone receiver from ear to ear while I'm talking. Surely this can't be the first time someone has left a family behind? I burst out. No, but I've never actually experienced a situation where people haven't been married or had time to sign a paternity certificate, I honestly don't know how to deal with it. The city court says you have to issue a summons, I say. Right. The way things are now, the Social Services is sending me demands, I continue. It looks like something's gone wrong, she says. Yes, but they say that they're only basing their actions on information held by the Tax Department and according to them Livia is an orphan placed in foster care with me. Where is the child now? Livia is here with me. So she is with you, then? Yes, of course, she's my child. Yes, exactly, yes, of course. I'm getting three demands every day, it's a full-time job going through all that crap and answering it, for instance now I have to attest to the Social Security Agency that Karin is dead, apparently the death certificate wasn't enough, I have to put it in writing how and why she died, above all they're wondering why the infant girl Unknown Lagerlöf is living with me. It sounds as if she's dropped the telephone, she mutters something to herself in Finnish. I have to ask if I can call you back, I have to talk to my colleagues here at the Family Law Unit, it's Thursday today, I won't have time before the weekend, I hope to be able to call you back at the beginning of next week, but quite honestly, I have never experienced this before. That doesn't exactly make me feel calmer, I point out. No, of course, but I'll prioritise this, she answers.

Mum is standing on a stool, a pair of kitchen scissors in her hand. She has just pruned Karin's butterfly bush. Two short, almost denuded twigs stick up. What are you doing? I ask. It was looking so awful, there were almost no leaves left, she answers. It always looks like that after the winter, I say. You have to prune these, she answers. God, Mum. It was wilted, Tom. I stand on the sofa and

unhook the hanging flower pot. You've ruined it, I say.
Tom, you're being silly now. God, I understand you want
to help, but with certain things you could just ask, I say,
sitting down on the sofa with the flower pot, looking at
the withered leaves. Karin watered it every day, it flow-
ered last summer, I add. Mum sits down next to me.
She has a large grip holding her hair in place behind
her neck, it's so tight that it looks painful. I think you
and Livia should come with us to the summer house,
she says. No, I don't want to be stuck out there, I answer.
Tom, we can help you with her, a bit of fresh air, I can
make up the bed in the guest hut, Dad would like it as
well. I replace the flower pot on its hook and take Livia
back to my bed. The flimsy umbilical cord hat is a little
too big, it keeps sliding down over her eyes. Mum follows
me inside and stands at the foot of the double bed. Tom,
I won't be able to afford the summer house once Dad
is no longer around, my pension won't be enough, I
won't even be able to keep up payments on the flat.
Mum, not now, sorry, I can't take it. She scrutinises me
and after a while she asks: Do you think about the
future? I suppose I do, but not right now. Is Hasse picking
you up? No, David, he's coming at nine, I want to be
there in good time before everyone shows up. How many
will there be? she asks. A hundred? I guess. Oh my
darling, she says and strokes my shoulder. She tightens
her lips before she asks: You haven't started taking drugs,
have you? Mum, please. Your uncle killed himself with
drugs. He stayed on his own rotting in a rathole, I say.
I just get worried, who knows what people are capable
of when life turns against them? I've become a father,

Mum. Yes, Tom, you have, but you don't have to be strong. Shit, everyone says that, what the hell does it mean? I ask and stand by the bookshelf. I'll stay here and help you, you need to take your tablet, she says. I can sleep without them now. It's Karin's funeral tomorrow. What the hell do you think, you think I'm going to hand my child over for adoption? Tom, no one thinks that, she says and comes closer. She looks at me. I suppose if one had known life would end up like this, it would have been better to turn around in the doorway, she says. Mum, I never even went abroad with her, she really wanted to go abroad with me so much. Mum places her hand over my neck. She presses her cheek hard against my forehead. Dear child, she says.

Livia lies next to me in bed, surrounded by high pillows and teddies. I adjust the reading lamp. Karin avoided pink. She found the colour inane everywhere except on geraniums. For this reason I have a hard time believing that she bought the little pink diary as an adult, but I'm not ruling it out. I fiddle with the broken clasp to get it out of its fixture. The padlock can't be mended. I look at the keyhole, about three millimetres high and half a millimetre wide. I go over to the desk and pull out the drawer, then empty the contents of the tin mug. The key that I found on the spice shelf belongs to the diary. Livia looks at me with her little luminous eyes. Hi there, are you awake? I say and put my hand on her forehead. It's warm but not hot, she's snotty. I fetch a spray bottle of saline solution from the bathroom. A squirt in each nostril, she cries, sneezes, and tries to lie on her side. I put my telephone next to her and put on 'I Drew My Ship' with Shirley Collins, repeat play. I adjust the volume and put my nose close to Livia's hair. She calms down, she listens. Collins was apparently about thirty years old when she recorded the ballad. A warm, wistful voice accompanied by slow picking on the banjo.

The phone battery is dead when I wake up. I crane my neck, put my head just in front of Livia's mouth, she's breathing, still snotty and warm. It's a quarter to four in the morning. Ten hours until the ceremony. I get to my feet and plug the phone in. The lamp is glowing hot, I pull out the plug. Karin's anaesthetists said that she was in a dreamless state during her sedation. She was knocked out with Propofol. I could still not accept that Karin was just lying there in the intensive care bed without any kind of inner life. That night, the same night that I came home from Karolinska, I started searching the Internet for dreams during anaesthesia, and I found a review of the anthology *Consciousness, Awareness, and Anesthesia* in an American medical journal. I immediately tried to get hold of the book but it wasn't available anywhere in Europe. I had to order it direct from the USA, from Harvard University Press. It came by post the day before yesterday. I fumble in the darkness, seek out a torch in the chest of drawers in the hall and fetch the book. Livia is sleeping deeply. The anthology is heavy, I have to lie on my stomach in bed to be able to read it. One of the essays, *Dreaming During Anesthesia*, is written by the Professor of Anaesthetics Kate Leslie. She refers to several large-scale studies in which between twenty-two and forty-seven percent of the respondents who had undergone anaesthesia were able to talk about their dreams directly after waking up, including those who had been on Propofol-based sedatives. Before I turn off the torch I mark the line: *Most of the patients dreamed of pleasant social situations.*

At Karolinska I used to talk to Karin every day, sometimes hour-long monologues about Livia and the basement passages between the wards. One such time I told her that it looked as if Livia was chewing on the milk in her feeding bottle, more or less like I used to chew my yoghurt in the mornings, which Karin always found comical – because I didn't put anything in my yoghurt – and exactly at this point Karin coughed up phlegm into the tube. The nurses explained that it wasn't an unusual reflex among patients on the respirator. Still, it did feel as if Karin had suddenly laughed. It was something I imagined, but at the same time I believed it. She was dreaming of breakfast at Lundagatan.

A NURSE COMES out of Room 404. She glances down at a clipboard then scans the room, which is very much like a living room. In addition to Livia and me there's an elderly woman in a wheelchair. Only the alarm lights outside every room distinguish the ward from a rudimentary hotel. Tom? she asks. She has chestnut brown hair, she peers out from under her fringe. Thomas's grandchild, I assume? she says and looks at Livia in my sling. Yes, Livia, I answer. She looks like you. Yes, she's probably a combination of me and her mother, I answer. Her mouth pulls into a smile then grows serious again, she offers me her hand and says: Carina, I'm a nurse here, one of the people responsible for your father's treatment. I'm Tom, but you already knew that, I answer. She sits on the fabric-covered sofa and looks at Livia. How old is she? she asks. Four months, or, well, she was born prematurely, so in real terms she's only two and a half months. Ah, okay, well it's a wonderful time, this. She puts her hands on her thighs. Have you been here before? she asks. I came as quick as I could, I've been on Gotland, I came this morning. Do you know Stockholm Nursing Home? How do you mean, do I know it? This is the Palliative Care Department, which means we treat patients with severe symptoms, and patients at the end of their lives – you know why your father is here? He's been ill for ten years, I've spoken to both Mum and Dad, I took the ferry from Gotland this morning. So you know your father is gravely ill? That's why I came home, I answer. The idea is that your father should be as well and as pain-free as possible in this last period, she says, but I interrupt her: How much time is left? She lowers her gaze and answers: It's difficult to say. Is my mother in there now? Yes, she is with your father, she wanted to come and get you, I said I'd like to have a little talk with you first. Why? Your mother is upset. She's my mother, you know. They're happy you're here, your father has spoken a lot about you. I've got my own views on that, but okay, thanks. He told me how you got lost in a restaurant when you were two, and when he found you, you were sitting calmly in the bar drinking juice with two Italian tourists. Is that what he said? Yes, she replies. I can tell you it's one of the few times he was taking care of me on his own, he must have thought a two-year-old would just sit still under the table. She taps her hands across her thigh and says: As a rule the patients here don't have much time left. Okay, I answer. So to answer your question: A week, or a couple of days, it could also go faster. What do the doctors say? That's our estimate, she answers. I look over at the woman in the wheelchair. She's being fed by a nurse who mashes the potatoes with

216

a fork and, between one forkful and the next, dabs the wrinkled mouth with a paper napkin. If you want to talk to Per Strage you're quite welcome, he's our senior consultant here, she says. No, no need, thanks. How is Dad now? I spoke to him yesterday, he was sounding fairly perky at that point. His head is clear, but he's tired, sleeps a lot, from time to time he has the strength to go to the balcony in the wheelchair so he can smoke, with someone there to help, of course, he's very weak. Does he know why he's here? Your mother doesn't want us to say too much, obviously he knows he's in palliative care. Dad probably doesn't know what palliative care means, but okay. She looks up when voices ring out in the corridor, and greets someone while kneading her left shoulder with her right hand. That's all I had to say unless you have any questions, she says. No, thanks. If anything comes to mind, don't hesitate to ask one of us. Okay, thanks. She smiles at Livia, then wanders off towards a kitchen.

Room 404 has a small vestibule with a large mirror, and a toilet with a shower to the left. Mum sits in an armchair in one corner of the room. She stands up. Two hospital beds, Dad lies in the one closest to the door. His eyes are closed but swollen, they bulge underneath the skin. His mouth is open, his teeth brown. Mum kisses Livia's head and goes up to the bed. Thomas, Tom is here now, she says. He opens his eyes wide and turns his head until he sees me. He raises his hand. So, you're happy now that Tom came, aren't you? says Mum and turns towards me. He's been nagging ever since he got here about when you're coming. Dad, I came as

217

quick as I could, it was hard getting a ticket home, how are things with you? He makes a rocking motion with his hand. It's up and down, he's been tired today, says Mum and pats him on the leg. He clears his throat and puffs. Thomas, Livia is here as well, says Mum. He gives her a thumbs up. Does he have to share the room with anyone else? I ask. No, we're the only ones here, she answers. I have such a bloody headache, is there anywhere one can have a coffee around here? I ask. Do you want an Alvedon? I've already taken a paracetamol and ibuprofen, it doesn't help, I just need caffeine now. There's a coffee machine outside, I can go with you. She blows her nose and pokes about with the handkerchief in her nostrils. Standing by the coffee machine, she kisses Livia again on the head and says: You didn't come with her like this, did you? Mum, it's summer. Is your headache that bad? Don't think about it now. You do have a bit of a background, Dad has his cluster headaches and I have my migraines. It's caused by other things, I say. You're not drinking, are you? Mum, please! Her face wrinkles up, her nose and one cheekbone have burned in the sun, I have the same type of skin as Mum, I also turn red in the sun, unlike Dad and his Walloon pigmentation. She scrutinises me, points out that my shoes are filthy and that I have a hole in my jeans, then says in a low voice: I haven't told him it's over, do you think I should have? I think so, I answer. Laila told me that Patrik's dad felt such anguish when he found out, I don't want to inflict that on your father, she adds. Is Laila your advisor? It's not about Laila, it's about your father. I think it's essential to be honest, but do whatever you think is best. But he doesn't ask. Maybe don't force it on him, but if he asks I think you should be direct. I don't know, it's so hard, I don't think he wants to know, she says, squeezing the locket on her necklace. On one side is a photo of Dad from their wedding at Huddinge Town Hall in June 1977, while the other side holds a picture of the family's spindly and long-since dead mongrel cat. Many years ago Mum had a picture there of herself, but she removed it. She has never felt comfortable with photos of herself, just as she's never enjoyed the least bit of attention. As a child I liked how Mum kept the wedding photos in her locket. It was as if they kissed every time the locket was snapped shut and the pictures joined. I was going to do a bit of shopping, she says and looks around, adding quickly: He doesn't read the newspapers anyway, but he still wants a copy of *Expressen* on his belly, will you stay with him? That's why I'm here, Mum. Moments later I have to call out to her: Mum, hello, the exit is that way, isn't it, to the right? She looks confusedly in all directions.

I put Livia in the bed next to Dad. He's torpid from the morphine. A catheter runs from the back of his hand to a drip-stand. I wish he'd say something. A couple of well-chosen words from the dying father to his son. He says nothing. Me neither. I take his hands in mine. He looks uncomfortable about it. But I don't let go of them. His dry, greyish yellow hands covered in hair like smudged printer's ink chafe against my skin with the same curious heat as those paper bags I used to carry about in my childhood. Their handles and weight gave me sores on my palms. Usually I had ten paper carrier bags lined up in the garage by the souterrain house on Björkängsvägen, filled with the week's newspapers: *Expressen, Aftonbladet, Dagens Nyheter, Svenska Dagbladet, Eskilstuna-Kuriren, Sydsvenska Dagbladet* and a load of sports magazines. At the recycling centre in Årsta we lifted the bags out of the car and lugged them up to a high ramp, then tipped them into a bulk container. Dad lit a Marlboro Red right by a big 'No Smoking' sign. He looked down into the jumble and said: So much bloody work went into that, all the trips, accreditations, interviews, conversations, pictures, articles, checking, editing text at night, soon there'll be nothing left of it but a lot of shit-smelling porridge.

Hello, Karl, you're looking more sprightly today, I see. Dad clears his throat and replies to the nurse: I want to smoke with my son. His name's Thomas, I add, Karl is his second name. The nurse stops, his bulky torso bulging out of his light blue uniform shirt. He gets out a bit of paper from his pocket, unfolds it, reads, and says: Yes, it's Thomas, you're right. Thanks, terribly good of you to admit it, says Dad. With his Södermanland dialect, his hissing voice, and his rejoinders at once snappy and poisonous, he brings to mind an aged spitting cobra. The nurse sniggers and starts fiddling to get the braces of the patient lift under Dad's legs. If you keep looking a bit longer you might find something really exciting there, says Dad. Yeah, that's right, no, I'm trying to find the attachments, I have a back problem, I don't have the strength to lift you, he says. I can lift him, I say. This will be fine, he answers and fixes a couple of braces. Dad is hoisted up by a motor on the ceiling and he stays suspended in a seated position half a metre above the bed while the nurse leaves the room. Some of them have the odd brain cell and some don't have any at all, says Dad. I suppose he got stressed, I say. Yeah, but what the hell, just leaving me here hanging, he's so muddled he makes people on the Disability Job Scheme look like a bunch of geniuses. Shit, Dad. What the hell, leaving me here, hanging? Isn't he a bit like Krutov? I ask. Who, that one who was just here? Yeah, I think so, something about his eyes, his cheeks. It hadn't come to mind but now you say it . . . Krutov was not muddled, that's for sure. Didn't he finish off his career at Brunflo Hockey Club? I ask. He had such problems with his weight, it was the end for him, he ate everything, even his own career. What about you, are you eating? I ask. He shrugs. The nurse comes back with a wheelchair and Dad looks at me and says: Krutov. I quickly turn to Livia. She's fallen asleep with her arms around a pillow. Dad breaks wind as he's being lowered into the wheelchair. Whoops, says the nurse. Dad shakes his head. It's natural, adds the nurse. Is it? Dad exclaims. Yes, he says. Sitting semi-naked in a chair lift, farting? I interrupt Dad and ask him where he put his pack of cigarettes.

Dad guides me through the corridors with terse commands: No, yes, good. He's afraid of heights. As a child I got to change the bulbs in the ceiling lights because he didn't dare get up on a stool, he was so at a loss, he was deeply impressed whenever I managed to get them back on. I park the wheelchair against the wall of the long, open balcony which my father refers to as 'the smoking gallery'. I lean against the railing. On the right is St Göran's College, a modernist building constructed of toughened glass, concrete, and steel. In the distance I can see Dad's old workplace, the skyscraper belonging to *Expressen* and *Dagens Nyheter*. Don't stand so near the edge, Dad hollers. She's attached, I say, tugging at the locked buckles of the sling. What difference will that make if you fall? he says. I help Dad light his cigarette and step a short distance from him. Livia sucks and gnaws at the dummy string. Dad's arms are so scrawny that the gold-coloured wristwatch he bought in the Caribbean in the nineties is strapped to his upper arm to stop it sliding off. He peers at me and says: What are those trees down there, are they poplars? Poplars? Well, I don't know, he says. *Don't you see, Leonor, the river poplars with their stiff branches?* I answer. Have you been drinking? he asks. Not a drop since March, I answer. That's good, he says. It's from a poem, Antonio Machado, he wrote it after his wife Leonor died, I explain. Oh, if you say so. She died young, I point out. I can't make any sense of poems like that. Who can? I answer. Why are you reading them, then? he asks. I really don't know, I say. Maybe you should have a glass of something with Krutov in there? Yeah, maybe I should. I like song lyrics, but they have to have a beginning, a middle, and an end, I mean your old lady was a bit sceptical about my wanting to name you after Tom T. Hall, then she listened to his lyrics, well, as I said: a beginning, middle, and end. He moves his left hand across his thigh and goes on, as if thinking aloud: A double gin, a slice of lemon, some bottled tonic, and ice. Shall I fix you one? I ask. No, he exclaims. It's easily done. No, sit down, I don't want one. Okay, as you wish, I say. Ice Man and Tommy Engstrand were here for a while yesterday, they brought the newspapers, I mean we meet twice a year for dinner, he says. Who is Borg to you, Dad? What do you mean, who is he? You often talk about him, who is he for you? Ice Man is legendary, he's the greatest one we've had, he answers, looking at me with a touch of irritation when I start laughing. Go on, you tell me then, he adds. I can't, but I can tell you who Borg is for me, he's a guy who can't write his own stuff. You've hung him out to dry there a bit, be careful what you say, he answers. That's how it is, I look up to you more for what you've written than him for his tennis. Dad crosses his arms and answers: When I was a kid I was very good at mental arithmetic. Uh-huh, is that in relation to what I was just saying, or what? No, just for the sake of saying it. I always have a feeling there's a subtext to what you say, some little jibe that I'm too dumb to pick up on, I reply. Stupid you've never been, but your temperament contributes to the greenhouse effect. You're bloody funny, Dad, you know that? He taps the ash off his cigarette and says: Mum got annoyed with Ammi the other day. Uh-huh, okay, what was that all about, then? I ask. I mean, when I say annoyed, Mum never says anything, but Ammi was sitting here with Börje and Hans and Harriet, talking about the parties they were going to and the trips they were planning. Yeah, I under-stand, yeah, it's not easy, she didn't mean any harm by it, but it sounds a bit self-centred, I suppose she's always

223

been one to open her mouth without thinking. Don't say anything to Börje, says Dad. Why would I tell Börje? You can say whatever you like, whenever, he answers and I laugh. A lot of people can't stand situations like this, they don't know what to say, or what to do with themselves, I've heard that Laila's been a real rock, I say. Yup, say what you like about Laila, she's a right old suburban bag, but she's good to Mum. Laila must have been about my age when Sten passed away? She was older than you, says Dad. Yeah, but she was left on her own to take care of two children. They were grown up, they weren't even living at home any more, he points out. Okay, whatever, my point is that to have the courage to meet someone in a difficult situation you must probably have some experience of death. Do you remember Boanäs? he says. Yeah, of course I do, I reply. It was always raining and if it wasn't raining the mosquitoes were swarming, he says. I have a great photo of you and Börje and Hans from Boanäs times, you're standing in a rowing boat, poor old sods, and then I worked out that you were actually about my own age when that picture was taken. Dad chuckles and answers: Mainly we just rowed out to get some peace, I guess we were moderately interested in the fishing. It's not for nothing that we used to call those weekends the Boanäs Race, fifteen grown-ups and twenty snotty kids sharing an outside latrine, well, you'll remember it of course, but we had fun, we caught a pike now and then, Christina minced it and made heavenly pike balls, and then the country music, the stereo was always on from morning till night, 'If Drinkin' Don't Kill Me Her Memory Will' and songs like that, it was classic, the parties we had, and the ladder up to the attic, remember that? Yes, I do, I answer. I mean the way everyone slept up in that attic, it was a nightmare going to bed, that ladder was slippery as hell, and I was drunk of course, and afraid of heights, and then there was that ladder to climb, carefully and without drawing too much attention to yourself, and then, wham, you and all the other kids would be standing there in your pyjamas, pointing, yeah, thank God that's over. I miss Boanäs sometimes, I answer. Dad chews on his cigarette and says: I was married once before. What? It's many years ago now. Okay, I answer. A Finnish photo model, and a nymphomaniac to boot, she wanted to do it everywhere, I was too old for it already then, I told Börje while I was walking out of the church: This won't last longer than a week. Is that true? Yeah, and I was almost right, it lasted three weeks. So why did you get married, then? I ask. You should know, though, Mum is superior to them all. Have you told her that? Yes, he answers, gazing out towards Mariebergsgatan. How are you, Dad? I ask. I've sat next to tough blokes with a lot of money who've said, a hundred grand on the next car being white. If you do that you have too much money, I reply. You can gamble on anything. I guess so. What colour will the next car be? he asks, then goes on: How much are you staking on it? I'm the bank, a very friendly bank, ten times your money back if you're right? Livia and I are throwing in a million kronor, red, I answer. Dad peers at the street. Grey, he exclaims, sorry, kid, you just lost your flat, lucky it wasn't for real.

What are you thinking about, Dad? I ask. Nothing special, he answers, then asks me to light him another cigarette. It's so blustery that he has to cup his hands around the lighter. Who's taking care of Bosse? I ask. Falken, he answers. How's Falken these days, then? He was here this morning, he says. Is he still coaching some team or has he stopped completely now? I ask. He's watching the telly and eating egg sandwiches, says Dad. Glowing embers are flying all round his head. Are you tired, Dad? I ask. Mum doesn't know that I know, he says. Know what? Why I'm here, he says. No, Mum doesn't want to tell you too much. It's finito, he says, nodding at me. Yes, it is, I answer. He looks down at Livia who's playing with my hand. You're good with her, he says. Thanks, Dad, and yes, I am. He breathes smoke through his nose and adds: All you can do is fall to pieces and then come back. Yeah, maybe, I answer. He looks down at my hands again. Tom T., he says. Yes, Dad? When you were small you liked to sit on my lap and tickle your palm on my shirt collar.

Klockarvägen 10 in Huddinge. Four floors up. A rocky outcrop is visible behind the apartment building. I also catch a glimpse of the industrial estate and the red brick of Huddinge Centre. Everything is covered in a layer of coldness. High above hang two parallel streaks of vapour from an aircraft. It's the first public holiday falling on March 2002 and the Public Early-Warning and Information System is being tested. Sirens are blaring everywhere. They make me shudder, I have to check the time and date to make sure that no nuclear power station has blown up or some other disaster has taken place. The sirens also activate something else inside of me. A sort of Pavlovian response, whereby I immediately start worrying about my future. This afternoon I am worrying more than usual. I am no longer in touch with Ellie, the relationship is over. My university education in literature and philosophy is also over, a four-year course that was vaguely entertaining but meaningless.

Only Dad and I are in the flat. Mum is at the theatre with colleagues from the council-owned Huge Property AB, whose flats she lets. Dad is wearing his greyish yellow chinos and the white T-shirt with the wasp emblem of *Expressen*. Neither fit him any more. Nor does he wear them with ease. The clothes have become too heavy, washed too many times and worn out, as if he's taken refuge in them. It's been a long time since Dad and I last saw each other one-to-one; in all my time in Uppsala I only saw him sporadically. He sits in the mint-green leather armchair by the matching settee. It's an off-putting colour, at least for a suite. It's cursing and yelling at all the other colours and sofa suites in the world. Not least at the more discreet colours picked by my mother. Dad bought the sofa in the early nineties and attributes enormous and immodest value to it. On the table made of glass and cherry wood stands a ceramic jug which he continually tops up from a wine box of red Castillo de Gredos.

Do you need money? he asks.

No.

Why have you come, then?

I live a hundred metres away, sometimes I pass by. He

gouges at his teeth with a toothpick, levers open his lean jaw with his fist. With his eyes half-closed he stretches his lips back, then studies the bloody toothpick in the glare of the chandelier and puts it on the table.

There's food in the fridge if you want some, he says.

Thanks, I'm fine.

How are you getting along with the ladies?

Dad, Ellie and I just broke up. He shuts his clippings book and gets out his pack of Marlboro. All the articles Dad ever wrote are cut out and carefully glued into these large, heavy ledgers, from when he was sixteen and wrote short notices for *Eskilstuna-Kuriren* to the years when he was writing headline articles for *Expressen*. His clippings books take up metres of shelving in his study. He plugs in a cigarette and stands up with his cryptic smile, the one that's always made me want to crawl into his arms, and in his laboured English he quotes one of Tom T. Hall's songs: *Friends are hard to find when they discover that you're down.*

I shower for probably an hour when I get home to Edsvägen, then sit on my bed and study my birdlike legs beneath the bath towel. They're as skinny as Dad's but not as evenly brown as his, just lifelessly pale and ugly. I have got water in my ears, which causes a sort of tinnitus. I even out the pressure and shake my head. I fetch cotton buds and I sit back down on the bed. I even out the pressure again but the sighing in my ears doesn't go away. I listen to it so carefully that in the end I start to pick up a structure: there's an interval, a seven-second-long dull sound blast, which then disappears for fourteen seconds. Then it starts again. The sighing ebbs away. Only the sound blasts are left. Thousands of sirens from far inside my head.

I answer my mobile in a driving rain that blows in under the umbrella. Livia is babbling into the south-westerly wind. She waves her arms, it looks as if she's opening her mouth and poking her tongue out at the heavy drops. It's Karin's haematologist, Franz Callmer. He explains that he usually gets in touch with the family after someone has died. It's easy to start brooding on what really happened, maybe you have a bit more distance to it now, it's common for people to build up questions, he says. Yes, I suppose it is like that, thanks, I answer and break into a run towards the front entrance of the hospice, leaving behind the temporary shelter of a garage roof. In real terms it's best to meet, he says. That could be diffi-cult right now, I answer. You're thinking about your daughter? It's not only that. How is your daughter? Livia is fine, thanks. Livia, yes, I can at least tell you that acute myeloid leukaemia is not hereditary; I know this very well, my mother had AML, so that was the first thing I looked into when I became a doctor. Do we know where AML comes from? I ask. We don't know for certain, in Chernobyl there were reports of many cases of AML, also in Japan after the radiation from the atomic bombs. And it's been shown that people handling benzene have developed AML, that's the sort of thing you have in petrol stations. Could Karin have got the leukaemia from the laser blade? No, he answers. I thought you just said you weren't sure where AML came from? I know enough to say that it was not caused by a laser blade; environmental

229

factors are usually the main reason for most of our cancers, the chemicals we release are absorbed by animals and plants which we then eat, hereditary factors obviously play a role as well. Tom, you seem to have a few questions. Wouldn't it be better if you wrote them down and then came here so we can talk under more relaxed circumstances? By the way I can't hear you very well either, you keep cutting out. I'm at a hospital, my father is in a palliative ward. What did you say, did you say palliative ward? Yes, at Stockholm Care Home. Has your father been sick for very long? He has GIST, I answer. Did you say GIST? Yes, GIST. Gastrointestinal stromal tumour? Dad calls it his Alien, it weighs in at two and a half kilos. It's a type of sarcoma, does he have it in his stomach? he asks. How did you know that? They usually get lodged there. How long has he been in treatment? Ten years, I answer. Well then, he's hung on for a long time, how old is he? I stop in a secluded waiting hall, abstract art on the walls, marble floors, a sofa in blue leather. I shake the water off the umbrella, work my feet out of my sandals, and sit down. Livia starts chewing my finger, she has no teeth but there's force in her jaws. Sixty-six, look, thanks for calling, it's very considerate of you. I can see you have other things on your mind, how are you coping with all this? Even grief has its lowest point, I answer. I should also just add here, GIST is not hereditary either.

I get myself a cola from the one café in the hospital, Restaurang Huss, and then hurry up to Room 404. I get my MP3 speakers out of my rucksack, put them on the table and put on Tom T. Hall's 'Old Dogs, Children and Watermelon Wine'. Mum is sleeping in the armchair.

She's snoring. I take off Livia's clothes and put her next to Dad. He holds her and watches me while I hang up the wet garments on the radiator.

The radio with the broken aerial is on the mantelpiece. It's been broadcasting the quarter-finals of Wimbledon all day. The door is held open by a hasp, windows towards Båtstigen, and the giant pines absolutely silent in the wind, the manured fields, damp and mould, between the pines I see Lake Henaren and the wet floating pontoon.

These last few years my father has been ghostwriting Björn Borg's tennis commentary in *Expressen*, and before every important tennis championship he gives *Expressen* his own opinions in the other man's name. In practice I'm the one who's been ghostwriting the articles lately, because Dad is so weakened by his illness that he has difficulties using his fingers.

Okay, what about this, then? I say, reading aloud from the document in Dad's computer: *When I was twenty-five years old I dropped out of top-flight tennis, well, twenty-five, old or young, just cross out what doesn't seem right, I was fed up with tennis, tennis was blah blah blah*. Dad interrupts:

No, you can't write that, *blah blah blah*, he wouldn't express it like that.

The parties, the injuries, Loredana? I point out. Dad rubs his arm and mutters to himself:

Blah blah blah.

Dad, I'm trying to write like you when you're trying to write like Björn Borg. He puts down the newspaper and groans:

You're making me break out in a sweat, with you it's always nought to a hundred in a blink. He grimaces at the empty fireplace, which hisses a little in the draught, and says: All right, then, heck, let's go for it.

I finish the piece and write Björn Borg at the bottom. Dad checks through the text with the surly scrupulousness of a proof-reader. Finally he says:

I'll call and okay it with Ice Man.

His shoulders tremble as he picks up his mobile. Borg doesn't answer right away, he never does. Dad leaves a message on the voicemail and then, with a whistling sound in his throat, he stands up.

Goddamnit, he pants and grabs his flies, whips out his penis, pinching it with his right hand. He hurries over to the kitchen door, he's dripping. Standing on the threshold, he pees onto the lawn. It's not a barrel of laughs, you know, having a leaky bit of tagliatelle like this, he says, turning his head towards me and adding: There was a time when I could bounce out of bed on my morning hard-on.

Borg calls back after twenty minutes and they chit-chat for a while. Dad reads out the piece. In the middle of the text he stops himself and takes off his glasses. The right-hand earpiece gets caught behind his ear for a moment, and he blinks to stop the other earpiece going in his eye. He recites with exaggerated clarity: Blah blah blah. He repeats: *Blah blah blah*. He adds: I could bloody swear you said something along those lines to McEnroe some time? Dad presses the tip of his tongue to his upper lip. He puts on his glasses and slaps his hand against his knee, bursting out laughing. Classic, Ice Man, bloody off the chart, you're going to get shedloads of mail again; Björn Borg, the internationally respected columnist. Dad gives me a thumbs up. I slip out of the kitchen door and then hear Dad's laugh ringing out all the way to the cellar in the garden. I get myself a cold beer and lie on the sunlounger.

Hi, darling, says Karin when I call.

Is everything all right?

Yeah, fine, I just wanted to check, I get off in Malmköping, right?

Are you joking?

I always forget, she answers.

Yes, in Malmköping, we'll come and pick you up, call when you get to Södertälje.

I've bought a bottle of wine and some flowers, will that do?

They'll just be happy to have you.

Is it too much, maybe it's enough with flowers?

Stop it now, it'll be great.

Oh good.

I miss you, I tell her.

I miss you too, but we'll see each other tomorrow.

I get so sentimental when I'm here, now they've moved to Tanto this is the only thing still left that feels like home.

Yeah, that's how I feel about Gotland, she answers.

Exactly, okay, I'll call later to say goodnight, I just wanted to check on you that everything was fine.

Can't we just say goodnight now? I'm already in bed.

What's the time?

Eleven, she replies.

Oh shit, I thought it was nine, okay, goodnight darling, I miss you, it's so damned difficult getting off to sleep without you, I went off at two o'clock and then woke up in a panic at four because you weren't there.

Darling, it's just one night.

It's more than enough to make you weep, I point out.

How's Thomas?

Okay, it's just that he looks so fucking old, he looks like he's eighty.

You say that every time you see him.

I don't need to talk about it, call me when you wake up, goodnight.

Are you annoyed?

No.

Sure?

Yes.

I just meant it's something you get sad about, his looking so old, she says.

Don't forget to call me right away when you wake up, I answer.

What if I wake up early? she asks.

If you wake me up it's a good morning as far as I'm concerned.

Darling, I'll call, love you.

Love you.

So . . . Malmköping? she asks again.

Yes, get off in Malmköping, I have a long beard, a dirty baseball cap, I'll be waving like hell, you'll recognise me.

Dad is sitting there looking out towards Båtstigen when I come back into the cottage.

How long has Mum been out with the mutt? he asks.

She left when I started writing, maybe an hour?

Dad points at his jacket hanging over the back of one of the kitchen chairs and says: Can you get me my wallet, inside pocket?

He's had it for as long as I can remember, awkwardly large, of dark brown leather. He takes something out of a compartment. At first I think it's a receipt but it's a faded and folded piece of lined paper. He holds it up, giving it a little shake. Do you remember this? he asks.

What is it? The corners of his mouth start twitching.

I was sixteen when I wrote it, he says.

Sixteen?

Yes, he answers.

I can't say I remember it, I can only recall two letters, the one you wrote so Mum got a job, and your fan letter to Hitchcock.

You'd make a good private detective, the letters to Hitchcock and to grandmother's boss were posted, I did it myself, I couldn't possibly still have those letters; I just said it was *you* who wrote the letter.

Me? I exclaim, no, you said you wrote it.

No, I did not.

What do you mean, no? That's what you just said.

Did I? he says, scratching his ear.

Yes, you said you wrote it.

My head's spinning today, in which case I made a mistake.

Anyway, what is this letter? I ask. He unfolds the paper, looks at it, and says:

You'd dropped the hockey, you wrote that I no longer

existed for you ever since the gambling scandal, Lia had just finished with you, isn't that right?

What is that letter? I ask again.

You've always had a sense of drama, he says.

Okay . . .

From the TV-Puck Tournament to that liver problem you had at that bar, and then your forged passport, don't you realise I still remember all that?

Clearly you do, I answer.

Have you ever listened to *anyone*? he asks.

I was eleven when I had to carry you to bed and console Mum, don't give me this shit. He folds up the paper, puts it back in his wallet, shakes his head, still apparently amused by the situation, but not in a disdainful way, he's genuinely amused. Have you been keeping that in your wallet all this time? I ask. He rubs his knuckles against his palm, then he presses his hand against his shinbone, puffing, and then with sudden determination he gets to his feet and stands next to me. His shoulders are swinging. It's as if he's unsure whether he's allowed to hug me, so he doesn't, instead he just pokes my cheek. He does it clumsily, his fingers are bent into a hard stump.

Tom T., the ghost of ghostwriters, he says.

The first grown-up book I decide to read is a Swedish translation of a French polemical text entitled: *A Book on Suicide: Motivations and Techniques*. I find it in a second-hand bookshop by Mariatorget. The title attracts me. I pay thirty-five kronor for it, but only leaf through it. I can't make head or tail of it, it's riddled with unusual words that I don't have the energy to look up. Allegedly written by two *Le Monde* journalists in the eighties, it contains many tips on how to kill oneself without excessive and unnecessary violence, such as swallowing a cup of apple pips. The pips contain a substance that can release a fatal dose of hydrocyanic acid. That afternoon I pedal along on Mum's bike through working- and middle-class areas, villas and terraced houses with dry lawns and garden figurines made of porcelain and plastic. It's a public holiday. No one's about. But now and then there's a light left on in an empty kitchen or living room. Not unusual in these parts of Huddinge. The timer plugged into the socket is supposed to create an illusion of someone being at home, which might deter burglars. I fill my rucksack with apples and cycle home.

Later that evening I jog down to Huddinge Station, a commuter train pulls in, I hide my face in my hood and slip through the revolving barrier. From Södra Station I walk down to Riddarfjärden and stop on an unlit quay. I've left my letter of farewell to Mum and Dad on the kitchen table. I squeeze the apple pips in the freezer bag. All night I sit there, leaning against a bollard, listening to the lapping of water against the granite blocks.

My father wheezes, I struggle to hear what he's saying. The white blanket with purple stripes is drawn right up to his chin and his dry-as-leather, brown-black face feels increasingly lifeless and inaccessible to me. He asks me to go and get him some cash from the cashpoint on Sankt Eriksgatan. Get some wine for Mum and Laila, and two copies of *Expressen* and an *Aftonbladet*, he adds. I can pay, I reply. You don't have any money. I can afford a couple of newspapers and a bottle of wine, I answer. No, he says. Yes, I can. Don't be ridiculous now, he wheezes. I pick up his wallet from the bedside table, peer inside it, run my finger over the bills and say: You have fifteen hundred in cash. It's good to have, he answers. Do you want me to pay with your Visa so you can keep your cash? Yes, do that, he answers. I buy the newspapers and wine in Restaurant Huss; I smuggle the bottle out under my jumper because the waiter looked murderous when I asked if I could bring the wine up to the room. I sit in the stairwell between the second and third floors, and I look through Dad's wallet. My letter is between two business cards, I recognise it at once, I rip it up without reading it and throw the scraps of paper in the bin outside the elevators, then I just stand there. Why has Dad carried the letter with him for twenty years?

Mum pays me no mind, she sits motionless in the armchair, her heels on the footstool, staring at Dad. Livia, wearing nothing but her nappy, is asleep on her. I leave the newspapers and the wallet with Dad. He's also sleeping. I put the bottle of wine on the windowsill among the cut flowers from relatives, colleagues, and friends. I read a few of the cards. We could have had another twenty years, she says. Mum? I'm so heartbroken, Tom, what am I going to do without him? It'll work itself out, Mum. It seems only yesterday he came up to me at Maxim, on Drottninggatan, that was the in place in the seventies, he lied about his name and said he was a private detective, do you know what made me fall for him? No, I answer, unable to stop myself from smiling a little. His smell, he smelled so nice, she says. How did he smell? I ask. He smelled of Thomas. You know, Mum, I remember the smell of Lypsyl and newsprint when I slept between you, I can't have been much older than five. He always used Lypsyl, she says. Mum, you have slept next to each other for forty years. He was away a lot, if it wasn't the Olympics it was some World Championship, but he always called, several times each day, I felt safe with him. Yes, Mum, he was there for you. He was. And you've been there for Dad, always, I say. She looks at the flowers and answers: And then there's this, all the journalists and their bloody reminiscing, their trips, their drunken nights, and all the sportsmen, it feels as if they are taking him away from me, it feels as if everyone is taking Thomas away from me, sorry, I'm so confused. Mum, he's your Thomas, you've lived with him for forty years. Yes, darling, you know, don't you? She takes down her legs from the footstool and says: Can you take her? I want to sit with him for a moment. I move to the armchair with Livia. Mum puts the side of her head against his mouth.

I haven't spoken to my counsellor since she went on holiday in early June. Hello, Tom, it's Liselotte, am I calling at a bad time? No, I'm sitting on a blanket with Livia, she's chewing a rubber giraffe; how have you been? I've had a nice relaxed time, she says, I've spent hours reading *DN* every morning, that's the sort of thing you value at my age. It sounds good. And you were planning to go to Gotland, weren't you? Yes, exactly, but I think it might be better if we get in touch another day, if that's okay? Yes, of course, if that's how you feel, we can arrange a new time right away if you like? I don't know. How are you, Tom? I don't think I have the strength to talk today. It's good you say that, shall I try to call the same time next Tuesday? My father is unwell, I say. I remember, how's he doing? It's been a real roller coaster with him, he was so bad at Karin's funeral that he had to be helped around her coffin, but at Midsummer he was fairly sprightly, I spoke to him on the phone, he'd had a shot of schnapps, him and Mum were at their country place in Dunker, I just blurted it out and said I was feeling like shit, he answered: Tom T., there'll be other trains. Yes, but Tom, how was your Midsummer? I was on Lidingö with Sven and Lillemor, I wanted to be close to Karin's grave, Lidingö was completely deserted, mainly I just read. You had enough peace of mind to read? I didn't have to think about my own shit, I lay in the grass by Karin's grave, it was beautiful, the trees, the water, I read all day, all evening, sometimes Livia woke up, I fed her, I played with her, I had time to get through several books, that was my Midsummer, have you ever read Sebald? No, but the name sounds a bit familiar. His novels come up now and then in the arts pages. That might explain it, she says. In one of the books he's sitting in a hotel window looking out over a park where all the trees have blown down in a storm, men with machines are digging them up by the roots, sawing up the trunks and driving them away, the park is turned into bare hectares of turned-over soil, he sees little tufts of grass coming out of the mud, he writes, *whose seeds have remained, who knows how long, deep down there.* That was lovely, you know, she answers. I'm just so tired, it makes no difference that Livia is sleeping through the night now. Tom, that's perfectly normal, remember it's only been four months since you lost Karin, and in the midst of all this you've become a father. The woman in charge here says he won't live through the night, I reply. It takes a while before Liselotte answers: Sorry, are you talking about your father now? Yes, I answer. I didn't realise it was so critical, are you with him now? I've been here for three days, I answer. Tom, being there must stir up painful things for you? My mother, I say. Yes, your mother? she answers after a while. It's difficult to talk, I say. Yes, I understand, take your time. It's so hard seeing how sad she is, I say. Yes, oh yes. She holds the back of his head, she gives him fruit squash through a straw, she's there from the time he wakes till he goes to sleep. He's as weak as that? It feels like that's what she's done all his life, all he could do was talk and write, Mum had to do everything else. I think I recognise that, maybe it's something to do with their generation? I'm glad I came here in time, it's good to just sit there and watch them, they laugh a lot, and then they put their foreheads together, I've decided to remember them like that.

My diary is lying on the bed, I didn't put it there. When I am not writing, I usually keep it hidden under a pile of comics on my bedside table. I leaf through it. In the night I wrote down my uncensored anger about Dad's injustices and alcohol habits and our relationship, he hasn't just marked the bad spelling and ambiguous use of pronouns, he's also critiqued sections in his upright handwriting. The marker pen has gone through several pages.

The lead-up to what is known in the media as the gambling scandal is that my father publishes a series of articles in *Expressen* at the end of the eighties and the early nineties. He claims that the results of some matches in Swedish bandy and ice hockey have been fixed. His information comes from a poker pal from his youth, with contacts in the underworld, that's what Dad tells me. In his articles he states that the Mafia has diddled the state-owned gambling behemoth Tipstjänst out of at least thirty-six million kronor by bribing key players from some of the leading teams to underperform in certain crucial matches. Before the articles go to print, Dad stands up at the dinner table in Björkängsvägen. He points at his big forehead and says: There's going to be a bloody big hullabaloo, this is massive, believe me, this will end with a Pulitzer.

No one comes forward to confess. The Office of the Chancellor of Justice sues *Expressen* for slander. Although *Expressen* wins on all 176 counts of the prosecution, Dad is treated with scepticism by his colleagues, even his closest friends are dubious about him. It makes me feel as if it's the Malmquist family vs Sweden and the Mafia. Murder threats add weight to that feeling. Two bodyguards sit in a dark Saab with blacked out windows in our drive, and another three of them are indoors, opening and closing the front door for us. There's a silent state of war in our home.

One morning there's a crackling sound of walkie-talkies. Two bodyguards order us upstairs onto the windowless landing, we run, we're told to curl up on the floor with our hands over our heads, one of the bodyguards has drawn his pistol. Mum hugs me a little too hard. She presses her hand over my eyes and whispers:

It's only make-believe.

I open the laptop on the table and start looking for a photo that Mum has been asking for. A group photo from the New Year's dinner on Jägaregatan in 2011. Mum remembers Harriet borrowing my phone and photographing everyone at the dinner table. If so, it will be the last photo ever taken of Karin and Dad together. I think Mum is mistaken, I can't remember the moment. Thousands of photos. I can't find it but I stop on another one of Dad, from the summer of 2003. Out of focus, badly composed, it's an image I should have erased, I have better pictures from that time. Dad is wearing a V-necked jumper, he's sitting in a wheelchair in the entrance lobby of Huddinge Hospital. His chain with the gold crucifix against his chest. He's unshaven. His glasses rest on his straight, sharp nose and the earpieces disappear behind his hairy ears. What makes me linger on the photo is a wrinkle under his right eye, which makes me think he's just about to wink at me.

In the evenings I wait until the sports programmes on the radio and his smoker's cough are silent, and I can hear his snoring from the study. I wrap myself in my duvet, I traipse into the bedroom, continuing to Mum's side of the bed. I shake her and ask if I can sleep Pompe. She always give me the same answer: Yes, but only if you promise this is the last time. I lie on the beige carpet and tuck my hands into my armpits. It's all quite different if Dad's in the bedroom and he hears me coming in. He rummages about for his glasses on the bedside table. He wants to be able to see me clearly against the brown woven wallpaper. I pull the duvet tightly around me.

Damn it, Tom, you're too old for this, he says.

I'm afraid of snipers, I squeak.

I'm the one they want to shoot, you're actually in more danger lying up here, he answers.

Pompe is taken from one of Barbro Lindgren's children's books about the dog that doesn't dare sleep by itself. I'm Pompe for one more year. I stop when I'm eleven, which is when the murder threats against Dad begin to subside, and the bodyguards are replaced by a large red emergency button, which I am told I should only press in cases of absolute urgency. The button is on a metal box connected to the telephone jack in the kitchen. I have so much respect for that red button that I take detours around it. In the event of an emergency I wouldn't dare press it, I'd be much more likely to stop anyone who tried. Rather than sleeping Pompe I read under the reading lamp through the nights. It's as if I'm inside a one-man tent made of light. Shadows and dark silhouettes have no right of entry. I read Tintin, Conan the Barbarian, The Phantom. But Superman gives me heart palpitations. There are so many people he could save but he doesn't have time for them all in spite of his immeasurable strength and speed. More than anything

I like to look at Bergvall's Atlas. Inside, I've marked with a felt-tip pen all the places I'd consider living in when I grow up: Tórshavn, Mahé, Isabela Island, South Orkney Islands, Yaren, Easter Island, Bouvet Island. The islands are unfamiliar to me as a child, exotic names in a well-thumbed school atlas, small, greenish yellow dots surrounded by immense, dark blue oceans. I picture them as untouched, safe places, free from the masses, free of people, and I populate them with my favourite creatures from fairy tales. I have to stay within the glow of the bedside light, every night, week in, week out. I run off to pee all the time, the darkness frightens me, I'm sure that it's because of the dark that I'm eleven and I wee the bed, because I never wee myself in the daytime. On my way to the toilet I run through the unlit hallway, past the kitchen, along the mirrored wall: there, in a room of seven square metres, he sits in a cloud of smoke. On the nicotine-yellow wallpaper hang photographs of him with table tennis players, boxers, wrestlers, runners, hockey stars, equestrians, and tennis legends. He's writing on the Tandy computer. Although I learn to hate my father I manage to convince myself that the darkness breaks up around his writing fingers, secretly he is a guardian against the darkness, he protects me with his own life, he and the islands, the fairy tale creatures, the immense oceans, the depths, the waves, the sun.

Room 404. By the open window there's a half-metre tall abutilon, just behind the sofa on which I am sitting. We have a similar one at Lundagatan. Livia makes big eyes at it as she drinks her formula, it has spindly branches, it moves in the draughts of air like a huge insect against the glass. Livia's nappy is heavy and warm. I change it for a new one and look for the clean dummy. My phone goes off and the tones of 'I Drew My Ship' ring out, the melody and Collins's voice calm Livia, she used to go to sleep to that every night on Gotland. I didn't have time to check the post before leaving the flat this morning, I just scrabbled together what was on the doormat and stuffed it all into my rucksack. I've had a reminder about the writ. Someone at Stockholm's City Court underlined the following in thick green ink: *If you do not acknowledge receipt the summons may be served in another way, for instance through a bailiff.* The City of Stockholm is summoning me on behalf of Livia, in a procedural notice it is written: *You are called to the City Court to respond to the petitioner's suit and additional assertions in the enclosed application, procedural appendices 1–4.* It also says that I have to provide an undertaking in writing to the City Court as to whether or not I am the father of the child.

At Stockholm Central Station Mum scans the departure times.

Are you angry? I ask.

No, but I would never have let him travel by himself, she answers.

Why didn't we go with him, then?

You know what, he was given an ultimatum, either stop drinking or you're out, that's what I told him. Her breathing becomes panicky. Now he's sitting there in

Båstad! Then she goes silent quite abruptly, looks over her shoulder, and adds: We shouldn't talk about it here, people can hear us.

We board carriage 3 of the train to Gothenburg and Mum checks our tickets against the numbers on the seats. Further down the carriage a man in a tracksuit reclines with his feet up. He's reading a newspaper. Apart from him, the rest of the carriage is empty. Mum is wearing light blue jeans, a white blouse under a loosely knitted jumper with turquoise wrists. Her hair is curled.

We have to run when we pull in, we have to change to Västkustbanan, the train leaves at 14:34, we mustn't miss it, she says.

You've said that a hundred times.

These are our seats, she says and sits down. She gestures towards the seat opposite.

I'd like to stand, I say.

Why?

Just because. She slides her suitcase under the table and looks out of the window as the train departs. It is lovely, though, Strömmen, she says.

I like the Bjäre peninsula, I answer and sit down.

That's something quite different, you've been there since you were six, well, that's half of your life, God, how time passes, she sighs.

Will you get divorced?

I don't know, it's complicated, he can't sleep at night, he's not feeling well, this whole thing with the gambling scandal has worn him out, he's not himself any more, he's self-medicating.

Self-medicating?

Yes, that's actually the right term for all this, she says, stretching. She squints at the man in the tracksuit and adds: We shouldn't talk about this now.

He cried when he called last night, I said you were asleep.

He called last night? she bursts out.

We talked about the tennis, he was drunk as a lord.

Tom, don't talk so loud.

Who can hear, who the hell cares?

Don't swear, she says.

I'm so bloody sorry, I answer. She sighs, tugs at her jumper, and asks:

Why didn't you tell me this?

You were sitting there talking to him when I woke up, you spoke for ages.

Yes, he called this morning, we had quite a bit to talk about.

Are you going to get divorced?

It's up to him, she answers in a clipped voice.

I'm on your side, he's a bloody drunk, I answer.

He's ill, Tom, it's not his fault, it was wrong of me to let him travel on his own. She leans forward and pats me on the cheek.

Stop that, I say and turn away.

You're just like Dad, no one's allowed to touch you.

Stop it.

Not so long ago you refused to let go of my skirt, she says.

You never wear a skirt, I say.

I do actually, but it's just an expression, it means you were very Mummy-focused.

What's going to happen now, are you going to fight, or what?

I've already told you, we're taking him home, he can't drive the car himself, we'll drive him home, we'll go home, I suppose we'll have to stop for the night, we'll get there so late, we'll leave right away in the morning, he mustn't be by himself.

The tennis doesn't finish until next week.

He can't work now anyway, answers Mum.

Are you getting divorced?

Darling, you're all I have, we'll have to see, Dad needs help now, there's been a lot of pressure on him lately, it's been difficult for us all, she answers.

People are talking about Dad at school.

Oh really? says Mum.

We have a supply teacher in woodwork, he asked loads about Dad, he said Dad's good at making stuff up, he said there's no gambling mafia here.

Don't listen to what people say, they talk so much rubbish.

He said we had bodyguards because *Expressen* wanted to sell more newspapers.

Sweetheart, don't think about it, people are naïve, don't give it another thought, I'm going to have a serious talk with your teacher when we get back, she says and takes off her jumper. Her throat is a livid red.

No, you mustn't.

He can't talk to you about those kinds of things, it's nothing to do with him, she says.

You mustn't, I won't go back if you do.

Okay, okay, let's leave it for now.

249

What does naïve mean? I ask after a while. She blows her nose into a tissue, then spits out her chewing gum and throws it in the bin under the table.

Just that people are really idiotic, she answers before going on: I've been doing a lot of thinking lately.

About me?

About us, about Dad, about me, about everything that's happened, I never had a family when I was growing up, I only got one with your father, I never had a mother or a father in that way, not like you, I grew up in foster families, I just longed to grow up and have a family of my own, family is the most important thing one can have, a real family, sorry, my head is a bit messed up at the moment, I'm a little confused . . . God, oh dear, I feel awful, I shouldn't have let him go. She snatches at another tissue and presses it against her nose.

Were you adopted?

No, I just lived with other people, it's hard to explain.

Dad is a bloody big baby.

Tom, don't talk like that.

Well he is.

Am I red here? she asks, touching her throat.

Yes.

I don't usually wear perfume, I have a bad reaction to it.

So why did you put it on, then?

Was it bad of me to let him travel on his own? she asks.

Don't know, he'll be fine.

We won't be, though, not financially at least . . . where would we live?

I'll be a millionaire one day from the hockey, you don't have to worry about money, in a few years we'll be rich.

Sweetheart, I'm thinking aloud, sorry, we're tired, we'll see how it all pans out.

Mum?

Yes, sorry, I'm not thinking straight.

When Dad left, didn't he want me to go with him?

I'd never have allowed that, she answers.

But did he want me to come?

There was never any question of that, I would never have let him take you in any case, but we have to get some sleep now if we're going to manage this.

You sleep.

Tom, put your seat down and close your eyes for a while, we need to sleep, she says.

I'm not tired.

It's a long trip, try.

Give it a rest, I'm not some bloody kid, I say and get out my Game Boy from my rucksack and start choosing from my game cassettes. Mum pulls on her eye mask and puts her feet on the seat.

Well I'll sleep for a while now, wake me if you need me, I don't sleep very deeply anyway, she says, then pulls down her eye mask to her chin and peers into her bag. There are sandwiches in the outside pocket if you want one, liver pâté and pickled gherkins in some of them, they're marked with a cross on the foil, they're your ones, she says. She adjusts her eye mask and uses her jumper as a pillow. I really do have to sleep now, I'm tired.

Evening has fallen when we get to Båstad. We take a taxi from the little train station to Kungsbergsvägen 25, the same two-storey house with the saddle roof we rented last year. On previous trips we rented other houses, always close to the beach and the Atlantic wind, it feels good being near the harbour, I like lying at the far end of the jetties catching crabs with a net, I can stay there for hours looking at the water ascending towards Hovs Hallar, or the wake of the ferry between Torekov and Hallands Väderö, but I lied to Mum, I can't swim at all, I run over the tiled bottom of the Malen Baths shooting my arms into the water and pretending I'm Matt Biondi, and if I like I can go with Dad to the Press Section at Centre Court and shake hands with the tennis stars, I hate seeing how Dad looks up to them, how he makes a note of everything they say and how he drops his shoulders and smiles at them, they're no better on gravel or grass than I am on ice, and I tell them that, they laugh and say I'm entertainingly bolshie, Dad takes me aside and whispers:

Tom T., learn to keep your mouth shut, listen, let others talk themselves silly.

The taxi driver lifts Mum's suitcase out of the boot. The ground-floor lights are on but the curtains are drawn. There are a few sticks and some yellowish-green pollen on Dad's company car, a red Honda Accord, parked in the drive.

Tom, wait for me, Tom, listen to me, wait, Mum calls out after me, but I continue to the fenced-in lawn and sit in the hammock. She hurries after me and hisses: You never listen, do you?

I'm just sitting down, I'm tired.

You've been sitting all day, she says, putting her suitcase down on the paving stones. She peers at the windows.

So what happens now? I ask.

We do what we came to do, she answers as she walks determinedly to the door, rings the doorbell, opens it, and calls out: Thomas, we're here now, we're coming in.

Final respects are paid in Högalid Church. Scarred, brown marble flagstones, lanterns suspended from chains, a gloomy beamed ceiling. I tuck Livia into the pram and lean against a sheet metal cupboard with 'Emergency Defibrillator' stamped on it. Hans and Harriet, Börje and Ammi, Göran, Laila, my aunt and cousins from Eskilstuna, Sven and Lillemor, my friends Hasse, Stefan, David, Alex. They stand in a huddle of heavy, dark woollen overcoats, cigar cases, the odd hip flask. A disappearing generation of newspaper men, big ears, pockmarked noses, proliferating eyebrows, flabby skin hanging in folds down their throats, eyes that seem to be missing their eyelids and are filled with judgement. Hard gentlemen who seemed to me, even when I was a child, to be of another age, another world. One of them stands with his back to me talking to three other elderly journalists or newspaper editors. I hear him say in a voice with a marked Stockholm dialect: The most refined roasting in newspaper history, without any doubt, carries the signature of Alf Montán, he had seen Ragnar Frisk's film *Åsa-Nisse Flies Through the Air* and he gave it a single crossed-out star, he only wrote three words: 'Enjoy your flight.' Their laughter sounds like smokers' coughs. A couple of younger journalists wearing flimsy suits are standing around another tall table making small-talk. That was in the seventies, wasn't it, Jamaica, in the middle of a match in progress against Peter Fleming, which was when Borg turns to Malmen on the stand and calls out: Malmen, this will be over in a minute, order a tray of pina colada, see you in the hotel room in twenty minutes. Another one answers: It's so bloody cool, they were mates with the stars in those days, imagine all the stuff that never got printed, whores, drugs, fights, shit, we're stuck behind the crowd control barriers with the kids. Stefan, Hasse and Alex stand next to me. David is talking to my aunt a little further off. Tompa, says Stefan. Yes, I answer. Sorry for saying this, but this stirs up a lot inside, I remember when my mother passed away, it was a while ago, but shit. Yes, I answer and turn to Alex: Stefan's mother Monica always brought Stefan in the pram when we were living in Mossbrännevägen when our dads were covering the world championships or Olympics; Janne is a legendary *Expressen* photographer. I know, I know Janne, answers Alex. His bald head is hard to miss, says Stefan, looking over at his father who's talking to Börje and Göran. Stefan became obsessed with my NYPD patrol car, I say, and Stefan grins. I go on: I started hiding it from him, that car was a present from my dad, I didn't want to share it with Stefan, I didn't want to share it with anyone, Mum and Monica always managed to find it, Mum wanted me to be generous. I was so anxious as a kid, says Stefan, I didn't want to come along unless I was allowed to play with that police car, and I add: In the end I buried it in the garden, then Stefan got the car at his thirtieth birthday party, I'd been hiding it from him for twenty-five years. Alex and Hasse laugh but Stefan looks a little upset. What's up, Stefan? I ask. I spoke a bit with Göran earlier, he answers. Who's that? asks Hasse. One of Thomas's best friends, an old journalist at *Expressen*, I mean him, Dad, and Börje have been colleagues on the newspaper for donkey's years, answers Stefan. Uh-huh, says Hasse. Did Göran say something unexpected, or what? I ask, and Stefan responds: When did his wife pass away? Anna-Karin, must have been the early nineties, I reply. So a long time ago, then, says Stefan, then adds: The way he talked about her it's as if it was only yesterday that she was put in the ground.

Lillemor moves forward tentatively, says hello to my friends, hugs me, and then bends over the pram. The princess is sleeping, she says and looks at me. Four months and already an old hand at all this, she adds. Thankfully she's unaware of what's happening, I answer, glancing at Stefan who's keeping his eyes on Alex and Hasse as they move through the crowd. Well, I guess the important thing is to keep your eyes firmly on the road, avoid looking into the ditch, she says. I don't know, at least there are flowers in the ditch, there aren't any on the road, I answer. In the summer, yes, but not in the autumn or winter, she says, and goes on: I can't stop myself, I have to touch her. She takes Livia's hand between her thumb and index finger. She looks up at me again: Sorry, I couldn't control myself. She's your grandchild, I say. Sven stands in front of me and pats me on the arm and shakes his head. I look at him, because I'd like him to say something, and then he says: The ceremony was beautiful. Yes, I answer. One of the younger journalists strides up and asks something about the gambling scandal but I don't have time to work out exactly what he's asking, because at the same time Lillemor says that she and Sven are going to slip off home while there's a break in the rain. The journalist is tall, with a shiny pageboy hairstyle, and he says: Maybe it's a hard one to answer, but that game fix in the table tennis world championships in Birmingham in 1977, that was a bloody big deal, your dad was the first one in the whole world to expose that. He has a staccato delivery, abrupt movements, his eyelids twitch. Sorry, I'm not really with it today, what are you asking? I respond. I get it, he says and looks around behind him. No, it's fine, what was your question? I'm probably disturbing you, he says. What was your question? I was asking which was your dad's biggest story, what do you reckon? The gambling scandal, I answer. Shit, there was some rough stuff there, I heard, bodyguards and all that? Afterwards we had bodyguards, also before, Dad had a talent for provoking people, I say. I suppose you hung out with him a lot when he was working? he asks. Yes, absolutely, I've been all over Europe with him, and the USA, tennis, golf, ice hockey, football, Formula 1, everything, I saw and heard a lot – he said he'd rather go out with a Romanian tank than watch Lisovskaya shot-putting, he referred to the wife of a colleague of his as Downpour, and he described one sports journalist in Skåne as a fivefold gold medal winner at the four-hundred-column metres for the talentless. Shit, that's just so Malmen, like, he was such a bloody smooth operator, I have to get this down, he says and gets out a little writing pad from his inside pocket, jots down a few lines and says: We had four pages about Malmen, well, I guess you must have read them, but we wanted to feature a page or so about the funeral as well, no big deal, but oh yeah, J-O Waldner picked Malmen didn't he, sorry, I mean your dad. He's also Malmen to me, I throw in. Really? he asks. To a degree, I answer. Cool, but that thing with J-O about his gambling addiction, that was massive. He didn't want to talk to anyone apart from Malmen, a billion Chinese sports fans practically did the splits at his say-so, J-O is like a demi-god over there. Sorry, it's been a long day, I need to collect myself a bit, I say, checking the locking mechanism on the pram chassis. I get it, shit, I'm pretty emotionally spent myself, I can understand you've got other things on, but we're going to the Press Club later, just so you know, Malmen's son is always welcome, he says. Thanks, I answer. He taps me on the shoulder and says: I've heard about it all, it's bloody terrible, unimaginable, and now your dad. Thanks, I answer and barge my way through with the pram, weaving between the high tables before I get stuck behind a vicar and a photographer with an *Expressen* wasp emblazoned on his waistcoat. I look for my snuff tin in my jacket pocket. The photographer twists a wide-angle lens onto his Nikon. The vicar points at the glass panel above the entrance and says: It's a P combined with an X, those are the first two letters of Christós in Greek. Damn, look at that, says the photographer and casts a harried glance at the door without apparently taking much note of the Christ monogram, being more concerned with getting a picture of the funeral guests. The vicar turns towards the nave and lets his scraggy arm hover in the air as he continues: There we have Torhamn's crucifix, the largest one in the Nordic region, we have thirty-two metres of headroom here. The large crucifix hangs on the wall above the altar, simple, in matt earth colours, strangely calming. Mum sits largely invisible on a stool by the piano and stares at the wreaths. She's wearing a black dress, boots, and a blouse as white as her hair. She holds two fingers on her left wrist. I imagine she's counting the intervals between each beat of her heart, as he taught me to count the distance between lightning and thunder. The officiating clergyman stands slightly behind her, watching an audio technician who's squatting and hauling in a cable by the microphone. One of the elder gentlemen holds out his hand towards me. He doesn't relinquish his strong grip when he says, in a low voice: My condolences for your grief, your father was one of the most important sports journalists of his generation. Thanks very much, thanks, I answer. He lets go of my hand, nods, and puts on a black fedora which he's been carrying under his arm. He wanders off towards the main door, using his umbrella as a walking stick. I back away, focus my gaze at a downward angle to avoid eye contact with anyone, and push the trolley towards the choir. The runner has been invisible to me until now, I bend down and touch it, it's made of coarse nylon, cerulean blue, sky-blue like Karin's nightie. I sit down with the pram next to me, a couple of rows behind my mother and my father's light-coloured oak casket.

FIFTY MILLIGRAMS OF Lergigan no longer help, I always wake up too early. I shine the light from my phone at the cot. Livia is sleeping with her hands behind her head. She's breathing serenely. I kick off my duvet, my underpants are wet with urine but the sheet is dry. A smell of ammonia. I stand in the shower with my hands pressed to the tiles. I fetch new underpants from the linen cupboard and fill a Duralex glass with water. Most of Dad's vinyl is still in cardboard boxes. The coal-black record shelf looked so vulgar in the flat that I had to paint it white. I sit on the sofa and drink the water. There's no one to call at half past two on a Monday morning. My eyes adapt to the darkness. The narrow hall with the metre-high stacks of books on one side and the hat shelf with the anchor hooks on the other. Karin's duffel coat on a coat hanger. I put it in the clothes cupboard and close the door. Tomorrow I'll probably hang it back up again. I bring my leg up and fold out my little toe, the cut from my athlete's foot is suppurating, my toenails have become dirtily yellow and porous. I fetch the Tupperware boxes from the fridge. In one is cucumber salad, in the other potatoes, in the third one Mum's ossobuco made from knuckle of lamb, tomatoes, white wine, olives, sprigs of thyme, laurel leaves. I eat it cold. Leaning against a flower pot is the photograph of my father and me in Cassis, we're standing in the lit-up harbour surrounded by the famous rocks and the night. I didn't want to be in the photo, I'm pulling a face. In a lot of the photos Mum took of me and Dad in the eighties our eyes are red because of the flash, I've read that it's the blood vessels that are visible, which doesn't happen on modern cameras thanks to red-eye reduction. I lie down on the sofa with Italo Calvino's novel *Under the Jaguar Sun*. His original intention was that it should be entitled *The Five Senses*, and be arranged in five parts, one for each of the senses. He never managed to finish the manuscript before he died. Three parts were completed: taste, hearing, and smell. I'm too anxious and tired to make any notes. The camping mat is petrol-grey and made of foam plastic. I bought it for Karin to exercise on during her pregnancy, she never did. I pull it out on the floor next to Livia and throw down my duvet and pillow. I thread my hand through the bars.

You tell me it's seven degrees outside and I answer that the milk is starting to run out. Not long after you come down from the attic with a cloth bag full of wool and tell me that the moths were shimmering like silver up there. You want to write a children's book about this moment and your cautious enthusiasm unnerves me –

the way you tag *maybe* or *but we'll see* onto the end of every sentence. I never told you about the squirrel on Mossbrännevägen, I'd forgotten about it myself, of course I hadn't really forgotten it, I just hadn't thought about it for a very long time, but this morning, when I was singing Alice Tegnér's song about the squirrel for Livia it suddenly pushed its way through my memories. I am three or four years old, the squirrel lies under the pine in the ditch by the road, I try to wake it, I go and get my mother from the potato field, in my mind at least she's wearing some sort of iridescent shawl that changes colour in the light, she's younger than I am today, she bends over the squirrel and says: We can't wake it up.

I have got rid of the television, I have cancelled the newspaper subscriptions, I read the books that you bought and think about the underlined bits every few pages, I quickly flip through the news on my phone, I can hardly deal with it any more, I hear the screams and the wailing sirens, even a minor forest fire thousands of kilometres away makes me feel frightened, immediately I start imagining the birds being burned to a crisp as the heat rises and engulfs them.

I have a nude image of you, heavily pregnant in the shower, your right arm inserted into the gushing water, your fingers splayed, your eyes looking up, your breasts large and heavy, and your belly, like a Venus figurine, I step out of my clothes and walk up to you, into my origin, into my incompleteness.

Your love for me in its rawest nakedness was when you said: You talk a lot about what sets you apart from your father, have you never thought about how you are like him?

At times I go back with him to the hot-dog stand in Huddinge Shopping Centre, to the picnic bench by the dog roses, we have Sausage Special with Boston gherkins and we drink refrigerated Pucko, it's wordless between us and even when I try to ask him something it gets drowned out by the noise we make as we eat. Only you know me, you understand why in the middle of the night I watch the bonus material of Michael Haneke's *The White Ribbon*, the making-of documentary, a sequence in which the director instructs one of the actors about how he wants him to open a barn door and discover that his father has hanged himself from the roof beam, the instruction only lasts a few minutes but it terrifies me into calmness.

I have started sleeping Pompe again, I lie on the floor next to Livia's cot, she wakes me at five every morning, pokes at me curiously, and in case I go back to sleep she pulls me hard by the nose and laughs so infectiously, so incomparably, that it's impossible to get annoyed. I have told you what Dad used to call me and Mum at the summer house, how he raises his fist and shakes it in the air. I want him to hit me, touch me, but he only rails and threatens, he has never hit anyone, he's afraid of violence, he's fascinated by violence, he's got several decades of championship bouts in heavyweight boxing, one and a half metres of VHS cassettes, he says that no one before or after fought more beautifully than Cassius Clay. I'm a hard bastard and stand in my skates and shorts in the garage and practise left jabs and right hooks against the brick wall, my knuckles toughen up, my wrists get thicker, and this must have been the same summer that you buried your guinea pig Sofie at Skyttevägen and discussed the poem you had written for her with your parents. Even today it is not unusual for me, when I'm feeling really bad and the words of consolation do not present themselves, to punch the wall as hard as I can.

Mum and Dad do not go back to Båstad after his collapse and a year or so afterwards they buy the summer place on Båtstigen. Dad feels good in Sörmland, his home country, the fields, the mixed woodland, the funnel chanterelles, the mosses, the rusty brown pond; I miss the Atlantic wind but I adapt myself. I steal a bottle of Koskenkorva and sit on the pontoon with my father's copy of the Swedish Academy Glossary, the pages smell of cigarette smoke, the sound of bush crickets, the bright night sky like an enormous reading room, and I learn two new terms: papillary lines and protuberance. Mum sold the country place the other day, she gave it up quickly and cheaply, she needed the money.

Just risen from the bed your scent is at its strongest, you stay in the kitchenette, you stretch and look out at Metargatan, moments later I get into the bathtub where you are, the water overflows, your toes against my thighs, knees sticking out of the foam, you look at me and tell me there's a unique kind of reality in the presence of death, a reality that erodes all protection until one is forced to confront life without any hope of mercy, I didn't understand you, I understand you, but you no longer exist, it's a nothingness beyond consciousness, and I have learned to live in an expectationless coolness.

It doesn't take long before you wake and notice that I am no longer there under the duvet, you find me on the floor in the hall with my back towards the cast-iron radiator, after so many years you know it's best just to sit down next to me and not touch me, or even ask questions.

Five drops of vitamin D on a spoon. Livia swallows and puts her hands in the yoghurt. No, Livia, not like that, we don't play with food, I say and wipe her with a damp towel. She clings to my neck when I lift her out of the chair. She toddles over to the basket of toys and throws teddies and wooden blocks into the air, then starts studying a doll Lillemor gave her. I scour the floor where she was sitting and finish off her leftover yoghurt. She drags the doll along the floor. Daddy, she says. Yes, darling? I answer. She tries to clamber onto the sofa. Daddy, she says again. Go on, you can do it, Livia, I say, and she does.

I can hold the front porch of Lundagatan open while pushing Livia through in the buggy. She sits up. In the yard is a steel bicycle rack. Most of the bikes haven't been used since last summer. Their tyres are partially buried in the gravel and need to be pumped up. Dry leaves have caught between the spokes. Only one bicycle stands out, it has purple plastic roses wrapped around its handlebars. Look, says Livia. She stares at the bicycle. Yes, Papa told you about it yesterday, you've such a good memory, Livia, you remember Mum's bicycle. I put on Livia's sunhat with the floppy brim and button up her spring jacket which I found at Stockholm Stadsmission's second-hand shop on Hornsgatan this winter, it's been heavily used but there are no holes in it, probably it hails back to the decade when Karin and I were born, it's milk-white with a floral pattern in faded red. I throw away the bin bags full of prawn peel and nappies then stop on the pavement on Lundagatan. I feel a resistance to taking the short route to Malmgården Pre-School, the route that leads to the right past Högalid Church, a walk of about fifteen minutes, instead I turn left, a detour of close to an hour, past the ice cream kiosk in Skinnarvik Park, under the elms on Ringvägen-Hornsgatan and the block known as Svärdet where my mother has moved. The park lawns smell stronger than the bins outside the restaurants. Livia lifts her chin into the breeze, litter is rising and falling and sand flying. Plane, she says and gazes up over the leafage of Tantolunden. I squat in front of her and say: Do you know, Livia, those are one of Dad's favourite things, vapour trails, that's what they're called, the lines behind the planes, ever since I was a little boy it's made me happy looking at them. She laughs because I'm smiling at her. Livia, today I'm not staying with you at the nursery, you'll be with Ulla and Irja and all the children, there'll be a right carry-on, you'll all have snotty noses and you'll throw soft toys at each other, most likely you'll be bloody furious when I come to pick you up. She takes off her sunhat, throws it on the ground, and makes a clucking sound when I pick it up. Livia, that wasn't fun, well, maybe a little bit fun. During one of my walks with her I stop by the traffic mirror, the one on the sharp curve outside my parents' house on Gotland. In it I see myself from above, looking down at an angle, I am filled with anguish of a sort that I also get from the works of Bruegel or Goya in your art books, I no longer have thinning hair, this last year I have been losing it, I am marked with a bald patch, I have become an emaciated human being, I have a grey beard and grey hair on my chest, you wouldn't recognise me if you ran into me in the grass by the deep pool at Eriksdal baths.

It's the end of summer and we swim four lengths, you don't like the smell of chlorine but I like it, there's a bottle of Chablis in the bicycle basket, Swiss hard cheese, a roast chicken, vine tomatoes, there's a high-level haze in the sky, you're ashamed to be drinking wine in the morning and I tell you it's always winetime somewhere. You have droplets of water around your throat, and there's nothing else we long for. Three weeks later I am sitting at a table in Bistro Amika scribbling down two lines on the back of a McDonald's receipt, you are on the operating table in the building next door, it's raining outside the window, a real downpour, the onslaught makes a booming sound as it comes down over the NeuroCentre. I had those lines published much later, but they did not fit in the poetry collection, they were diminished among all the epic lines there. I think about them sometimes, not every day but often, and I want so much to wander back to 29 August 2004, and sit next to the Tom who wrote them: *It's not the rain that's falling, it's the lakes rising.* I wouldn't have the capacity to console him, but I would tell him that these two lines are still very important to Tom, ten years on.

I change nappies, wash clothes, I go shopping at Hemköp and tie the carrier bags onto the buggy and fill the rucksack with vegetables and fruit, I cook, I bathe her, vacuum the floor and listen to Argerich's interpretations of Chopin and Ciccolini's interpretations of Satie but always come back to Richter's recordings of Beethoven's piano sonatas, I scour the floors, I let her sit on my shoulders, I talk to her, I explain why I am doing what I am doing, like a sort of sports commentator, she listens, she understands, she has a sense of humour, she learns many words although she has trouble pronouncing them, she prefers Miyazaki's films to Teletubbies, and Shaun Tan's fairy tales to picture books, I realise that she is gifted but I think it's mostly about her need for closeness, she is socially minded, intuitive as you were, she notices that I get more involved if I also enjoy the film or book, I pay the bills, I can only write when she's asleep but not more than a couple of hours, I can't manage more than that, I go to sleep with the laptop resting on my belly, and then she gets a high fever, she shivers and wakes in the night, she vomits and shits in the bed, I get the winter vomiting disease myself, I still have to force myself up and wash the bedlinen, I get on all fours scrubbing the toilet bowl, I try to get her to drink something, I fetch wet towels, I fan her with a T-shirt, I make an attempt to keep my thoughts of impending disasters to myself, and then she recovers, I change nappies, go shopping, cook, console and bathe her, I brush her golden-coloured hair, cut her nails, vacuum, I change the soil in the flower pots and read on the net about plastics that disrupt hormones and reproduction and can also be neurotoxic for little children, I feel like an irresponsible parent, I throw out all the plastic that I suspect may be dangerous, she calls out for me, but I am tired now, I have never been so tired, I even have trouble reaching for the books on the top shelf, I push the toys into the corners with my foot, I forget to flush the toilet, I open the fridge and then just stand there facing the zinc-white innards, the cold light radiating from fifteen watts.

I have nightmares about her not existing anywhere, I launch myself out of bed and call out for you, I roar something about how she is gone, I realise that I am dreaming about the time before she existed, while you were still here, and I no longer know what's a nightmare and what isn't, a few times more recently I have woken up with memories of that intensive care nurse, the one at Söder Hospital, who shut me out of Room B and stole time from us when it was its most important, in my dreams I meet him alone in an open space of artificial ice, I let go of my club and take off my hockey gloves.

Your mother often gets in touch via text, she writes: *Grateful for a sign of life, I worry so much these days.* I don't get irritated about her anxieties as much as you used to, I just answer: *All is well with us.* Once or twice I punch in the door code of the Neonatal ward when I'm outside the house in Lundagatan, it's as if it's lodged in my muscular memory. Does it make any sense to you when I say that I miss Karolinska? The midwives and Neonatal nurses who lift me up, my friends who stay the night with me in Family Room 1 and cry when I cry and the long corridors that always lead to something important? Livia's tears run remarkably slowly when she gets upset, it reminds me of liquid glass, she's so real, beautiful, true, she has a smile that acknowledges not only me, but everything about me, good or bad, she looks at me with eyes that have known me all of her life. You know I love her with all the weight of us, still it feels as if I have the best behind me and the most important in front of me, some nights I only want to lie naked in a cave like Mikael in Huddinge, curl up in the mother's womb and close my eyes until I am unborn. I lay my hand on your breast and ask you not to call it sad.

I say: Sshh.

And I say: My daydreams of you are beautiful.

Livia wakes up with the sun and sits up, my name is Papa, she calls out for me again and I don't have time for brooding or even feeling. Like you, she takes note of the small things in life, the spectrum of colour in spilled oil, the gooseberry mite on the end of a broom handle, a scratch on my elbow, a spider's skein between the crystal lobes of the chandelier on the ceiling, even a rusty bottle top is something magic to her. She knows that the photos of you are valuable, I keep them next to me in bed and I say good morning and goodnight to them, she touches them and I have learned to say: Darling, Daddy is not sad because of anything you have done.

I stop outside one of the allotments and adjust the buggy's handlebar. Four women sit at a garden table, they talk loudly, all have short white hair and black sunglasses, they seem to have just had their breakfast, I see two empty bottles of rosé in the grass under the table. Livia has learned that there's an echo between the pillars of Liljeholmen Bridge, she hollers, listens for the response, bends back her head towards me, she wants me to make a noise as well. The willows lean over the water and, in the light breeze, trail their long sprays across the footpath. Livia holds onto the bar with both hands when I run with the buggy through the leaves all the way to the pontoon swimming baths. Again, she says.

I get out a tissue from my pocket and wipe her nose. No, Papa, she says and pushes me away. She looks at the mallards under Reimersholme Bridge. The sailing dinghies recently put in the water at the sailing club jetty smell of wood tar and turpentine. Livia wants to throw a willow leaf that has caught in the buggy into the water. I help her.

Last Thursday I found a letter you started on your computer, dated January 2012. They are the only words where you directly address her. *You move in my belly. It's grey outside, no snow, mainly sleet, but soon it'll be spring and then you'll be here! Don't think you're kicking as yet, mainly you just turn around. You move quite a lot, especially when I am lying still*. It is not difficult to memorise the essential part, and I become one with the letter as one day she will also become one with it, just as you two were one.

She is naked and jumps into a cloud of water from a sprinkler, she stands with her legs wide apart behind a forsythia bush to pee, she has a black ant in an insect tin, she wants a plaster on her finger. I love listening to her role-playing, the shifting nuances of her voice when she plays on her own, I remove the stabilisers of her bicycle and run behind her as your father once ran behind you, and she makes drawings and asks me to send them to you.

I have never hated as I hate now, it has no direction, no meaning, and every time I try to understand it, attach words to it, define it, control it, I start crying so violently that I am afraid of waking her even if I am in a different room, and I put my hand over my eyes and I hear myself saying: It's only make-believe.

I ask you not to call it sad, either.

Other women will come into her life and hug her on her birthdays and offer advice, we'll move away from Lundagatan to another street, another city, another country, she falls in love with an older boy or girl, she skives off school and goes swimming in flooded mine shafts and smokes marijuana on a roof, over long periods she does not ask about you, she calls home while on a trip abroad, she misses home, I meet her at the airport, she says she thought she saw you, she loves your clothes, she finds a receipt in the pocket of your duffel coat from a shop that no longer exists, she finds me critical and unfair, she cites Simone de Beauvoir, she pulls the duvet over her head.

She says: Sssh.

And she says: I often dream about my mother.

Then she turns thirty-five, and, getting married in your red dress with white dots, she has your fingers, they feel like your hands when I let go of her, and she gets older, our daughter walks with a crutch over the chalk-white pier towards the stone house, she lets the cat out and goes inside. She looks at you, thinking that the photo is old.

The pre-school is housed in a manorial building from the eighteenth century. Patinated roof-tiles, brown ochre pointing and white columns at the entrance. It has been a nursery since the forties. Parents and children enter at the back of the building. A tall, white-blooming cherry tree stands in a corner of the courtyard. In the little vestibule I put on some light blue shoe covers and carry Livia into the section they call The Frogs' Room. Livia presses her nose into my throat. Ulla, one of the older and more experienced teachers, catches sight of us. Good morning, Livia, she says, crouching towards her. Livia peers at her, and she adds: And good morning, Livia's dad. Hello, I answer. She takes down a folder from a shelf above the sofa, where two nappy-wearing children are sitting. They glare at Livia and at me. I just want to check with you, if something comes up and we can't get hold of you, who should we contact? she asks. I'm the one to contact, I answer. She looks a bit puzzled. One of Livia's grandmothers, I'm pretty sure I left their numbers with you, aren't they there? I ask. She looks in her folder. No, doesn't look like it, she answers. I put Livia down, she immediately wants to be picked up again. She clings onto my leg as I drag myself over to the table to have a look. I'm fairly sure I gave them to you, I say. Ah, well, no, we only have your number, she says. Okay, right, can I write here next to that, or . . .? Yes, that's fine, she answers. Hello, Livia, says Irja, another teacher, and then goes on: Do you have some favourite song, something you like? 'I Drew My Ship' by Shirley Collins, also Nina Simone, there are others, Joni Mitchell, I answer, and Irja interrupts me with a laugh that she only seems capable of offloading by bending her head back and opening her mouth very wide. I was thinking of some children's song, 'The Bear is Sleeping' or 'Heads, Shoulders, Knees and Toes' or something like that, she says. She has raven-black hair, she could be about twenty years younger than Ulla, both of them are short and slightly rotund. Yes, I got that, I answer. I was thinking we could start with some song that you recognise when we sing at the morning assembly, she explains, making a face at Livia. Oh right, okay, that's nice, no, I really don't know, I answer. So we'll just go ahead as per normal, she says and gives Livia a pat before she goes back to reading a book for the children on the sofa. Livia hugs me hard. Ulla clasps her hands together over her stomach and asks me to go with her. She walks into a cloakroom and stands by a wall decorated with drawings. She pulls out a blue plastic storage drawer. This is Livia's, if you could bring in a change of clothes that would be great, an extra pair of trousers and a jumper, it's good to have some rain clothes, wellies are useful to have, the yard can turn into a real mudbath, she says. I've brought clothes in the buggy bag, I answer. Would you mind leaving them in the drawer, we don't want to dig about in your bag, she says. Okay, yeah, but I haven't brought any rain clothes, should I go and get them now? I ask. No, you can just bring them in tomorrow. Sure, of course, oh and I was wondering one thing, I say as we walk through the hall towards the yard. Ulla stops, looks at me, and I continue: I read that there used to be a textile factory here and some chemicals were dumped, do you know anything about that? I don't, I'm afraid, but we've had the court-yard checked on several occasions, there's nothing dangerous here, not at the pre-school anyway, she answers. I mean, Livia puts things she finds in her mouth, I point out. Children do that, no, there's nothing to worry about, as I said, the yard's been checked several times, she says, and looks down at the sandy slope, stamping her foot and adding: It's just mud here. She makes eye contact with Livia and says: You're going to have so much fun here when Daddy's working. Livia pokes the tip of her tongue out, and her cheeks go all rosy. I always have my phone on me, if anything comes up just call me, I'm nearby, it'll take me ten minutes, max, to get here. She nods at my shoes and blinks: Livia, now your papa has forgotten about his shoe covers. I take them off at once and I'm already heading back to the vestibule when she says: You can just give them to me. Uh-huh, okay, thanks. She stuffs the shoe covers into the pocket of her mustard-yellow windbreaker and slaps me on my back: This will be just fine. She leans towards Livia: You're a very sociable and secure girl, you're going to make lots of new friends here, and the weather's nice too, this'll be just perfect. I squat down and give Livia a hug. Darling, Papa's going home now to work, but I'm not far away, I'll only be gone for a little while, I say. Livia pinches her lips together when Ulla picks her up. Shall we wave to Papa? she asks.

A teacher from another group stops me by the gate. Livia's dad? he says. I nod at him. You have to fill in what days you're on holiday, he says, handing over a few stapled papers, and then goes on: We're closed from week twenty-nine up to and including week thirty-two, if you need a pre-school spot at this time we pool our resources with other pre-schools. I don't think we're going anywhere, I tell him. Fill it in and hand it in once you know, it would be good if we could have it this week, he says. Okay, thanks, I answer and secure the gate. I fold down the cover of the buggy. Ulla holds Livia up by the fence at the closest point to the gravel path. She's placed her feet on the crossbar. Livia doesn't seem to know how to wave, she just stares at me, it strikes me that I have never been away from her for so long that waving has been necessary. Behind the stone wall by Anders Reimers väg I stop again to wave, but they've gone, I take off my sunglasses, I squint at the yard, the sandpits, carts, buckets, toy cars, spring animal rockers, teachers with skipping ropes, climbing frames, cones, a slide, three-wheelers, children everywhere; but then she's there in her sunhat with the floppy brim and her jacket with the floral pattern. She's waving, under the cherry tree.